THE FIRST INSTRUCTIONS

"You will receive a package at your home in a few days. Do not allow anyone else to open it. Do not tell anybody its contents. The package will include a map and directions. It is the *where*. It will not include the *when*. That I will tell you now. Please listen carefully. Are you ready?"

"Yes."

"December 10. Twelve midnight. Come alone. Don't be late. Don't park within 100 feet of the destination. Do you have that?"

"Yes."

"The Circle is closed, we are ready to begin…"

VENGEANCE

BRIAN PINKERTON

LEISURE BOOKS  NEW YORK CITY

A LEISURE BOOK®

April 2005

Published by

Dorchester Publishing Co., Inc.
200 Madison Avenue
New York, NY 10016

ISBN 0-8439-5532-5

Printed in the United States of America.

Visit us on the web at www.dorchesterpub.com.

ACKNOWLEDGMENTS

Special thanks to my partner in crime Jill Pinkerton for her invaluable assistance and loyal support. I would also like to acknowledge Mike Calcina and Jon Ford for valued editorial input, and Nancy Pinkerton for courtroom insight.

VENGEANCE

Prologue

Former NFL fullback Justin Hoyt, six-foot-four and 288 pounds, wept like a small child.

The big Texan clutched the sides of the podium, lowered his head, and watched his notecards smear into a hopeless blur. He could not stop the tears.

The packed auditorium fell silent. Little sounds became magnified. The shuffle of a coat. A small cough. Someone with the sniffles.

The sniffles continued, scattered throughout the crowd, and Hoyt realized: *Some of them are crying, too.* He could feel his own heartbeat and the wetness on his cheeks.

"Please pardon me," he choked. "It'll just be a minute."

Hoyt wiped his eyes. He ran a hand through his gray buzz cut. He looked up into the bright lights, away from the sea of faces. He imagined Tommy looking back at him, urging him, "Go ahead, Pop. You can do it. You're doing fine. Don't fumble the ball."

Until now, everything had gone well. Hoyt arrived

early, a little after six, and met with high school administrators, village board members, and the Community Affairs Officer from Benton Park. They were all very nice and appreciative. They told him how valuable it was to have a former Chicago Bear speaking to the kids and parents. People would look up to him. They would listen. He was *cool*, said Emily, the perky young student counselor and event coordinator.

He could help save lives, said Principal Meg Evans.

The evening had a full agenda, and Hoyt was the closer. So he sat in the back row, off to the side, joined by his wife, Sandy, and watched the parade of speakers.

Principal Evans opened with the unveiling of a large, student-created banner that read "Freedom 2 B Drug Free." Decorated in red, white, and blue, the slogan and artwork would also be available on T-shirts and baseball caps after the program, with proceeds supporting the community's substance abuse program. Evans condemned pop culture for celebrating drug use and introduced a group of students who performed an anti-drug rap song.

The students were followed by a somber medical expert who rattled off statistics about drug use among youth and gave a crash course on the different types of recreational drugs—from marijuana to ecstasy—and their effects on the brain and body. When the expert referenced heroin, Hoyt shut his eyes and tightened his grip on Sandy's hand.

Emily, the student counselor, bounced on stage next with a box of drug paraphernalia.

"Parents, these are your red flags." She displayed

pipes, rolling papers, and a hypodermic needle. "This needle can not only give you a drug overdose, it can give you AIDS," she said, punching out the word "AIDS" with dramatic emphasis. Then she discussed some of the behavioral signs of drug abuse: drastic changes in weight, sloppy speech, withdrawal, depression, and mood swings.

She's describing Tommy, thought Hoyt.

Next, a former student from Benton High talked firsthand about the horrors of addiction. Mumbling and regretful, the skinny young man told the crowd about his past struggles with cocaine. He wiped his palms against his pants. Every admission was clearly painful. "Man, take it from me, it's not fun and it's not glamorous. It is sheer hell."

When Crime Prevention Supervisor Bryan McGowan from the Benton Park Police took the podium, Hoyt's emotions shifted. He felt the sadness in his heart replaced with anger. Before McGowan spoke a word, Hoyt had folded his arms across his chest and fixed the stage with a skeptical stare.

The police talk a good game, but they don't do nearly enough, thought Hoyt. The drug dealers have a free pass. The cops are lazy, the courts are sloppy, the lawyers are crooked. That's the real reason our kids are falling victim to this poison. We let scum run loose in the community.

McGowan made a few basic requests. He told the audience to dial 911 if they suspected drug dealing, and reminded them that fighting drugs was a shared responsibility.

"You are the eyes and ears of Benton Park," said

McGowan. "You can help us identify the source of these drugs."

Right, thought Hoyt, so you can slap them on the wrist and put them back into society.

When Meg Evans introduced Hoyt as the evening's special guest speaker, the auditorium came alive with loud applause. Hoyt kissed his wife and began the long walk up the aisle in his snakeskin cowboy boots.

On his way to the stage, there were butterflies in his stomach, followed by an unusual sensation of fear. It sent him back nearly twenty years to his first professional game with the Redskins. He remembered how he had taken hold of the fear then and turned it into aggression. Aggression against the enemy, which had been the Detroit Lions.

Tonight, the enemy was drugs and drug dealers.

"I appreciate the warm welcome," he told the audience. "Frankly, I'm amazed anyone remembers me. I had a short career, but a good one. There's a joke among players that NFL stands for Not For Long. You get banged up, fresh talent comes up through the college system, and they put you out to pasture. I played pro ball for four years with three teams. As you all can tell from my drawl, I come from the South—brought up in Texas, a die-hard Cowboys fan. Before you boo, I also love the Bears.

"I lettered in football at Alvin High School, went to Texas A&M, played for the Aggies, opening holes for Damian Terney, who became a finalist for the Heisman and went on to fame and fortune with the Kansas City Chiefs. I got picked up by Washington in the sixth round of the 1987 draft. Also played one year for the Cardinals, and then ended my career here in Chicago, where I had one good year, and one not-so-good year. I got banged up with some injuries, knee problems, and then I got released.

"Overall, I had a pretty good run. I had a reputation for going into every game with a tough mental attitude and being a very physical player. I'm proud of the numbers on the back of my football card, but life goes on. As you all know, my last two years were with the Bears, and although I grew up in Texas, I now consider Chicago my home. I have lived in a community just south of here for almost fifteen years."

Hoyt glanced down at the podium. He saw that his hands were shaking.

"Chicago is my home," he continued, "and it is your home. Unfortunately, we have a most unwelcome and deadly intruder in our home. That is why I am here tonight to speak with you. We have a fight before us, and winning this is more important than any game—football, basketball, baseball. Those are just sports. I'm talking about life. And losing your life. I'm here to tell you about the drug pushers. These people poison our neighborhoods. They destroy our families. They—"

Hoyt felt his throat tighten and stopped, then forced the rest out.

"—they killed my son."

He looked out at the expressions in the crowd. Every pair of eyes rested on him in rapt attention. Parents sat alongside their children, most of them high school students, but many of them younger. He could see a small girl who must have been only five or six. Her face was pure innocence.

Tommy was that young once, pure, unspoiled, with a bright future.

Hoyt charged forward with his prepared remarks. He saw Sandy in the back, deep lines etched in her face, and drew strength from her. She had been a rock during his home rehearsal, helping to craft his speech.

"Don't hold anything back," she had said. "Don't be afraid to scare these kids, if that's what gets their attention. You are addressing a room full of Tommys. You can make a difference."

Hoyt told the crowd, "My boy was a real good kid. He loved football—the acorn doesn't fall far from the tree. Loved the Bears. He also loved to read, got good grades, had girlfriends, loved rock and roll. In that respect, he was like most of the kids in this room. He didn't start out bad, but somewhere along the way he walked through a wrong door. He fell in with a bad crowd. It was something I didn't recognize until it was too late. If I had realized it earlier, who knows. But by the time I got involved, he was already pretty far gone. It's something that haunts me to this day.

"In football, I could rip a hole in some of the finest defensive lines in the game. But I couldn't make a dent in my son's addiction. These drugs are strong. Kids, you must be stronger.

"You have choices. Think about what your goal is. In football, we just wanted to win. To have the best score. In life, your goal is to have a good career, a loving family, friends, some money and success, sure. Big house, nice car. You want to get all that, but what are you doing today to get you there? What's your game plan? If it's drugs, forget it. You will lose. You will get beat.

"Now, I understand about peer pressure and all that. But a strong person doesn't crumble to peer pressure. You just don't.

"As I'm up here talking to you all, I see a lot of heads nodding. You agree with me. That's good. But it's not enough to nod your head. Because the enemy is out there, and nodding your head doesn't send them away. To combat the drugs and the drug dealers, we need a good defense *and* offense. It's just like football. You can't win with only one or the other. And I am instructing you all, tonight, to put on your gear, become warriors, and FIGHT the enemy: *The evil scum who get our kids hooked on drugs!"*

Hoyt realized he was shouting now, his words booming from the speakers hung throughout the auditorium. He was straying from his notes.

But he didn't care. These kids and their parents had to hear it. They had to learn this one important lesson.

"We cannot sit back and expect our law enforcement and legal system to take care of things for us. I don't mean to offend anyone here, but the system has problems. It's broken and it needs to be fixed."

Hoyt hesitated. Now came the most difficult part. But he had to tell the story. Tommy's story.

"Two years ago, I had to struggle with the fact that my son had become a drug addict. His grades went down the toilet. He lost interest in sports. He sold his stereo equipment. He stole from me and from his mother to pay for his habit. We tried to help him. He *wanted* to get better. 'Dad,' he said, 'I don't like this, but I don't know how to stop.' The sickness was very bad. You can't just turn it off when those drugs infest your body. Tommy's source for drugs—the drug dealer—kept finding ways to get to him, to keep him hooked. He hung around outside the school. He came to our house when we weren't home. That cockroach of a human being deliberately got my son addicted, so he could profit off his addiction. He lured my son away from rehab, sucked away all his money, and then he took away Tommy's life."

Hoyt took a deep breath, then continued. "On a Saturday night, my boy came home late from a party, lay down in his bed, went to sleep, and never woke up. He was seventeen years old, same as many of you in this room. He died from a heart attack caused by a 'speedball,' a deadly combination of cocaine and heroin. It went into his body and stopped his life."

The room was hushed. Hoyt's voice started to crack. "The only . . . the only consolation I have . . . in my boy's death . . . is that the doctor told me he didn't suffer. He fell asleep and went into a coma, and his body gradually shut down. When I found him, it was the next morning. I was going to get him for breakfast. We were having pancakes, his favorite. I knocked on his door, but there was no answer. I walked inside and saw him lying on the sheets. His face was relaxed and peaceful. But he wasn't breathing. He was all pale. His heart had stopped. My boy Tommy was gone . . . our only son . . . lifeless in his own bed . . . and he's never coming back."

That's when the tears came. Hoyt had blinked them away several times, but now it was impossible.

The big Texan crumbled.

Fifteen seconds passed, then almost a minute.

When Hoyt had some composure back, he apologized. He had to finish his speech quickly. He had to make his final push into the end zone. He knew he should stick to his game plan—but his rage had taken over.

His final words were driven by raw passion, not speaking points.

"The man who destroyed my son continues to go free. He should have been locked up for life for manslaughter. He was arrested for selling drugs. He went to court and received a ridiculous sentence. It was a slap on the wrist. His lawyers said his apartment was searched illegally, so some important evidence got thrown out. This creep only spent a few months behind bars . . . took my boy's precious life . . . while Sandy and I now spend a *lifetime* devastated that our son is gone."

He was shouting again now. He brought it down a notch, but the fury continued to shake his words. "Today, this destroyer of lives is running loose, back in business. I can't get the police to stop him. He's out there, at this very minute, working to destroy someone else's children. Maybe yours. Are we, as a community, going to stand there and let it happen? When will we finally get fed up and clear the streets of this filth? *When?*"

The word reverberated around the auditorium. Hoyt crushed his notecard in his fist. He shut his eyes and took a deep breath. Then he spoke very softly.

"No family is immune from these beasts. It can happen to anyone. It doesn't matter your color, your religion, where you live, how much money you have.

Please, for the sake of your families, protect your loved ones. Don't let what happened to my boy happen to you. Look out for your friends, your sons, your daughters. Thank you."

Hoyt left the podium drained. The audience applauded, loud and supportive. Hoyt could barely hear it. All he wanted was to return to Sandy and embrace her and go home.

Hoyt patiently waited offstage as Principal Evans finished the program with a rundown of counseling services and after-school activities, concluding with a pitch for the T-shirts and caps.

With that, the Benton Park anti-drug rally came to an end.

Hoyt tried to work his way back to Sandy, but people rushed up to thank him for his stirring speech.

"No problem. Thanks," responded Hoyt, shaking hands, still dazed.

Emily, the event coordinator, approached with a box containing several footballs and asked him to sign them for a raffle to benefit the Benton Park substance abuse center. Hoyt obliged, signing the balls and offering to autograph any other items, whenever they wanted.

As Hoyt was signing the footballs, the Benton Park police officer walked past him and gave him a blank stare, but that was to be expected. Hoyt really didn't care about how the police felt. They had blown it worse than a ref missing a critical call on Super Bowl Sunday.

After Hoyt dealt with Emily's request, a man in a suit shoved a business card in his direction. He was an attorney. "Mr. Hoyt, I want you to know that under the Drug Dealer Liability Act, you can sue the dealer for damages in civil court. Not a lot of people are aware of that in Illinois—"

"I know," said Hoyt. "But I'm not interested."

"Can I ask what you're doing now? Outside of football?"

"I'm a sales representative for a glass replacement company," responded Hoyt.

"Well, I can't promise you NFL-type compensation, but I am confident that we could get a settlement that would be a very nice supplement to your current income."

Hoyt's tone grew firm. "Listen, I don't want his money. I want that bastard taken out of society."

"Understood," said the attorney, continuing to extend the business card. "But if you have a change of heart . . ."

"No," said Hoyt. "Sorry."

The attorney left and Hoyt was ready to finally make his way to the back of the auditorium. However, one last individual waited patiently for his attention.

Hoyt sighed and greeted him with a weary smile. "Hi."

"Mr. Hoyt, I was deeply moved by your words tonight." The man appeared to be in his early thirties, wearing round, wire-rimmed glasses and a full beard. He was several inches under six feet tall, appearing even smaller under the shadow of Hoyt's sturdy build and cowboy boots.

"Thank you," responded Hoyt. "I apologize for breaking down up there. It's only been a year, and I still have a hard time talking about it."

The man nodded. His eyes had an unusual intensity. "I understand. I sympathize with you, sir. In fact, that's why I wanted to talk with you."

The man leaned in, addressing Hoyt in a low tone. "I can help you."

Hoyt responded with a sad smile. He regarded the man politely. "I doubt it . . ."

"I'm talking about Douglas Decker," said the man.

Hoyt immediately felt a jolt through his heart. Just hearing the name, spoken out loud, felt like a dagger.

Hoyt stared at the man. "That's . . . the name of the dealer who killed my son."

"Yes, I know," the man responded, keeping his tone lowered. "Mr. Hoyt, would you like to see Douglas Decker go away?"

"You mean to jail? We've tried . . ."

"No," said the man. "Go away. Forever."

Hoyt examined the man. He could see from his face that he was dead serious. Hoyt took in a deep breath. He nodded slowly. He spoke softly and absolutely truthfully.

"More than anything in this world."

One

Chalk in hand, Rob Carus stood back from the vocabulary list he had just written on the blackboard and gave the students in his summer school class a moment to copy the words in their notebooks. The room became busy with scratching pens and pencils. Rob's eyes went to the clock on the wall. *Five more minutes.* Then he looked out the window for possibly the five-hundredth time. *Sky still blue.*

A TV weatherman last night had frightened Rob with a slight chance of rain, but so far, so good. He hadn't even spotted a stray cloud.

It was a bright and perfect summer day in July, and Rob Carus wanted to scramble out of Evanston Township High as desperately as any kid in the room. His mind was not on the curriculum this morning, and his students could probably sense it—the long pauses, his jumbled train of thought, and that obsession with looking out the window. No doubt, they could see the wandering in his eyes.

Ordinarily, Rob was more engaged in his teaching, but on this day he was getting engaged to be married.

Beth Lawter was destined to become Beth Carus; she just didn't know it yet. Here's what she did know: After Rob's second period class let out, freeing him for the afternoon, he was going to meet her at the bike rack behind the school. Then they were going to bike together to Lake Michigan, follow the lakefront into Chicago, and spend the rest of the day at North Avenue Beach.

As far as she knew, simply a fun summer day. Then, at sunset, the ring.

Rob was enthralled, intimidated, delirious, ecstatic, and about a dozen other words he could add to the kids' vocabulary list. He couldn't think of a bigger moment in his life, ever.

After reading about love in famous literature for many years, dismissing it as something abstract and conceptual, love had now reached in and grabbed him with a tight fist, with no signs of shaking him loose.

Beth was it. She was everything he had imagined when he used to mentally sketch his perfect companion—smart but not stuffy, funny but not silly, beautiful but not vain—

"Mr. Carus."

Rob shook away the daydreaming and saw that Jamie DaMask had been raising her hand, now tiredly propping it up with her other arm.

"Yes, Jamie?"

"I think you spelled *idealistic* wrong."

"No, I don't th—" He turned to the blackboard and

saw *idealitic.* That was embarrassing. "Holy cow, you're right."

"Do I get extra credit?" she asked hopefully.

"No, but I just flunked."

Some of the kids laughed. Rob grabbed the eraser and quickly fixed the spelling. Then he turned and faced his students.

What the hell, tell them.

"As you can probably sense, I'm a little distracted today. Tomorrow, I can tell you why. So that's an added incentive to be here. Don't worry, it's good news."

"Did you win the lottery?" asked Jimmy Alp.

Rob smiled. "Could be."

The bell rang.

The entire class lurched out of their seats, a collective force. Most of them had already closed and stacked their books several minutes ago.

Rob grabbed his large black gear bag from behind the desk. He waited until the last of the students filed out of the room, then followed into the hall.

Rob went into the faculty washroom and changed into swimming trunks, placing the engagement ring inside a plastic, waterproof inner pocket. He zipped it shut. He pulled a pair of khaki shorts over the swimsuit. Then he changed into a cream-colored T-shirt and gym shoes. As he emerged, the summer school dean, Theresa Crowe, saw him and said, "Hey! Cute knees!"

"Thanks," he responded cheerfully. According to the school grapevine, Theresa found Rob "hot," and he often caught her checking him out. She was a looker, too, but no Beth.

"I'm out of here," he announced. Rob walked the central corridor between the courtyards, headed to the back of the school and out the west exit.

The sun dumped heat on his neck and shoulders. It felt both good and uncomfortable. There would be no rain today.

Beth stood by the bike racks—her green Schwinn propped next to her—watching the activity on the outdoor running track. She wore orange shorts and a black tank top, her short blond hair pulled back into a tiny ponytail. She looked as youthful as the nearby students.

As Rob walked up, Beth saw his shadow approach and turned, then grinned. She took off her sunglasses.

"Hon," she said. He kissed her. "What a great day."

"The water temperature is sixty-eight."

"Always doing your research."

"I figure we'll be ready for a dip when we get there, to wash off the car fumes."

"I brought my swimsuit." She motioned to the bags on her bike. "I've got our lunch, too. We should probably fuel up."

"You think of everything."

"Somebody has to help the absentminded professor. You'd forget to eat, if I didn't remind you."

They found a grassy area near the athletic field and had their picnic. Beth brought out the sandwiches from Sig's Deli and cans of Coke. As they ate, she talked about her morning at the Skokie Rehab Center, where she worked as a physical therapist. Every day brought new anecdotes about the familiar cast of characters, ranging from stroke victims to hobbled athletes. He loved to listen to her dramatizations. They were funny, sad, inspiring, touching. She was a great storyteller.

During the recent weeks of planning this day, Rob had drilled himself with second-guessing: Is the timing right to get engaged? Should I wait? Will she be ready? Am I ready?

But now, sitting with Beth on the perfect afternoon, sharing laughs and conversation and Sig's sandwiches, watching her smile with the immaculate sky behind her, he knew that everything was right.

Rob checked his watch. Almost one o'clock. Probably another six or seven hours until he popped the question . . . and his life changed forever.

After lunch, they tossed their cans and wrappers. Rob attached his gear bag to the back of his bike, a sporty Trek 980. They encountered some students he knew and he introduced Beth to them. "Mr. Carus is cool," one of the kids told Beth. "He's not like the other teachers."

"I think he's pretty cool, too," said Beth.

Within minutes, they were in their bike helmets and heading east on Church Street, the journey underway.

They rode their bikes in single file when cars crowded the road, and side-by-side whenever there was opportunity.

"Pothole!" alerted Rob when sections of the road turned crumbly.

"Bad driver!" alerted Beth when inconsiderate vehicles approached too fast and close.

When they reached Sheridan Road, Rob and Beth took the Evanston Lake Shore Trail south. The glimpses of beachfront filled Rob with excitement. The lake breeze took the edge off the heat. The sidewalks were busy with Northwestern University students, many of them paired off in couples holding hands.

Entering Chicago's Rogers Park neighborhood, past the cemetery, the traffic—both cars and bicycles—became heavier, but they were ready for it, it was nothing new. This was the punishment that preceded the reward. Most aggravating was the stop-and-go succession of traffic lights and, of course, the fat, sluggish CTA buses with the hapless strings of cars behind them, brake lights popped on. Most of the cars had their windows rolled down, each blasting a different song to celebrate the summer, heads bopping inside, even as traffic sat motionless.

When Rob and Beth reached Chicago's lakefront bike path, it was like arriving at a party. Rob felt submerged into something big and wonderful and alive, a panoramic, pulsing energy. The climate seemed to bring the entire population outdoors. Rob and Beth joined a community of people taking the day off, all ages and races tossed together in a supersize salad: bikers, joggers, in-line skaters, baby strollers, dog walkers, tourists, big families, intimate couples, cops, the homeless, and others who defied categories. East of the path, huge crowds hunkered down to enjoy the beaches that stretched all the way downtown and beyond.

Rob and Beth passed Montrose Harbor, Waveland Golf Course, the Addison Totem Pole, the Fullerton "Theatre on the Lake," and came to a stop at North

Avenue Beach. It was already bursting at the seams, buzzing with chatter. Vendors hawked sunglasses, beach jewelry, and bottled water. Lifeguards sat in towering chairs. Food simmered on barbecues lined up on the grass. Police circled on horseback.

Finding a private patch of sand would be a challenge. Rob and Beth locked their bikes, and brought their bags to an area that was relatively calm, away from drunk yuppies, hip hop blasters, and diaper changers, and not in the path of a game of frisbee.

"My butt is sore," said Rob, dropping into the sand. "As my physical therapist, you have a duty . . ."

"Yeah, right," said Beth, wiping sweat from her forehead. "You can't afford what I charge my patients."

"I got medical insurance."

Rob removed his shoes and fell back on his elbows. Behind Beth, he could see a canyon wall of skyscrapers, with the black Hancock building reaching highest among its peers.

When Rob first met Beth, she was attending classes not far from the Hancock, at Northwestern's Chicago campus. She was studying for her Doctor of Physical Therapy degree at the Medical School.

At the time, Beth lived in an apartment in Evanston with a classmate. The two of them would frequent KAFINATE, a coffee shop on Central Street, where Rob often picked up a cup on his way to school.

He noticed Beth one day because she was laughing uproariously over something her roommate had said. Beth made an instant impression on him because he found her to be very, very cute.

In the weeks that followed, Rob probably saw her

seated at that same table eight or nine times before approaching her. His opportunity arrived when she sat alone one morning with a book.

Confederacy of Dunces by John Kennedy Toole. One of Rob's favorite novels—and definitely his favorite funny novel.

If you ever wanted to approach her, now is your chance, he told himself.

Shut up, don't pressure me, he responded.

He ordered his coffee and then wandered near her, pretending to notice the book in her hands for the first time.

"Hey, that's a great book," he said.

She looked up, and she smiled.

On that smile, he was sold.

They talked a little bit about the book, then about some other favorite books, shared recommendations, and after he stood there for five minutes, she invited him to sit down, and then the conversation really flowed, and he wound up staying half an hour.

Back at the high school, he found that his first period Freshman Humanities class had waited only fifteen minutes before freeing themselves.

Mary Pat, the department chair, wasn't pleased about his tardiness, but Rob managed to make up an excuse about car trouble, and it probably didn't sound good because he was a terrible liar, but that was okay, because . . .

. . . *he had gotten coffee girl's name and phone number*.

The next seventeen months were a wonderful ride, a romance that continued to reveal new layers, new joys. They both loved good books, analytical conversation, biking, and no bullshit. They discovered that they shared compatible tastes in music, movies, food, art, and sexual positions.

And she was that rarest of beauties: She didn't recognize her own good looks.

Intentionally or not, she often hid her beauty behind glasses with dull frames or oversized clothes, like a disguise. But when she dressed to the hilt for their first extravagant date—a Chicago Symphony Orchestra concert and French dining—it nearly caused his knees to buckle.

Stop that! he wanted to tell her. *If you keep that up, somebody's going to steal you away.*

Sometimes, in fits of self-consciousness, Rob didn't know what she saw in him. Physically, he considered himself nondescript—neither attractive nor unattractive, neither heavy nor thin—with average features and straight brown hair. He was always surprised when told women found him handsome.

On personality, he could be too reserved and analytical. He wasn't a good "party" person. In fact, he preferred the company of one person or a small group. At parties, he typically connected with a couple of people, stayed with them, and didn't mingle the rest of the night.

Rob's prior dating history was spotty at best. He had been hurt by women with a half-hearted interest in him. He had also dragged himself through relationships where he couldn't muster the appropriate level of enthusiasm.

When Beth came along, she was a revelation. She

wiped away a lifetime of cynicism about finding the right partner.

Rob's parents were divorced, and their subsequent relationships didn't fare much better. It created a cloud over his own expectations. He found deep and satisfying relationships with books, but women were a challenge.

Hank Thigpen, a geometry teacher at Evanston High and one of Rob's closest friends, once told him, "Your perfect mate is out there, somewhere. You just have to get off your ass and go find her."

Later, after Rob introduced Beth to a very impressed Hank, Hank told him, "Damn it, you screwed up, Carus. You didn't find your perfect mate. You found *my* perfect mate."

Rob knew the relationship had become serious when Beth wanted to bring him to her hometown to meet the parents. Rob spent a three-day weekend in Canton, Ohio, and her parents couldn't have been nicer. Mr. Lawter was an auditor at an accounting firm, and Mrs. Lawter worked in purchasing for an electronics manufacturer. They were down-to-earth and cheerful. Beth later told him that they gave him "two thumbs up." Much of the weekend was spent returning to her childhood haunts, looking at the homes of old friends, exploring parks and schoolyards where she once played, and revisiting her favorite hiding places at the library for retreating with a good book.

During the drive home from Ohio, on a long, dark stretch of highway, in a totally spontaneous moment that was also somehow perfect, he told Beth he loved her. She said she loved him.

Within a mile, he was convinced this was the girl he would one day marry.

And now weeks of anxiety had led to this day at North Avenue Beach. The engagement ring remained zipped in his swimsuit pocket. Every now and then, he touched it through the fabric to reassure himself that it was still there.

The ring accompanied him throughout the afternoon and she had no clue. They wandered up and down the beachfront, checked out the volleyball contests, watched the fishing on the breakwaters, and waded into the waves. At the beach house, a huge structure shaped like a steamship, they bought snacks and checked out the view from the upper deck. They roamed an open-air fitness center, a roller hockey rink, and the nearby chess pavilion.

Finally, they returned to their spot on the sand for some extended people-watching. As evening approached, the noise level dropped. There were fewer boomboxes booming and kids screaming. Pedestrians swarmed west on the Lincoln Park footbridge, which crossed over a congested Lake Shore Drive. Rush hour commuters merged with departing beach-goers.

Beth and Rob stayed. For dinner, they returned to the beach house and snagged seats at Stefanie's Castaways Restaurant. They feasted on Jamaican jerk chicken and several tropical drinks. They returned to the sand with a nice buzz. The sky remained clear.

A portable radio at a nearby blanket was blasting

"Now Is the Day," a new pop hit that was as irresistible as it was disposable. "I love this song," exclaimed Beth. "I don't know who does it and I don't care. It's just great beach music, don't you think?"

Rob had to agree that it had hooks, an infectious blend of reggae and bubblegum. He watched Beth dance in the sand, giddy and uninhibited. It made him happy to see her so happy.

Beth dropped, laughing, into the sand.

"How late do you want to stay?" she asked.

"Let's watch the sun go down."

"What a romantic," she teased.

"Are you in a rush?"

"Absolutely not." She smiled, eyes half-closed. "I'm so relaxed, I could crash here overnight."

They continued to people watch and talk, while Rob kept one eye on the sunset. He timed the big moment with the perfect visual accompaniment: as the sun hit the water just right and the waves sparkled against a stunning splash of orange and pink in the sky.

"This is so gorgeous," said Beth, and Rob was already reaching into the swimsuit pocket. He brought out the ring and kept it hidden in his hand.

"Beth."

She turned and faced him. Some of her short blond hair was flopped forward. He could see his reflection in her sunglasses.

"I have a question I want to ask you."

"Yes, teacher? Is it multiple choice?"

"Actually, it is."

"Okay, what are my choices?"

"Yes, no, maybe, don't know . . . does not apply."

She laughed. "I can pick one of those."

"Actually," he said, "this is serious. I'm joking because I'm nervous, but this is totally serious."

She dropped her smile, and actually appeared alarmed.

Shit, I didn't set this up right, thought Rob. No turning back, here goes.

Rob showed her the ring.

Before he could say a word, she gasped. Her mouth opened.

He handed it to her and she took it gingerly.

"Beth," he said, "would you marry me?"

She remained focused on the ring—half a carat, set in a white gold band.

She made no response. The silence caused Rob to feel an entirely unexpected pang of fear.

Then she reached up and removed her sunglasses. There were tears in her eyes.

"Yes," she said, voice cracking.

Rob felt his own eyes water and swallowed hard. *Damn it, I'm not the one who's supposed to cry.*

Beth put on the ring, admired it, then gave him the tightest embrace he had ever felt.

"Yes, Rob," said Beth. "Yes, I want to marry you. The answer is yes, yes, yes."

Her affirmation filled him with an overwhelming warmth and happiness. They remained on the beach, arms around one another, until the sky went completely dark and the moon came out. They talked about calling their parents the next day, and telling their friends. They began to plan their future together: a wedding the following summer, honeymoon in Hawaii, and, ultimately, trading two rents for home ownership.

"You know," said Rob, "this means we're going to turn old and gray together."

"I can handle that." Beth smiled.

The bike ride out of the city was serene and romantic. Their headlamps cut small paths of light. The moon followed in a race down the lakefront. The waves crashed to their right, the skyline glowed behind them, and sprawling trees stretched high above.

The trip back into Evanston zipped along at twice the speed of the journey into the city, with a diminished flow of cars, pedestrians, and other bicyclists. It was easier to shout conversation back and forth as they traveled the streets. Both of them were pumped up, giddy.

"Let's wake up my roommate and tell her," said Beth. "It will blow her mind. She was just asking me, 'So when's he going to pop the question?' "

"What did you tell her?"

"I told her I was going to give you until the end of the year, then *I* was going to propose."

"Really?"

"Serious," said Beth. "This is the twenty-first century. You think I can't propose? Except I would have done it in the middle of one of your classes, just to freak everybody out."

Rob laughed. "Then I could make them write a paper about it."

She mimicked his voice: "A 500-word essay on matrimony in contemporary society, due by Friday, graded on a curve, with bibliography and footnotes."

Rob suggested, "We could come up with a good vocabulary list. Prenuptials. Conjugality. Monogamous . . ."

Rob and Beth took a turn off Sheridan Road and headed west into a residential area. The streets became darker and empty, with only occasional motorists.

As they came within a mile of Beth's apartment building, they were met with a flashing arrow and diamond-shaped sign alerting "Road Work Ahead." The street quickly narrowed, crowded by silent excavation equipment and sawhorses with blinking lights. The lanes in each direction were squeezed, separated by concrete barriers. Rob and Beth moved into single file.

"Careful," said Rob, staying a good distance from the drop-off at the edge of the original pavement. Beth was close behind. A strip of road had been broken apart into rubble, exposing metal grids. Rows of cement rails alternated with stacks of sewer pipe inside the work zone.

"They're always tearing up the roads around here," said Beth.

Rob could hear a vehicle approaching, its engine humming. Large beams of light spilled ahead of them, gradually intensifying.

"Car," said Beth, hugging the side of the road. Rob turned his head to take a quick look.

A large, silver Range Rover was gaining on them. Rob realized it wasn't about to slow down.

"He's going fast," said Beth.

"There's nowhere to go," responded Rob.

"Hey!" She extended her arm and waved it frantically for the driver to see.

The front of the SUV came just short of the bikes, then reduced its speed, remaining very close.

Then the driver flashed his brights.

"What a jerk," said Beth.

"He'll have to wait until we get past this construction," said Rob.

The driver blasted the horn, loud. It sent the blood racing through Rob's veins. Exactly what did this guy expect them to do?

The SUV got closer, flashing its lights again.

"He won't back off!" exclaimed Beth.

Rob pumped his legs hard, peddling fast, and Beth kept up behind him. But the vehicle continued to bear down on them, its grille appearing like big, clenched teeth. This is dangerous, this is crazy, thought Rob.

As the front bumper of the SUV pushed closer to her rear tire, Beth became forced to the very edge of the road, inches from toppling into the excavation and crashing into one of the construction horses.

The SUV began to push alongside the bicyclists. The front of the vehicle squeezed past Beth, then reached Rob.

Rob frantically looked back and forth between the road's edge, the construction obstacles, and the oncoming SUV. He could see the outline of the driver, but nothing more, behind the tinted glass.

"There's no room you son of a bitch!" shouted Rob.

The massive silver vehicle continued to squeeze alongside both cyclists. The roar of the engine filled Rob's ears. The side door brushed his elbow, causing his balance to waver.

"You crazy—!" shouted Rob, infuriated. He

snatched his plastic water bottle from his bike frame and flung it at the vehicle. The bottle bounced off the passengerside window with a *thunk*.

The driver's response was immediate and deadly.

The Range Rover deliberately swerved to the right, sideswiping the cyclists with a loud *thud*. The impact propelled both bicycles out of control and off the road, crashing into the roadside construction. Rob was thrown headfirst over the handlebars. His eyes filled with a whirl of sky and pavement and lights. Beth's scream filled his ears. Their bodies skidded across the gravel and broken pavement, flung like rag dolls, bicycles tumbling behind them.

Rob landed against a section of sewer pipe, pain tearing through his body. He tried to quickly get back up, but his body wouldn't cooperate, fire ignited up his leg and spine, and he fell back down.

Rob's left arm was completely useless. He grabbed it and it felt like somebody else's arm. Lying on his side, he saw the SUV. The vehicle had stopped about thirty yards ahead.

"Beth," said Rob. He tore off his helmet. He forced himself to partly sit up, grimaced through the pain, and looked around. He saw her green Schwinn, horribly mangled, which petrified him.

"Beth!"

She was a dark shape, limp, curled against a concrete barrier rail.

Rob shouted away the pain and stood up, one arm limp at his side, one leg screaming. He staggered over to Beth. He looked down at her.

She was not conscious.

Rob spun toward the SUV, which remained stopped up ahead. He took several steps toward it. He screamed, *"We need an ambulance! Please! She's hurt! She's hurt bad!"*

The response was instant.

The SUV drove away.

Rob watched in horrified disbelief. He stared hard at the vehicle before it disappeared.

Illinois license plate: GX 113.

He recited it out loud. He burned it into his memory.

The road lit up. Another vehicle was approaching.

Rob stumbled into the road, dragging his bad leg. He waved an arm, blocking out the pain, screaming: "HELP!"

The lights engulfed Rob. The vehicle reached him and stopped. Rob stumbled to the driver's window.

The motorist opened it halfway. It was an older black man with graying sideburns.

"Please," said Rob, and he could tell by the man's expression that he was terrified. "My girlfriend has been hurt very bad. She needs an ambulance. It was a hit and run. Please . . ." Rob felt the blood on his face, a wetness covering his cheek and ear.

"I can call 911," said the driver, quickly grabbing a cell phone. "Hold tight. I'm calling 911."

"Tell them license plate GX 113," said Rob. "Don't forget."

"GX 113," repeated the driver. "Are you—?"

Rob left the car and staggered across the roadway. He fell, got back up, and forced himself over to where Beth remained motionless.

Rob collapsed in front of her, hitting the ground

hard. Her face was pale. Her limbs were twisted the wrong way.

"Beth . . . Beth . . ." Rob murmured. "Please be okay . . ." He started to choke on his words. The entire horrible scene started to dissolve, breaking apart into spots.

Then he passed out.

Two

Rob awoke in motion. He could see a steady succession of white squares, some of them illuminated.

Excruciating pain painted half his body. He was on his back, strapped and unable to move. The lack of control brought instant panic. His neck felt tight, like something was choking him.

Then he saw young men, two of them, at ninety-degree angles, walking hurriedly on either side of him. They wore dark shirts and pants, patches on the shoulder. Paramedics. The white squares and lights were ceiling panels.

He was being wheeled through a section of Evanston Hospital between the ambulance bay and emergency room. He could hear the swoosh of electronic doors opening.

"MVA coming in," called one of the paramedics. "Bicyclist hit by car."

Rob immediately felt a surge of horror overtake his confusion. It all came back and hit him like a punch:

the silver Range Rover, the construction zone, the sudden sideswipe.

"Beth," said Rob weakly.

After several turns, the gurney stopped. Rob was inside one of the curtained trauma rooms.

A new face peered over him. A woman with braided red hair. She wore a blue lab coat. Rob strained to get a better look at his surroundings and immediately felt new shockwaves of pain.

"Try to keep your head still," she said. Then, to someone outside of view: "Michael, get X-ray in here."

Rob realized he was wearing a neck collar.

"Do you know where you are?" asked the woman.

"Hospital."

"What's your name?"

"Where's Beth?"

"Please, sir, can you state your name?"

"Rob Carus. C-A-R-U-S. Her name is Beth Lawter."

"Can you feel or move your toes?"

"I don't think . . . Not on my left. Is my leg broken?"

"You've got a number of brokens."

"This thing is choking me."

"We don't want to remove it until we see a clear X-ray of your neck."

"Can you loosen—?" His words trailed off and his eyes drifted from her to the ceiling.

"We're going to give you an injection of Lidocaine for the pain."

"Thanks," he mumbled.

He never felt the injection.

Another doctor leaned over him, a man with big

glasses, big nostrils. Like the red-haired woman, his expression was blank, analytical.

"Vital signs are stable," said the woman.

"We need to clean him up," said the man. "He's still bleeding."

"My face itches," said Rob, and he couldn't do anything about it. The sheer helplessness made him want to scream. His face felt puffy, raw.

"He'll need a head CT," said the male.

"Where's Beth?" Rob asked. "I need to go see her."

"Sir, you need to stay right here."

Rob tried to sit up. Agony shot through his limbs. The two doctors quickly put out their hands to stop him.

"I'm sorry, but you can't—" said the male doctor.

"Just for a minute, I need to see Beth."

"Not now," said the red-haired woman, but Rob continued to struggle.

"Stop it!" the woman said, as if addressing a child.

Rob felt a fury wash over him. *"Take me to her, now."*

"Haldol," the male doctor said to someone Rob could not see.

"I just want to see my fiancée!" shouted Rob, with a final surge forward. Then he fell back on his pillow. His strength was quickly evaporating. Pain gripped him everywhere. He wanted to cry.

"I just want to know where she is," he said weakly.

Someone started cutting open his T-shirt. "Hey . . ." said Rob.

". . . broken left humerus . . ." said a voice.

Yes, thought Rob to himself, becoming delirious. Broken humorous. That describes it perfect.

". . . compound fracture . . . right tibia . . ."

"Broken humorous," muttered Rob, shutting his eyes. Beth would find that funny. He would have to tell her.

Another passage of time vanished into a black hole, longer this time, and when Rob awoke he was alone in a hospital room, laid out on a bed. Half of his body was immobilized. He wore a paper-thin, blue hospital gown. The neck brace was gone. Stiffness and aches covered his body.

Light came in through a window. Must be daytime, thought Rob, groggy. He could hear some small sounds in the corridor, chatter.

Beth?

He thought hard, but could not remember seeing her in the hospital or hearing about how she was doing. He had no information since finding her unconscious. Maybe she was in the next room? Or already discharged, waiting in the visitors' lounge?

"Hello!" said Rob.

No one came. Then he saw the button for the nurse and pressed it. And waited.

A nurse finally entered, a woman in her fifties with her hair in a bun and bags under her eyes.

"I need to see Beth Lawter, my fiancée."

The nurse simply said, "Let me get a doctor," and left.

Rob sighed. He couldn't get out of bed if he wanted to. His left arm was tightly wrapped and in a sling. His left leg throbbed in a cast that stretched from his toes to his upper thigh. There was a dull ache inside his head and a dryness in his mouth, having been asleep for the last fifteen hours. The only part of his body that was exposed was his right hand. He held it in front of his face. His palm was covered with cuts. He flexed the fingers.

Hey, something that's not broken.

A balding man in a white lab coat entered the room. He had glasses perched low on his nose. He carried a clipboard.

"Hi, I'm Dr. Bernardi, orthopedics," he said.

"I'm Rob, patient."

"How do you feel?"

"Hurts."

"Where's the pain?"

"Leg, mostly."

The doctor began touching different parts of his body, applying gentle pressure, moving limbs and joints very cautiously.

"That hurt?"

"No."

"Feel this?"

"Yes."

"How about that?"

"Ow."

"Okay."

Dr. Bernardi pulled up a chair and sat alongside the bed so Rob wouldn't have to strain to look up at him.

"The worst of it is your leg, as you can probably guess. You've got a compound fracture of the left tibia and fibula. Those are the bones of your lower leg, below the knee. It's going to require surgery to make an incision and access the bone. We think we can get you into surgery late this afternoon, fingers crossed."

Tibia, fibula, thought Rob. Vocabulary words.

"Your upper left arm is fractured, the bone between the shoulder and elbow, the humerus. Now, you probably have some pain in your upper back. That is the broken scapula."

"Scapula?"

"Your shoulder blade."

"I didn't know those break."

"Everything breaks."

"I learned that the hard way."

"Luckily, the joints are not affected, but your arm is going to have to remain in a sling for a few weeks. I don't think it's going to require surgery. We also closed an open wound in your back."

"Great."

"You've also suffered a concussion. The good news is there is no brain injury. There's no spinal cord damage."

"Okay."

He looked at his clipboard and found one more thing. "Oh, and a cracked rib."

"Why not . . ."

"Right now, we have your leg in a temporary plaster. In surgery, we are going to need to insert pins to stabilize the bone."

"Pins? Do you put me to sleep for that?"

"Oh, yes. We'll explain all that to you. You'll meet with the anesthesiologist."

"Is Beth doing okay?"

"I'm sorry?"

"My fiancée. We were both hit by the car. I haven't seen her since the accident."

"The police are going to talk to you more specifically about the accident."

The doctor stated it so plainly, that Rob took it as a good sign. She must be okay, otherwise the doctor would have said something or reacted to Beth's name with a cringe, or some kind of clue . . .

"When can I talk with the police?"

"They wanted to talk with you as soon as you were able."

"I'm able." Rob felt a rush of adrenaline. His head felt clearer, the world was coming back into focus.

"Okay then," said Dr. Bernardi, rising from the chair. "I'll get them. We'll talk some more this afternoon."

The wait was about ten minutes, but felt like an hour. Sitting there, staring around the room, became increasingly agonizing. His head filled with apprehension. *Beth had to be okay, not any worse than he was. She had her helmet on. But what if something happened to her spine? What if she was paralyzed? Or in a coma? Whatever the case, he would take care of her.*

He forced himself to be optimistic. She would show up in his room with bruises, bandages, maybe a crutch, but be okay. Her smile would remain intact.

Let me be worse off than she is, prayed Rob. Mess me up, but not Beth. Give it all to me.

Two police officers, both overweight, one with a mustache, entered the room.

Rob immediately tried to read their faces.

One of the officers shut the door.

"Have you talked to Beth?" asked Rob.

"Mr. Carus, I'm Officer Quiles. This is Officer

Bartholomew. Officer Bartholomew reported to the collision scene and is working on the accident report. I'm the detective assigned to the investigation, because we have some unanswered questions."

"So do I," said Rob quickly. "I need someone to tell me about Beth Lawter. She was riding with me, and I know she was hurt. The doctors and nurses won't tell me anything."

"Mr. Carus," started Officer Quiles, and he hesitated and looked at the wall. His face changed.

In that moment, Rob knew it was bad. The officer's tone, his eyes—if the news was good, there wouldn't be this awful silence.

Rob felt trembling ripple through his body. Then the police told him his worst nightmare.

"I'm very sorry, Mr. Carus. She was pronounced dead at the scene."

At the word "dead," Rob squeezed his eyes shut. He clenched his lips together.

"Her neck was broken," said Quiles. "She hit one of the concrete barriers."

"No no no," murmured Rob. This couldn't be happening. It was impossible. Less than twenty-four hours ago, the beach, the engagement, the perfect sky . . .

Officer Bartholomew spoke up quietly. "If you'd like some time to yourself, we can come back."

Images invaded Rob's thoughts. He kept seeing the silver SUV. Approaching fast. Headlamps bright, horn blasting. Hitting them in a single, swift movement.

"Don't leave," Rob said firmly. He swallowed hard. "We have to talk now. You need to understand this. Beth was murdered."

The two officers just looked at him, not saying anything. Did they doubt him?

"She was killed deliberately," Rob said, louder. "It was a silver Range Rover. The driver hit us on purpose. I know he did. It's a fact."

"Why don't you start at the beginning," said Quiles. "Go slow. We'll take everything down. Just take your time."

"The license plate . . ." Rob searched his memory. He began to panic. "I can't remember!"

"We have the license plate," said Bartholomew.

"You do?"

"Well, we have *a* license plate number from the motorist who found you and called the police. He said you gave it to him."

"Yes! I did!" Rob look at them both. "Then you have the person who did this?"

"Again—Mr. Carus. I think it's important that you tell us what you know. Every detail."

Rob replayed the entire event in his mind and recited everything he could remember. Some of it was a blur, some of it remained frozen and vivid, like snapshots. He described the construction zone, the huge Range Rover, the driver's eruption of road rage, the intentional sideswipe that knocked them off the road.

When he talked about finding Beth unconscious, curled up in the dirt and rubble, he broke down. Hearing it out loud in his own words made it more real and final.

The crying consumed him. It shook his chest and shoulders.

Beth was dead.

But he wouldn't let the officers leave to continue the conversation later. He pushed his way through to the very end. And he made sure to tell them again and again, in a shaking voice, until they were no doubt sick of hearing it:

"This was a homicide. This driver killed my fiancée. He wanted to harm us. He hit us with his car and drove away. I want you to arrest that killer and imprison him for the rest of his life."

The officers didn't offer any words of agreement. Not even an affirmative nod. They simply listened and took notes.

When Rob was done talking, he felt drained. He was soaked with sweat.

"Thank you for telling us what you know," Bartholomew said.

"Are you coming back?"

"One of us will be in touch after your surgery."

After they left, Rob looked around at the sterile emptiness of the hospital room and felt more alone than he had ever felt before in his life.

He broke down, this time into loud sobs. He prayed for someone to come and give him an injection that would put him to sleep and allow him to wake up somewhere else, in a different reality, safe and sound and back with Beth.

Rob spoke on the phone with both parents, his brother, and Theresa, the summer school dean. The conversations felt surreal and he barely understood the people on the other end, instead hearing his own horrible news. "Beth died yesterday . . . we were hit by a car on our bikes . . . it was a hit and run . . . no, I'm fine . . . I'm going into surgery for some broken bones . . . no, don't worry about me . . . it's Beth . . . I know . . . there's nothing you can do . . . I just wanted to tell you, so you know . . ."

He convinced his father and brother not to fly out, but his mother and stepdad were going to come see him, regardless of his protestations that he wasn't ready to host visitors. He finally allowed them to help out when he returned to the apartment. He was going to need assistance getting around, handling the basics—eating, sleeping, getting dressed.

Surgery lasted for several hours. It was another period of blackness, a sweet neutrality that ended with the shocking return of reality.

Beth is dead.

Those three words wouldn't leave his mind. They seemed to bounce off the walls and ceiling of his hospital room and swirl around him. He couldn't focus on anything else.

The surgeon inserted corrective pins into his leg: five screws and a titanium nail. He couldn't feel them, but could sense their presence under the morphine. Bandages saturated with plaster wound their way up his left leg. He had been told not to touch the cast, it would take a day or two to dry.

It already itched like crazy.

He ate Jello and a muffin when forced, but had no appetite. A heavy nausea hung deep in his stomach and he didn't know whether it was the medication, hunger, or shock.

Rob drifted in and out of short periods of sleep. His

sense of time was completely askew. At nine P.M., he was wide awake. He tried watching television, but the prime-time programming seemed more banal and irrelevant than ever.

Make-believe land. Laugh tracks. He watched an entire episode of something and absorbed none of it.

The television remained on for a newscast, and then something happened that he had never contemplated:

Beth's death was news.

The segment was short, sandwiched between a shooting and a rape, given equal gravity.

A hit-and-run "accident" leaving one woman dead and a man "seriously injured."

Then a brief snippet of videotape showing police officers talking to a gray-haired man in front of a large suburban home in the daylight. It was followed by footage of a police vehicle pulling out of the driveway—with the man sitting in the backseat.

The news anchor said the resident was Richard Shepherd of Glencoe, partner in a large downtown law firm.

"Shepherd was taken for questioning. No charges have been brought. Police say they are still investigating."

And as fast as the segment came, it disappeared.

Rob felt some relief. They found the driver. The police took him away.

Dear God, I hope they throw the book at him.

The next morning, a public relations representative for the hospital told Rob that the media had been inquiring about him. "We've given out just a basic update of your condition, that you're going to make a full recovery."

She made it sound unreasonably optimistic, when the truth was that he could never recover from what took place.

"A couple of reporters have asked if they could talk with you," said the P.R. woman, raising her dark eyebrows at him to encourage a response.

"No," said Rob flatly. "I'm sorry, but I'd rather not. Just have them talk with the police."

After lunch, Rob had started to doze off when he heard someone say:

"Knock knock."

Rob looked at the doorway. It was Hank, accompanied by Adrienne, the school principal, and Mary Pat, the department chair.

"Is now an okay time?" asked Mary Pat cautiously.

Rob shrugged. "Sure."

They lined up at his bedside. Adrienne had tears in her eyes.

"I want to hug you, but I don't want to hurt you worse," said Mary Pat.

"I probably wouldn't feel it anyway," said Rob. "I've got more drugs in me than Elvis Presley."

"Buddy, I am so sorry," said Hank. "I don't know what to say. I wish I could turn back the clock. This is horrible."

"Horrible," echoed Adrienne.

"She was such a great person," said Hank. "She didn't deserve this."

"How are you feeling?" asked Mary Pat.

"It hurts," he said simply. Pain inside, outside, everywhere. He described the pins in his leg and Mary Pat grimaced.

"You'll be setting off airport security and store alarms all the time now," said Hank, and it gave Rob his first smile since waking up in the hospital.

Hank displayed a large envelope. "The kids made a card. They really miss you, and they're all thinking about you and rooting for you."

Hank opened the envelope for Rob. Rob took the card with his right hand and skimmed the list of signatures.

"Appreciate it," Rob said. "Tell them thanks." Then he realized: "My classes. Who is going to—?"

"Already taken care of, don't worry about it, forget about it," said Mary Pat rapidly, holding up a hand.

They stayed for fifteen minutes, which was about all the conversation he could handle. When they left, he was exhausted.

Throughout the rest of the day, flowers began to arrive. They came from people in every facet of his life. Teachers from the school, students, friends, family, and even one of the neighbors in his apartment building. He received cards, too—a few of them were identical, probably bought at the same drug store.

Phil, a physical therapist from Evanston Hospital's rehab unit, came by to introduce himself and discuss Rob's rehabilitation exercises.

"We're getting you a modified walker with a brace for your left arm to rest in. You'll probably be able to use a crutch before too long, but for now you need the extra stability."

"How long before I can walk on my leg?" asked Rob.

"Hard to tell yet," said Phil. "But you should be able to graduate to a cane in eight to ten weeks, if all goes well."

After Phil departed, two more visitors arrived.

They caught him totally off guard, as he was not used to seeing them outside of Canton, Ohio. Not used to seeing them without Beth.

Her parents.

From their puffy faces and bloodshot eyes, he could tell they had been through a hellish forty-eight hours.

The three of them could barely keep a conversation going because someone was always breaking down. Rob told them about the afternoon at the beach, Beth's playful mood, and the marriage proposal. Mrs. Lawter asked his permission to bury Beth with the ring. "I can't imagine removing it," she said.

Rob agreed. The sudden thought of Beth always being "engaged" to him, even in some afterlife, gave him a sad spark of happiness. "I'd like that very much."

"I'm certain it's what she would have wanted," said Mrs. Lawter.

When Beth's parents finally left the room, Rob was more exhausted than ever. He slept through part of the evening and woke up shortly after ten P.M.

Check the news, he immediately told himself. Maybe the driver had been charged. An arrest with very high bail. He grabbed the remote and found one of the local networks.

The "Evanston Bike Tragedy" made an appearance after the first commercial break. After a quick recap of the situation, a distinguished-looking "spokesperson" for Richard Shepherd appeared on camera, talking to reporters.

"Mr. Shepherd is very upset," said the man who wore a crisp white shirt and yellow tie. "He is cooperating fully with the authorities. He was completely unaware of the bicycles. He heard a noise and thought he had bumped one of the construction sawhorses. Visibility was very poor."

The interview clip ended, and the story returned to the anchors, who wrapped it up with a brief comment about police continuing their investigation.

Rob stared at the television in disbelief. "That's a lie!" he shouted. He thrust the remote toward the television and switched across other newscasts until he found the Shepherd spokesman on another channel.

It got worse.

From a different angle, the spokesperson delivered his statement. Same setting, but another news crew, another well-rehearsed soundbite.

"This tragedy resulted from poor lighting and visibility in a city construction zone," said the spokesman, defiance rising in his voice. "When you combine that with cyclists who stray too far into a narrowed roadway, you have a recipe for disaster. There was nothing Mr. Shepherd could have done to prevent this terrible accident."

The segment ended and Rob screamed, "Bullshit!" He couldn't believe what he was hearing. It was lies. The SUV driver struck them deliberately with intent to cause harm. The driver even stopped to see the results and then sped away when Rob pleaded for help.

Who was this spokesman and where was he coming up with such nonsense?

Rob grabbed the telephone and dialed the Evanston police. He had to set things right as fast as possible.

When the front desk picked up, Rob asked for Officer Quiles—not available—what about Officer Bartholomew—not available—"It's important!" said Rob desperately. "I need to talk to them about a murder case."

Officer Quiles returned his call after twenty minutes.

"I understand your passion to get this resolved," said Quiles.

"Passion?" said Rob.

"But please trust us. We're still collecting facts. The accident report hasn't even been filed yet."

"*Accident* report?" shouted Rob. "This was intentional assault."

"Mr. Carus, we don't have the evidence at this point to file such a charge."

"How can that be?"

"First, we don't have witnesses."

"But what about me?" shot back Rob. "I'm a witness!"

"We don't have independent witnesses. We have a lack of evidence. We can't prove that he acted with recklessness or negligence. We can't even say he was speeding. It's a bad stretch of road. You hit the side of his vehicle. That's all we know right now."

"What about leaving the scene of an accident?" Rob was shouting.

Two nurses came into the room. "You're disturbing the other—"

"Richard Shepherd intentionally swerved to hit us," exclaimed Rob. "He stopped and watched us go down. What more do you need? A videotape?"

One of the nurses started reaching for the phone. "Sir—"

Rob tossed the phone to the floor. He wanted to thrash about in the bed, but he could barely move half his body. He fell back against the pillow.

"The other patients need their rest," said a nurse.

"I'm sorry," said Rob, breathing heavily, trying to calm down. "I don't want to disturb anybody. I think I'm losing my mind. I just found out that—" He decided to drop the details.

"Do you need something to help you sleep?" asked the older nurse of the two. She had a kind, round face.

"Yes," sighed Rob. "Knock me out."

Even when the accident report was complete and Rob obtained a copy, it offered no help. It was simply a list of facts about the location and parties involved with a little diagram. There was no blame attached.

After his discharge from six days in the hospital, Rob hounded the police on a regular basis. He rarely spoke to Quiles or Bartholomew anymore; usually he got stuck with the Public Information Office. They typically gave him the same response: No charges had been filed. The investigation continues.

"When you say 'the investigation continues,' exactly what is being done?" Rob would ask.

He wouldn't receive any significant answers, just the occasional remark about the police being very busy with a lot of cases.

Out of frustration, Rob finally reached out to the press. He spoke by phone to several newspaper reporters, telling his side of the story.

That brought out Shepherd himself. In the media, Shepherd vigorously disputed Rob's accusations of "road rage" and maintained that he was unaware that "bikes struck my vehicle."

On his computer, Rob researched Shepherd and confirmed his worst fears. Shepherd was a powerful attorney with a ruthless reputation. His law firm was characterized as a "juggernaut" that won most of its cases. He was a "five-star general" in the courtroom.

Rob's first few weeks back in his apartment were miserable. He couldn't get around and do anything. He could hobble, with pain. He wasn't scheduled to return to the high school until the fall semester. So he spent most of his days on the couch with ice packs, while various people came in and out of the apartment to help him with his recovery.

Hank visited often and delivered groceries, movies, library books, and Rob's Percocet prescription. He proved to be not only a good teaching colleague, but an invaluable friend.

A physical therapist named Kara came over once a day to help him with rehabilitation exercises. He had to maintain muscle tone and keep the blood flow feeding the tissues around the injuries. She also worked with him to establish careful procedures to accomplish simple necessities, such as bathing and using the toilet. Kara had known Beth from the PT program at Northwestern, and she offered heartfelt sympathy.

Rob's mother visited for a week with her second husband, a potbellied man named Herman. At least they provided entertainment. She harangued Herman constantly, with remarkable insults, but Herman was too slow-witted to respond or care.

"You sure have a lot of books," Herman said one afternoon, marveling over the packed shelves of Rob's bookcase. "Have you actually read all of these?"

"Most of them," Rob answered.

"I don't like to read books," said Herman. "Except books about TV."

Somewhere, Beth is laughing, Rob thought to himself.

Rob's mom and Herman stayed at a nearby hotel during the nights, and hung out in his apartment during the days.

When they finally left, his relief was quickly replaced by sorrow. As goofy and aggravating as they could be, they were a good distraction. Now he had more time alone with his thoughts. Not a good thing.

Over time, Rob gradually was able to put more weight on his bad leg. His upper body became sore from using the crutches and hoisting himself around. When his leg cast was replaced by a smaller one, starting below the knee, he got a look at how badly his gimpy leg had shrunken from muscle atrophy.

"That's what happens when you don't use it," Kara said. "Now it's time to learn to walk again."

When she took him for a stroll outside, he realized he hadn't been outdoors in a long time. The sunlight felt unusually bright. For weeks, most of his life had been confined to his living room sofa with books and newspapers. The twenty-six steps leading up to his second-floor apartment had been too much of an obstacle.

It was following one of his walks around the block that he returned to his apartment to find a message waiting for him on the answering machine. Since he was rarely out of his apartment, the blinking red light looked like a foreign object.

It was Officer Quiles, calling back with genuine news. He was turning the case over to the District Attorney's Office for review.

Rob called him back. "That's good, right?" he asked.

"Well, the D.A. still needs to decide whether to pursue prosecution."

"How long does that take?" asked Rob, feeling a sinking feeling.

"A few days, a few months," said Quiles. "Hard to say."

So Rob waited it out some more, keeping Beth's parents updated through e-mails.

In late August, Rob returned to Evanston Township High on crutches, and received a warm welcome from the teachers and students. He had a lighter class load than normal, and Hank was a gracious carpool partner, handling the driving chores until Rob could return behind the wheel.

"I'm going to pay you back when I can drive again, mile for mile," Rob promised.

"Buddy, you don't owe me a thing," responded Hank. "Just grow your leg back."

On a cool Friday morning in September, Rob received a call at home from a *Chicago Tribune* reporter, who informed him that the District Attorney's Office had dropped the case. The reasoning was "insufficient evidence" to file criminal charges. The reporter pointed out that a senior partner in Shepherd's law firm used to work in the D.A.'s office. Then he pressed for a comment.

"My comment is unprintable," said Rob.

Later, in the teacher's lounge, Hank could sense something was wrong with Rob, and the two of them went outside to talk.

Rob told him about the D.A.'s decision not to take action, and about the connection with Shepherd's law firm.

"Attorneys protecting attorneys," spat Hank.

They stood to one side of the basketball court, watching some kids in baggy shorts shoot hoops. Rob searched for words. "I'm shell-shocked. I'm too tired to even be enraged. Whatever happened to justice? My God, what is wrong with society? Is this some freakish situation, or is this the norm?"

"We live in strange times," said Hank. "This country has great ideals, but can't execute. The goddamn system's broke."

"Beth is dead, and Richard Shepherd doesn't even get a traffic ticket."

"You got screwed. You had the bad luck of going up against a legal gorilla. He's connected, he's rich. It's a no-win situation. It's a friggin' brick wall. Sometimes, I don't know, I guess you just gotta . . . move on."

"No," said Rob.

Hank looked at him.

"No, I'm not going to move on. I can't keep living

with this knowledge that Beth was killed, and her killer can just lie to everyone's face and go free. I can't put that in the back of my mind, ever. He took away her life. He took away my fiancée. He took away a daughter. Without any consequences. Nothing."

"So what are you going to do?"

"I'm going to file a civil suit against him."

"Against Shepherd?"

"Absolutely."

Hank grimaced. "Rob. You know I'm a straight-shooter. So let me just lay it out. You will be going up against deep pockets and an army of lawyers. They're not going to roll over for you."

"I don't expect them to," said Rob. "But I'm not going to give up the fight."

Hank gave Rob a long look, then smiled. "If it's a fight they want, then it's a fight they'll get."

"It's going to get ugly," said Rob.

Three

In his spring English Honors class, Rob assigned *The Count of Monte Cristo*. To keep his head in his schoolwork, he regularly assigned novels that had parallels with his mental state. The story of Edmond Dantes, a young man torn from his fiancée and imprisoned for life for a crime he did not commit, was a natural fit. In the novel, Dantes was condemned to the Chateau D'If prison, from where men never returned. However, Dantes escaped. He methodically extracted revenge on the people who destroyed his life, and ultimately reunited with his fiancée. A happy ending.

Rob was still struggling to find any kind of ending—happy or otherwise—to his own trauma. In a few months, it would be the one-year anniversary of Beth's death, but the horrible five-minute ordeal with the Range Rover continued to replay in his mind like it was yesterday. The civil suit was inching toward a trial. He had high expectations and great anxiety. The preparation exhausted him, but he continued to find fuel in his outrage that Richard Shepherd remained a free man.

Rob still found it utterly unbelievable that the malicious driver escaped charges of any kind. Not homicide, not reckless driving, not failure to render aid, not even failure to reduce speed to avoid an accident. Nada. The D.A.'s office had defended its decision not to pursue criminal prosecution by citing a lack of evidence that Shepherd had acted with negligence or a "willful and wanton disregard for safety."

"I cannot in good conscience approve felony charges based solely on the injured party's version of events," stated a Cook County Assistant State's Attorney.

Richard Shepherd was a free killer, but like Dantes in *The Count of Monte Cristo*, Rob was committed to extracting justice no matter how long it took.

He assigned his English Honors students an essay on the moral justification of Dantes's revenge.

Being in the classroom made his days easier, but the nights alone in his apartment continued to weigh him down with anger and depression. He studied the details of the upcoming civil suit with an academic fervor. He obsessed over Richard Shepherd's easy escape from prosecution. He thought about Beth.

Often, he dreamed about Beth in his sleep. Sometimes they were good dreams, reunited as if nothing had happened, sharing in some activity or conversation. But other times, it was a gruesome return to the accident scene and finding her dark and crumpled in the construction, not moving, not breathing.

Sometimes, he touched her, and she turned and

looked at him, alive and okay, and he flooded with relief and wept with joy and—

—then woke up to reality.

For several months, Rob had gone to Beth's former employer, the Skokie Rehab Center, for treatment to recover from his leg injuries. At first, he considered going elsewhere, worried that the spectre of Beth would be too much. But he learned to embrace her presence, not run from it.

The staff helped his recovery beyond the broken leg. He could talk freely with them about his pain on the inside, and that helped just as much. They, too, missed Beth greatly. They kept a picture of her in the office, and she watched him through his rehabilitation exercises, blue eyes warm, mouth corners turned upward into a slight smile.

He met several of the patients she had worked with, including a carpenter with a messed-up back and the parents of a little boy with leg braces from a birth defect. Most of them knew he had filed a civil suit. They offered their support and prayers.

"Anything for Beth," said Alice Brunner, a seventy-seven-year-old stroke victim Beth had aided to recovery. "She was an angel."

After the many months of physical therapy, Rob was able to get around on his own two feet with minimal limping. He could drive his car. He had achieved every goal in his time line. His visits to the Skokie Rehab clinic became less frequent, then ended altogether.

Meanwhile, his visits with attorney Donald J. Levin, Jr., became more frequent as they prepared the wrongful death civil lawsuit against Richard Shepherd.

* * *

Throughout the spring semester, Rob would meet with Levin at the high school during his free periods. They would sit in student desks in the back of an empty classroom, door closed, and discuss the case.

Despite ongoing intimidation from Shepherd's team of attorneys, the threatened countersuit never materialized. Shortly after Rob and Beth's parents filed the initial complaint, Shepherd had indicated he would file defamation and slander charges to protect his reputation and his law firm's business. When the countersuit never showed up, Levin speculated that Shepherd realized it would only feed the perception that Rob was a victim and Shepherd was the aggressor.

After Rob filed the complaint, Shepherd's team of lawyers responded with their own documentation of the "facts," citing Rob and Beth's "negligent conduct" and stating that the bikers "voluntarily and knowingly exposed themselves to danger" by traveling on a dark roadway under construction.

"They will do everything in their power to spin this as your fault," warned Levin. "The jury is going to feel sympathy for Beth and her parents. That's a given. They'll want someone to blame. So the defense is going to divert attention from Shepherd by making *you* the culprit for leading Beth to that construction zone. They will do everything in their power to make you the bad guy. It's going to get heavy. They are very aggressive and they are very smart. Don't let them blow your focus. These guys are professional assholes."

The civil suit sought compensatory damages for

Rob's medical bills, his rehabilitation, Beth's funeral expenses, and grief counseling for Beth's family, but it was the punitive damages that made headlines: two million dollars to punish Shepherd for his deadly and deliberate attack. "He's got the money, so if we win, we should collect," said Levin. "He might have to sell off some of the antiques in his Glencoe mansion, but he'll pay."

"It's not about the money," said Rob, and he didn't even fantasize about what he would do with his share of two million dollars. "It's about justice and letting everybody know the truth. It's for Beth. It's the only thing I can do for her and her parents."

That summer, prior to jury selection, Shepherd's attorneys made an attempt to settle out of court. They offered to pay some of the compensatory damages. "Basically," said Levin, "they will reimburse the expenses that you and Beth's family incurred. Hospital bills, the funeral, the bikes . . ."

The mention of the bikes set Rob off.

"They think they can make me go away by buying me a new bike?" he said, rising from a classroom desk, unable to sit still, shaking with fury. "That's all this is about? 'We'll pay you back for the bike.' *What about Beth's life?* How do they intend to pay that back? 'Mr. and Mrs. Lawter, sorry about your daughter, but we'll replace her Schwinn.' No. He is going to pay for killing Beth. It's that simple. Richard Shepherd is going to get crucified for the whole city to see. That will be our justice."

Jury selection began, and Levin remained optimistic Shepherd would be found liable. Following an afternoon of screening jurors, Levin met with Rob at the school, pumped with fresh enthusiasm.

"We did the right thing. A jury trial is definitely the way to go," said Levin. "We have an emotional case. The sympathy will already be on our side. It's not going to be with some rich attorney in a fat SUV. Today, the defense was working their butts off to try to eliminate anybody that might have even a slight bias against attorneys and law firms. Let's get real, who doesn't mistrust attorneys? I don't trust attorneys and I am one."

Apart from the jury, Rob had another advantage that he was not afforded during the pursuit of criminal charges: a lower burden of proof. There was no longer the need to prove Shepherd guilty beyond a reasonable doubt. Instead, Rob simply had to show greater evidence to prove his case than Shepherd. It would be a contest of persuasion.

"I feel good," said Levin. "But we can't let down our guard. They have an all-star team and deep pockets. It's David versus Goliath. But don't forget, David won that battle. He had his slingshot, and we have our secret weapon. We have the truth."

The civil suit was the most exhausting experience of Rob's life. The hit-and-run, as horrific as it was, happened at once and without warning. The trial, however, was preceded by a year of preparation and anxiety and strong emotions, culminating in a highly charged confrontation in a public setting.

In the early fall, the case was heard by the Law Division of the Circuit Court of Cook County under Judge Stuart Adams. The trial took place in downtown Chicago at the Richard J. Daley Center and attracted a strong showing of reporters from the city's media outlets.

Levin struck first in his opening statement, which Rob helped to craft. As Levin spoke, Rob stole glances of the jury's reaction, hoping for some clues to what they were thinking, but they remained impassive.

"The defense is going to bombard you with the word 'accident,'" said Levin. "They want you to believe this was a most unfortunate traffic 'accident'"—Levin drew air quotes—"like a fender bender. They are going to imply that the bicycles struck the vehicle. Let me tell you two things. First, the bicycles did not strike Mr. Shepherd. Mr. Shepherd struck the bicyclists. This is an important distinction. Second, Mr. Shepherd's actions were not accidental, but deliberate.

"In a classic case of road rage, Mr. Shepherd accelerated and assaulted two people with a deadly weapon, his eighty-thousand-dollar, 6,000-pound sport utility vehicle. With malicious intent, he swerved hard to his right, and in an instant, as swiftly as a gunshot"—Levin sharply clapped his hands—"he struck the bicycles and crashed the two riders into the construction, severely injuring Rob Carus and *killing* his fiancée, twenty-six-year-old Beth Lawter. Mr. Shepherd stopped his vehicle, coldly surveyed his two victims lying sprawled broken on the pavement . . . and then he sped away."

Levin stopped for a moment to let the imagery settle in. Then he said, "Why, you may ask, did Mr.

Shepherd choose to hit Rob Carus and Beth Lawter with his Range Rover? What provoked him to commit this heinous act, ending Beth's young life and destroying Rob's hopes and dreams? The answer . . . a plastic water bottle."

Levin then outlined Shepherd's motivation for the assault, replaying the sequence of events from Rob and Beth's point of view: being approached from behind by the bulky SUV, the SUV's refusal to slow down in the construction zone, the honking and flashing brights, followed by the SUV's mad attempt to squeeze past the bicycles. He described the vehicle's door striking Rob's elbow and Rob tossing the plastic bottle, which led to the fatal sideswipe.

"Rob Carus bounced a plastic water bottle off the passenger window of Mr. Shepherd's car," said Levin. "In turn, Mr. Shepherd reacted with spontaneous yet deadly road rage, striking the bicyclists with his SUV. It was that action that caused the two bikes to crash, and young Beth Lawter to break her neck."

Levin mimed holding a gun. "Just as a finger squeezing a trigger can end a life . . . the flick of Mr. Shepherd's wrist at the steering wheel ended Beth's life."

When the defense presented its opening statement, Rob knew what was coming, but it still blew him away: blatant lying. Shepherd's lawyers had created an elaborate fiction, and they were going to serve it up to the jury with all the manipulation and psychology of a public relations campaign.

The lead attorney for the defense was "Arnie" Hews, a soft-looking older man with glasses, thinning gray hair, and a decidedly dressed-down appearance. The slick and rich attorneys were going to do their damnedest not to look slick and rich. Hews addressed the jury in a folksy, grandfatherly manner, speaking to them in a voice that suggested they were all old friends. It made Rob sick to his stomach, because under this charming guise, Arnie Hews was dispensing cold-hearted bullshit.

"My client, Mr. Shepherd is not a spring chicken," Hews chuckled. "I hope he doesn't mind me characterizing him that way, but the point is this: He has fifty-three years of a stellar reputation. He has a long and impeccable driving record. No speeding tickets, no parking violations. He has a long and very dedicated track record of serving his fellow man, donating his time and money to charitable organizations and community needs, serving on boards, rallying behind fund-raisers, always going the extra mile to make people feel good. Richard Shepherd is an exemplary citizen, and the plaintiffs are trying to reinvent him, if you will, into a person he is not, never was, and never will be.

"They would like you to believe that Mr. Shepherd is some kind of blood-thirsty killer who runs down youngsters on their bicycles when they get in the way. The plaintiffs are hoping you will buy into this portrayal, and they have a lot at stake. They have sued Mr. Shepherd for two million dollars. So you will hear a lot of selling from the other side.

"I don't have to do much 'selling' myself. All I have for you are the simple facts, backed up by experts, and you will hear from them, independent analysts, about what really happened that night on Wesley Road. So please, put your emotions in check, because this will be emotional, and focus on the facts when you judge this case."

The witnesses for the plaintiffs testified first. An evidence technician from the Evanston police department took the stand. Rob's white plastic water bottle was put on display. The technician described his duties: measuring, mapping, and identifying physical evidence relative to crime and accident scenes. Then Levin asked him questions about the water bottle, and the technician described where he found it—forty feet up the road from the scene of the collision.

"Would you say the location of the water bottle was consistent with Rob Carus's account of throwing the bottle at the SUV prior to being struck by the vehicle?" Levin asked the technician.

"It is," said the technician.

However, during cross-examination, Hews deftly worked the technician over, getting him to agree that the mere placement of the water bottle didn't establish that it provoked a collision or that the object even struck the SUV.

"Essentially," said Hews, "are you telling the court that there is no real linkage between the water bottle and the accident, that the bottle proves nothing?"

"No direct link," said the technician, and Levin's fingers fidgeted nervously with his pen, while his face tried to remain unaffected.

The next witness, the African-American motorist who arrived at the collision scene, offered his account of finding the injured bicyclists and recalled Rob's horror-stricken description of a "hit and run" accident.

"I don't disbelieve your testimony for a minute," Hews told the witness during cross-examination. "However, you are merely repeating information that Rob Carus presented to you, is that correct?"

"Yes."

"And you have no real way of knowing whether this information was truthful or some fabrication?"

"Yes, I suppose."

Beth's mother took the stand next, and she broke down frequently as she described the emotional anguish, depression and fatigue caused by her daughter's death. She talked about Beth's dreams for the future, her PT job, her love for helping people, and her love for Rob.

"Beth was our only child," she told the court. "Every morning, I now wake up with a hole in my life. I hope no one in this room ever has to experience the pain I have in my heart, every single day."

The defense declined to cross-examine her. Mrs. Lawter offered no evidence regarding the collision, and merely outlined her family's grief to justify the damages they sought.

After medical staff from the hospital testified to Rob's injuries, sharing X-rays, the time came for Rob to take the stand. The courtroom became very quiet. He could feel his heart pounding in his chest, and a sea of eyes watching him—both sympathetic and hostile.

The clerk swore him in. Then Levin approached. He looked Rob directly in the eyes.

"Mr. Carus," said Levin. "Please tell the court what happened that evening of July 16 on Wesley Road."

For a moment, Rob feared he would not remember his well-rehearsed testimony, but once he started, it flowed. He told the entire story, beginning with the engagement at the beach, continuing with the bike ride north, and leading to the arrival of the silver Range Rover.

As he spoke, the images flashed before his eyes, an old movie flickering to life, silent, with abrupt cuts. When he described finding Beth's body, he broke down. Levin gave him a look, *good show*, but it wasn't a show, the tears were 100 percent real.

During cross examination, Hews did not have an attack tone. He still sounded grandfatherly, even sympathetic. But his words were going for the throat. Rob had drilled for a tough interrogation. But he soon realized Levin had not been tough enough.

"Let me understand something, Mr. Carus," said Hews. "At the scene of the accident, you suffered a concussion, is that right?"

"Yes."

"During your testimony, you provided us with a great amount of detail. Minute by minute, second by second, all with tremendous clarity. However—" Hews made a face like he had just swallowed a bitter pill. "Typically, we associate memory loss with someone who suffers head trauma. Is it at all possible—"

"No," said Rob firmly.

"Let the defense finish the question," said Judge Adams.

"Thank you, Your Honor," said Hews graciously.

"Mr. Carus—is it at all possible that you don't have a full and clear remembrance of the sequence of events just prior to, and directly after, your major head trauma?"

"No," said Rob.

"That's a pretty strong assertion."

"Yes," said Rob.

Hews kept going, picking away at Rob's testimony, point by point, and it seemed like it would never end. He got Rob to discuss the dark and dangerous conditions of the roadway and construction zone. He got Rob to discuss what Beth was wearing—a black tank top.

"*Black* tank top," said Hews, looking over at the jury. "Wouldn't it be reasonable to expect serious bicyclists, at night, to wear some kind of reflective clothing?"

"It was eighty degrees," responded Rob.

Hews spent an unusual amount of focus on the bicycles' safety equipment. Why only rear reflectors? Why no rear flashers?

And, finally, "When you saw the construction zone, which you admit to being dangerous, why didn't you just take another route? You're with the love of your life, it's dark out, you've admitted conditions weren't the greatest, why not simply find a better bike path?"

"There were no cars," said Rob.

"That was your thinking at the time?"

"Yes."

"That proved to be wrong, didn't it?"

Rob looked over at Levin, who was frowning. He looked back at Hews. "I suppose so, yes."

After a long and determinedly dramatic pause, Hews said, "One final question, if I may. Mr. Carus, you talked earlier of going to the beach with Beth, enjoying the sun, going to the clubhouse, and so on. You got engaged. You were in a celebratory mood, am I right?"

Rob stared at him and shrugged. "Sure . . . Yes."

"Did you consume alcohol?"

Rob felt his throat tighten. *Oh shit, that's where he's headed.* Rob opened his mouth, but no words came out.

"I'm sorry," said Hews. "I didn't hear you."

"Please answer the question," said Judge Adams.

"Yes," said Rob.

"Yes, you consumed alcoholic drinks?"

"Yes."

"Do you remember how many?"

"A few."

"How many is a few?"

He thought hard. It was over the course of an entire afternoon and part of an evening. "Three?" he said.

"Three apiece?"

Rob said, "I believe so, yes."

"Six drinks altogether," said Hews. "These six drinks, were they beers . . . ?"

". . . and margaritas."

"Six beers and margaritas," said Hews loudly, then turned to Judge Adams. "Thank you, Your Honor, I have no further questions." Hews left the final image of six alcoholic drinks hanging in the air as he returned to his seat with the defense team.

The next day began with the rollout of witnesses for the defense. They were professionals who made a living selling their "expert testimony" to trial lawyers. A construction scene safety expert showed slides of proper and improper construction zones and made the case that the conditions were ripe for an "unfortunate accident." He suggested the bikes' rear reflectors became "lost" in the flashing lights of the construction.

He was followed by a Traffic Accident Reconstruction Specialist with degrees from a Traffic Accident Institute. He was bookish and overwhelmed the jury with complicated analysis and jargon to support his simple findings that the collision scene was dark and it was entirely possible that Shepherd did not see the bicyclists and did not realize he had hit them.

Pointing to locations on a diagram with a red laser dot, the witness described Shepherd's field of vision.

"The Range Rover, as you know, is high off the ground. The point of impact clearly indicates the bicyclists were in the motorist's blind spot—a very risky place to be. There are numerous indications that Mr. Shepherd could not have seen the bikes."

When Richard Shepherd took the witness stand, he appeared humble and concerned, yet very dignified. He sat up straight and answered the questions clearly and firmly, with great conviction.

Hews asked him about his driving record. Immaculate. Hews asked him if he had been drinking alcohol prior to the accident. "Not at all," said Shepherd.

Hews paused, looked at the jury, then back to Shepherd.

Ever been charged with assault? No. Ever been charged with a felony? No. Ever been involved in a case of road rage? No.

After establishing his impeccable character, Shepherd eloquently described the events of July 16, making it sound like a mundane drive home from the office. He said he was not aware that "bicycles veered against the side of my vehicle."

"I did hear a thump," Shepherd told the courtroom. "I heard something bump against the right passenger door."

"What did you think it was?"

"I believed that the car had knocked against one of the construction sawhorses."

"Why didn't you stop to see? Weren't you concerned?"

"I was concerned," said Shepherd. "But I also realized it would not be wise to stop my car in the construction zone. It wouldn't be safe. The lanes were very narrow. So I cursed my misfortune about getting scraped and kept going. I wanted to keep the lane open to traffic."

"Were you aware that you had struck the bicyclists?"

"Goodness, no."

"Did it ever enter your mind?"

"No, it did not."

In his chair, Rob squirmed. He despised how casual the lies sounded. He looked at the jury. Were they buying this?

"If I had known that people were hurt, I would have stopped *immediately*," stressed Shepherd. "I had a cell phone. I would have called 911 to get emergency assistance to help those two kids. Make no mistake about it—I feel very, very bad about what took place. I wish *I* had taken a different route that night. I don't like construction zones any more than anyone else. Especially at night."

During cross-examination, Levin worked hard to grill Shepherd, sweating profusely, rushing his words out. Shepherd sat back, cool and collected, and batted away the questions like flies.

He denied everything. He never honked at the bicycles. He never flashed his brights. He never tried to hit anyone. He never knew they were there. He didn't stop his vehicle after striking the bikes to see the injuries and speed away.

Through it all, Shepherd made faces, clearly designed to influence the jury. There was his *is this guy serious?* face; his *what a silly question* face; his *of course not* face.

Levin chipped away, but could not get any new or useful information out of Shepherd, who took control of every question to spin things back to his own rehearsed answers. Levin looked weak.

After dealing with Shepherd, Levin was wiped. Rob wondered if he even had enough energy for closing arguments.

Fortunately, Levin's closing statement was strong, and lifted Rob's morale. Levin was reaching into a well of reserve energy. He was finishing on a powerful note.

"When a motorist kills with a vehicle, we tend to automatically label it as an accident," Levin told the jury. "But what happens when that motorist deliberately uses that vehicle to kill? Shouldn't that be homicide? Why should it matter that it was a Range Rover and not a gun? The result is the same: serious injury, loss of life. Two young people, engaged to be married, their entire lives in front of them, now ruined. One life shattered, one life ended. And what happens to the driver of the vehicle? Well, he drives away. And now he wants you to believe that it was all some sort of misunderstanding. He thought he hit a piece of plywood. And obviously he didn't bother to look in his rear-view mirror, because if he did, he would have seen the twisted bicycles and broken bodies in his wake.

"You cannot allow this man to call his actions an accident, ladies and gentlemen. We cannot shrug and say, 'Gee, that was too bad. No one's to blame.' Because a man *is* to blame. He sits before you. A man who became consumed by road rage. We have all heard stories about road rage, motorists who snap for a moment—and a moment is all it takes to end a life. To swing a three-ton SUV to deliberately hit two young bicyclists. It only takes a moment of rage, a moment of action, and you have a lifetime of devastation for Rob Carus and the family of Beth Lawter. Don't let them down. Show them you understand. Richard Shepherd is liable. And now it's time for justice for Beth Lawter."

In the closing arguments for the defense, Arnie Hews picked away at the plaintiffs' testimony, citing "expert analysis," and reiterating Shepherd's innocence.

"Folks," he told the jury, "the plaintiffs and defense can agree on two things. First, two bicycles collided with the side of my client's vehicle at dark in a construction zone on a dangerous road. Second, that this was a very tragic and sad accident. No one denies that. And anyone can understand the plaintiffs' desire to find a bad guy in all this. However, my client did not act in a manner that was deliberate, negligent, or reckless. He had the misfortune of being on a bad stretch of road at the same time as two bicycles. These bikers did not have rear flashers or wear reflective clothing. They had been drinking alcohol.

"Please remember what you heard in this courtroom. You heard expert testimony that described the probable positioning of the bicycles prior to the collision. The collision took place off to the side, where it was hard to see two bike riders who barely reached the window level. Two bike riders in the dark of night. Two bike riders on a narrowed roadway, among the confusion of excavation equipment, sewer pipes, blinking sawhorses, and other commotion.

"Mr. Shepherd had not been drinking. He was not speeding. *He broke no laws.* He cooperated fully when the police notified him that his vehicle had knocked the bicycles off the road. As you have heard, Mr. Shepherd did not know he hit the bicyclists. Such a horrible circumstance never entered his mind. If he had been aware that such a thing took place, he would have done everything you would have expected of a decent man. He would have helped the victims and contacted the police. This is a sad story with a sad ending. But it is a story without a villain. Often, we want villains. It makes it easier to accept tragedy. But sometimes bad things happen, and only good people are involved."

* * *

The jury deliberated for close to twenty-four hours and returned its judgment on a Tuesday afternoon in early October. Hank and several others from the high school were in attendance to lend their support.

Rob believed that although both sides presented their case convincingly, the truth would win out in the end. Everything came down to the simplicity of the facts. He was telling the truth, and the defense was not, and surely the jurors were able to pick up on that somewhere along the way. They could sense it, hear it in the voices, read it off the faces . . .

At 3:10 P.M., the jury foreman informed the deputy sheriff that a decision had been reached. The twelve jurors returned to the courtroom, and the foreman read the verdict.

Richard Shepherd was found not liable in the death of Beth Lawter and injuries of Rob Carus.

In an instant, Rob felt consumed by rage. Cheers erupted in the courtroom—Rob saw Shepherd exchange high-fives with his attorneys—Beth's mother erupted in tears and her father turned pale—then there was a string of boos, Hank's voice heard loudest—and the judge shouting for order—

"Nothing's over," said Levin, leaning in toward him. "We have a couple of routes we can take. We can appeal. We can try to sue the construction company for—"

"No," said Rob. "No." He couldn't continue this insanity. He had to get out. More than anything, Rob wanted out of the courtroom, away from Shepherd and his team of professional liars, away from the misguided jury, and away from Levin.

As soon as he was able, he made a direct line to Mr. and Mrs. Lawter, hugged them, and apologized. "Don't blame yourself," said Mr. Lawter. "You did everything you could."

Rob moved toward the exit, submersing himself in the wave of people leaving the courtroom. He heard Levin call his name. Then he heard other people call his name—voices he didn't know—reporters.

Rob avoided the reporters until he got outside the building. They seemed to be multiplying quickly, and all the commotion was somehow only fueling his anger.

He finally agreed to talk to NBC Channel 5. They had questions, but he didn't hear them. Instead, he delivered the only thought he had in his head at the moment.

"A man just got away with murder. Richard Shepherd murdered Beth Lawter, and he is a free man. He never even got so much as a traffic ticket. He's a murderer, that is a fact. There is nothing else to say."

Rob pulled himself away from the Channel 5 crew and began heading for the parking lot. He knew he had to get out of there before he said something really crazy. He was all raw emotion now. He couldn't focus clearly.

Then, out of the corner of his eye, he saw Shepherd. Richard Shepherd was speaking to a circle of reporters and camera crews. He was jovial, chatting away, and Rob started to walk toward him.

". . . obviously I feel sorry for this young man," said Shepherd, "but you can't ignore the facts . . ."

Rob lunged for Shepherd. Several hands grabbed at Rob and pulled him back. Someone said, "Whoa, buddy!" Cameras whirled to face him. Rob made one more lunge for Shepherd and bodies blocked him.

"That man is a killer!" shouted Rob. "Richard Shepherd is a liar and a killer!"

Even as he shouted the words, Rob knew he was losing it—and losing it on camera, no less. He shook free, turned away from Shepherd, and headed for the parking lot.

This isn't me; I'm becoming a lunatic, thought Rob, panting as he moved swiftly across the street, ignoring the cries of several reporters who wanted more of his flip-out performance for the 10:00 news.

When Rob made it inside the parking lot and through several rows of cars, people stopped following him. Rob climbed into his Nissan, fell against the seat, and rolled down the window to get some air. He closed his eyes. He was hyperventilating.

I can't drive like this, he told himself. *I need to calm down. I need to regroup. I am in control. I am in control.*

He had been sitting there for several minutes when he heard someone say:

"Hey."

Rob opened his eyes and turned, and there was a wavy-haired man with sunken cheekbones looking in his window. He looked angry. It was one of the lawyers on Shepherd's defense team. He had sat to one side of Shepherd, with Hews on the other side.

"Listen and you listen good," said the man in a tense, low tone. "You just lost the case. It's over. I suggest you get used to it real quick. Because if you're going to continue to badmouth Mr. Shepherd in front of television cameras, you will be sued. Your attack on Mr. Shepherd is not only a personal attack, it is an attack on his business. You hurt the practice and you're going to be signing over your teacher paychecks to us for the next ten years. If you say another inflammatory word, we will come after you for slander and defamation of character, and it will make this trial look like a picnic. *Comprende?"*

Rob stared at the man. He struggled to find words and finally uttered, "It's not enough that Beth is dead, now you have to start threatening me? Is that what you're saying?"

"I am saying you are lowly dirt. You have no one to blame for your girlfriend's death but yourself. So shut up and go away, or we'll come after you, and we won't stop coming after you. Maybe we can start with damages for the big dent you put in Mr. Shepherd's car."

The lawyer gave a pat to the side of the window, pulled back, and walked away.

Rob trembled. He felt something then that he had never before experienced in his entire twenty-eight years. It started deep in his belly, pounded through his chest, sent tremors through his arms and legs, then buzzed inside his head, spinning like madness.

Rob Carus, the soft-spoken high school English teacher, was mad enough to kill.

Four

The spin doctors went into overdrive.

Shepherd, while victorious in the civil suit, remained cognizant of his tainted image. He launched a reputation-management campaign wherein money was no object.

Hank brought a clipping to the high school one morning and shoved it at Rob, exclaiming, "Shithead's in the news."

Rob took it and read it. Two lines of copy buried in the Marketing Watch column of the *Chicago Tribune*.

The law firm Shepherd, Sundern and Hirsch had hired Zoppi and Associates for an undisclosed sum to oversee public relations for the practice.

The columnist wrote: "A spokesperson would not comment on the deal, but the reportedly lucrative agreement comes only two weeks after Richard Shepherd was found not liable in an emotionally charged and highly publicized 'road rage' civil suit."

"Must be nice to have your own P.R. firm to tell

others what they should think of you," said Rob, shoving the article back at Hank.

Hank took the paper and crumpled it. "All the P.R. in the world isn't going to make him a decent human being. He will always be a piece of shit."

One morning, when Rob was eating breakfast while reading the newspaper, he turned to a page of the Lifestyles section and nearly threw up his Cheerios.

Richard Shepherd grinned back at him. His face was smug, shoulders back, standing front and center in a group photo of Chicago's elite at a charity benefit. The men wore snappy suits; the ladies were draped in elegant evening gowns.

Rob read the caption—a fund-raiser for a city animal shelter and pet adoption program. Curiously, one of the women in the photo appeared to be wearing a fur around her neck.

Shepherd, the caption noted, had contributed a prize to the evening's raffle, a weekend getaway at his firm's suite at a swanky Manhattan hotel.

Soon, Shepherd's face was popping up everywhere. Clowning around with a magician at a party to raise money for a children's museum. Co-chairing a silent auction to support leukemia/lymphoma research. Grinning ear-to-ear, kneeled alongside a frowning older man in a wheelchair at a dance benefit for "mentally and physically challenged adults."

Then there was the lengthy article in *Chicago Business*, where Shepherd was positioned as a staunch advocate and provocateur of pro bono service. "Every attorney in this city has an obligation to allocate a portion of his or her professional services to the community," he said. "Our firm proudly leads the way and I hope others will follow. Too often, we just focus on billable hours. Sometimes you have to think about the legal struggles of the less fortunate."

There was a quote from somebody at the American Bar Association praising Shepherd as a role model for the entire legal profession.

Every word Rob read only made him madder, but he couldn't stop absorbing each story and reference. It was like staring into some strange, alternate universe where everything was backwards.

References to the wrongful death suit virtually disappeared as if it had never happened, except for one mention in *Evanston Life* that made Rob so infuriated he screamed out loud, probably scaring the hell out of every neighbor in his apartment building.

The article discussed new road construction in Evanston and measures the city was taking, like additional lighting, to avoid another "unfortunate accident." The reporter had called Shepherd for a comment. Shepherd praised the city's efforts and then commented on his heart-wrenching ordeal of being sued.

"I was under attack, and it was very traumatic for me and my family. You had a young man who was trying to finagle financial gain from his fiancée's death. It's the worst kind of greed."

Rob kept waiting for the day his anger would subside. But it wasn't diminishing . . . it was steadily rising.

He realized he was becoming obsessed. And at the core, he felt hopeless. All enjoyment of life had been sucked out of his soul. He couldn't find comfort or distraction in books, music, or television. Everything was a neutral wash.

Sometimes, he would stare at the phone and fantasize that he could pick up the receiver, dial, and become reconnected with Beth. Together they would discuss the absurdity of it all—laugh, maybe—and find a way to rise above the blackened moods.

Many times, he tried to burn off his anger through physical exertion. He biked north, often into Wisconsin, adding up miles and ignoring pain. His bad leg would ache insanely. He would exhaust himself. Brain pain would be overwhelmed by physical pain. For a while, he might forget, a little bit.

Rob continued to correspond, via e-mail, with Beth's parents. They were the only people on the planet who could relate to his sorrow. One afternoon, he returned from school to find a package from the Lawters in his mail. He brought it into his apartment and promptly opened it.

Her parents had sent a stack of photos belonging to Beth. Photos from their relationship. Many of them he had never seen before. Pictures at random parties, at holiday gatherings, and from his Ohio visit.

On the back of most of the photos, she had handwritten little blurbs in felt pen. They were funny and colorful, pure Beth. He stared at her familiar penmanship, rereading the comments again and again, savoring them. It was like a brand new conversation, a reconnection. He spoke out loud, responding to her observations, and it made him feel good.

That night, Rob had a very vivid dream. He had his hands around Richard Shepherd's throat. Shepherd's eyes bulged. He was choking Shepherd to death.

While Rob had hired Levin on a contingency fee—a percentage of the potential award—Rob still had a chunk of out-of-pocket legal costs to pay. There was an itemized list of filing fees, deposition fees, service of process fees . . . all adding up to a sum he could not easily cover on a teacher's salary.

Rob began to juggle his monthly bills, postponing payment on those items with the lowest interest rate. Often, he didn't send checks until he received threats of disconnected service. Through it all, he managed to keep the phone, electric, and gas going.

Rob had added more classes to his teaching load, and that helped. The kids in his courses were unusually well-behaved and responsive, which was good because his fuse had definitely been shortened. He was "the teacher whose girlfriend got killed."

It was hard, but he managed to bring humor back into the classroom. And he continued to assign books that spoke to his inner state. He baffled his Freshman Reading students with Camus's *The Stranger*. They were too young to comprehend its grim, existential tone and absurdist trial. They didn't get it. They didn't have the necessary war wounds.

For most of his students, trauma meant pimples, or curfews, or being picked last for softball in P.E.

Ah, youth.

Aside from his first week back, he didn't talk about

the tragedy, and they didn't ask. But there definitely was a vibe in the air. The kids acted differently. In most cases, that was fine.

But then there was Maureen.

Maureen was a junior, and she was in two of his classes, Expository Writing and English Honors. She was quiet, introspective, and an excellent writer. On more than one occasion, he had read her essays aloud to the class.

Sometime during the fall semester, Rob realized Maureen had a crush on him.

It began with staring. He simply noticed she was looking at him all the time. He saw it most during class writing exercises. Most of the kids would be focused at their desks, scribbling away, or chewing on their pens and pencils, deep in thought. Maureen would be stealing glances at him.

When their eyes connected, he would smile back. *Hello.*

Her smile would widen. Then she would look back down at her paper.

Thirty seconds later, she would glance at him again.

He couldn't resist the urge to check to see if she was looking . . . but he didn't want to appear like he was reciprocating.

Early on, it just amused him.

Later, he grew worried.

In Expository Writing, he asked his students to write an essay about something they were passionate about. He received the usual papers about the Bulls and the Cubs, PlayStation, TV teen dramas, chocolate, or the latest Christine Aguilera CD.

Maureen wrote about her "secret love."

"He is an older man with eyes that contain great wisdom," she wrote. "He has deep feelings and a sad heart. Sometimes, I want to hold him, and him to hold me. We are two broken pieces that could join together to form a beautiful picture. He knows I exist but does not know the deepness of my feelings. I am afraid to speak out, but sometimes I think I will burst. My passion hurts because it is trapped inside."

Rob read the four-page, single-spaced essay and tried to convince himself it wasn't about him. He didn't know how to grade it. Writing-wise, it was probably an "A" . . . but would that somehow send her the wrong signal?

He gave her a B+.

Before long, she started to hang back after class in order to walk out the door with him and share some conversation.

At first, it was simply, "That was a great lesson today about dangling modifiers."

But every day, she grew a little bit bolder, a little more personal. "Are you doing anything fun this weekend?" she asked on a Friday.

"No, not really, just . . . stuff," he said, trying to keep moving. But a couple of chatterboxes blocked the door, and he was stuck alongside Maureen, and she kept the conversation going, despite his attempts to lead it into dead ends.

One afternoon, she told him she wanted to be a short story writer. "Can I show you one of my stories?" she asked. "I know this isn't a fiction class, but you're the best writing teacher I know."

He agreed to review her short story. She eagerly gave it to him.

The story was about a young high school student who romances an older man following the tragic death of the man's wife in an airplane crash. The young student's love heals the older man's pain, and after she graduates, they become married.

Oh shit, thought Rob.

He agreed to meet with her during a free period the following Monday to provide his "critique."

They met in his office. He kept the door open. She wore a very short skirt and a tight sweater that made the most of her junior curves. She had applied an overdose of lipstick. She sat next to him in a cloud of perfume.

She was undeniably a pretty girl, hair parted in the middle, cascading long and flat on either side of her oval face. She wore her sleeves long, practically down to her knuckles.

She leaned in.

He leaned back.

She continued to try to shorten the gap between them.

He told her the truth, that the story was well-written. He said the writing was a bit flat in places and instructed her to better utilize all the senses. He pointed out descriptive redundancies, struck out unnecessary verbosity, and circled awkward word choices.

His criticisms, while delivered delicately, appeared to sting. She didn't nod or say anything. She bit her lip and leaned her chin on her palm.

After a few more suggested edits, he said, "There's a lot of feeling behind this, and that's good, it's just the mechanics of bringing it to life."

She was staring at him. An uncomfortable silence passed.

Then she asked, "Mr. Carus, how come you don't have a picture of Beth on your desk?"

He looked at her, stunned. He didn't know what to say. "I do at home."

"Do you still love her?"

"Yes."

"I'm sorry about what happened," she said. "I cried when I heard about it."

"Thank you," he said, and he quickly found a run-on sentence in her prose and brought it to her attention.

Rob later told Hank about Maureen, and Hank asked, "Is she cute?"

"Cut it out," said Rob. "It's a delicate situation."

"I know, buddy," said Hank. "But believe me—it's not uncommon around here. Do you want me to spread a rumor that you're gay?"

"Only if it's with you," said Rob, and Hank laughed heartily.

"You just made a joke!" Hank exclaimed triumphantly. "That means you're on the mend."

Hank's mission in life became to find Rob the next Beth.

He began to introduce Rob to new women and set him up on dates. At first, Rob was reluctant, but he knew that he had to make the transition sometime. He couldn't mourn forever. He knew that Beth would want him to seek new companionship. It was truly time to let go.

And, who knew, maybe lightning would strike twice.

His first post-Beth date was a pale graphic designer named Janey who didn't smile or talk much. Janey was a coworker of Hank's girlfriend, Ellen. They worked together at a small company that published trade magazines for manufacturers.

The four of them went to a restaurant in Chinatown and picked Szechwan and Cantonese dishes out of an illustrated menu. Hank talked a lot to fill the awkward silences. When Rob asked Janey about her job, she simply said, "It's boring, really."

After dinner, they went to a blues club to catch one of the local legends. The music drowned out conversation. Janey stood rock-still, while everyone around her bopped to the music. Rob stole frequent glances at Janey and drank several beers, but came up feeling empty.

The next morning, in the teachers' lounge, he told Hank he wasn't interested in Janey.

"We have nothing in common. The chemistry's just not there," he said.

"I'll find you chemistry," promised Hank. Then he proceeded to fix Rob up with a morose woman who recently lost her boyfriend in a tragic accident. The boyfriend worked for the electric company and had been electrocuted.

"Don't ever do that again," Rob told Hank after the date failed dismally.

Hank swung the pendulum in the other direction

for the next set-up. He introduced Rob to Lorraine, an outgoing and vivacious kindergarten teacher. He promised she would be "fun."

Rob took Lorraine to the Chicago Museum of Contemporary Art. She wore a cashmere V-neck sweater with aggressive cleavage. She was short, but made up for it by wearing dramatic heels. She stepped around the museum as if tottering on stilts.

She kissed him, without warning, when they were alone in an exhibit room, observing "Untitled part 2." There were slides of faces projected on big white pillows on the floor. A small stereo hummed with something like insect noise mixed with a dripping faucet.

It was a bizarre setting, and not particularly romantic. The kiss, too, was bizarre and not particularly romantic. She bit his tongue.

Lorraine left him messages four times in the next five days, and when he finally called back it was to politely bring the relationship to a close.

"Forget about Lorraine," said Hank. "You're going to go crazy for Ericka."

This time, it was another double date with Hank and Ellen in tow. They had drinks at a piano bar, then dinner at a bustling Italian bistro.

Ericka bragged about drinking five cups of coffee a day and never stopped talking. She had tousled black hair that looked permanently wet, and wore a black pantsuit. As she gulped red wine, she talked about her job with a kitchen cabinetry company and seemed to be delivering a sales pitch.

"My kitchen is very small," said Rob.

"Then I can get you a good deal," she responded.

Each glass of wine turned up her volume one notch. Rob tried to probe for a common connection—books, biking, philosophy, old movies—and came up empty. Eventually, he found himself talking more to Hank than Ericka. They started talking about the latest budget cuts at ETHS.

I might as well be in the teacher's lounge, thought Rob.

As he sat there, Rob did feel the evening was succeeding on one level—he was starting to relax. Each date felt less tense. He could almost imagine sitting across from someone he could be crazy for. But who would that be?

Then, just before dessert, the restaurant tortured him.

A steady drone of pop music had been playing through ceiling speakers, and he hadn't paid it much attention, but all of a sudden as fast as a slap—

—he heard Beth's song. "Now Is the Day." The reggae-bubblegum tune that caused her to dance lightheartedly on the sand at North Avenue Beach. The sky had been sheer blue, they were moments away from engagement, the whole world was exhilarating and sublime, and the future was big—

The song sent his emotions crashing. Rob put down his drink. "I have to get up," he heard himself say.

Rob left the table. He moved quickly through the restaurant. The music seemed to follow him—it seemed to get louder—

Beth Beth Beth.

He pushed through the men's room door and stopped at the sink.

There were speakers in the men's room, too. The song, exuberant and sunny, continued to play.

In the mirror, he saw the tears on his cheeks. He turned on the faucet and washed them away with cold water.

The song ended, but remained in his head. It was like a mounting, brutal pressure. It shook him. And there was no relief in sight.

Rob stood in the extravagant lobby of One North Franklin, hands in pockets, watching the elevators. It was the end of the day, and the elevator doors were regularly splitting open and spitting out office workers headed for home. Bodies in business suits weaved past marble columns. Loud footsteps criss-crossed across the granite floor.

It was perhaps six o'clock when Richard Shepherd emerged from the second elevator bank. His gray hair was neatly slicked across his head. He wore a black tuxedo with a festive, powder-blue bowtie. His arm was around an older blond woman in a sleeveless red dress. From afar, she was very pretty. As she neared, Rob could see the unnatural tightness of plastic surgery, the phony frosted hair, and the way her teeth seemed bared in a permanent grimace.

"Mr. Shepherd," said Rob, approaching their path.

Richard Shepherd's head jerked in attention. His steps shortened.

Rob felt his heart hammering in his chest. This was

the first private encounter between them since the night Beth was killed.

Rob saw Shepherd's gaze go from blasé to recognition to alarm.

"Mr. Shepherd, my name is Rob Carus."

"We're on our way to a function," said Shepherd curtly. The woman joined him in delivering Rob a cold stare.

"I only want a moment of your time," said Rob, and then he delivered the line that he had been rehearsing for weeks, the root of everything that had been tormenting him for more than a year, the catalyst that had driven him downtown to track Shepherd to his law firm's headquarters.

"Look me in the face and tell me it was an accident," said Rob.

Shepherd turned away, tugging the blonde with him. He headed for the revolving door leading outside.

"Tell me it was an accident," repeated Rob. Then he shouted, full blast, "LOOK ME IN THE FACE AND TELL ME IT WAS AN ACCIDENT!"

People in the lobby turned to stare. Rob heard his voice echo back at him. He raised it to a new level of intensity, his words raw with fury.

"Richard Shepherd, I demand you stop and look me in the face and tell me that Beth Lawter's death was an accident!"

"Security!" hollered Shepherd, stopping to signal to two men in silver vests.

Rob caught up with Shepherd, nearly breathless with emotion. "All I'm asking . . . is for you to look me in the face and tell me that it was an accident. I want you to *LIE TO MY FACE.*"

"Congratulations," responded Shepherd cooly. "You will soon be the proud recipient of a restraining order. You will not intrude on my personal space again. If this happens again, I will have you arrested. I will prosecute. And may God have mercy on your pathetic little soul."

Rob heard footsteps clicking behind him. Two men each took ahold of an arm. They began shoving him toward the exit. A pool of observers had gathered by the doors.

The security men brought Rob outside the building and then stayed with him to make sure he didn't try to follow Shepherd. Rob saw Shepherd and the frosty blonde blend into the pedestrian traffic. They headed down the street and disappeared around a corner.

"Don't come back, or you'll be in real trouble," said one of the security men, a young guy with a weak mustache over his lip. They backed off, while keeping their eyes on him.

Rob left the front of One North Franklin Street. He left the financial district. He left the Loop. He kept walking northeast.

He returned to North Avenue Beach.

Rob sat on the sand at the spot where he had proposed to Beth. As the sky surrendered blue to black and the wind blew cold, he looked heavenward and spoke to the night.

Rob begged Beth's forgiveness for failing to bring her murderer to justice.

Five

Shortly after the lobby confrontation with Shepherd, the headaches began. Sometimes he woke up with them and they lingered all day. Other times, they snuck up on him during school, growing steadily throughout the succession of classes, until he was a wreck by tenth period. It was as though a giant pressure was building in his head. A pressure he could not relieve.

Sometimes the headaches got so bad, he felt hallucinatory. One afternoon, moving between classes, he saw Beth leaned into a locker, hugging a three-ring binder to her chest, talking to a small circle of friends, letting loose with her glorious laugh.

Of course, it wasn't Beth, but some fresh-faced student with the same short, wavy blond hair, bubbly voice, and lanky frame.

She continued to haunt him.

In efforts to get Rob to let go of Beth, Hank had been setting him up on dates, but they were consistently disappointing and only reinforced his longing for his lost love. The capper to his dating spree was Theresa Crowe, the summer school dean. Everyone from the administration down to the freshman class knew that Crowe was interested in Rob, and now, with Hank as her coach, her light flirting graduated to a full-blown campaign to launch a relationship.

"Go for it," urged Hank. "What's not to like? She's curvalicious."

"That would be a nice vocabulary word for my students," said Rob, "except that you made it up."

When Rob and Theresa finally went out for a Cajun dinner, things began okay. But then, Theresa, perhaps trying to showcase the depth of her empathy, brought up Beth. It was the wrong door to open because Rob spent the rest of the dinner talking about Beth in such extreme terms that Theresa felt humbled. By dessert, she gave up any hopes that romance was possible.

"You can't let go, can you?" she said to him, sadly.

"I'm sorry," was all he could say in response.

In his mind, no one could measure up to Beth. Beth had become an angel. Richard Shepherd had become the devil. And everyone else had basically dropped off the face of the earth.

One afternoon, as Rob drove home from school, one of his raging headaches burned a fire behind his left eye, forcing him to shut it. Cyclops behind the wheel, thought Rob. *Now all I need is for the other eye to go, and I can drive off the road into Lake Michigan.*

It had been another day of struggle. The students in his eighth period English Honors class were starting to rebel against the relentless series of heavy and morose books he was assigning. They wanted escapism. Perhaps they wanted Harry Potter.

Instead, they got Sylvia Plath's *The Bell Jar*, a harrowing journey through a young woman's severe depression and descent into insanity. He had asked the students to research and write a paper on Ms. Plath's mental state and personal experiences when she wrote the book. He let them discover for themselves that Plath committed suicide one month after *The Bell Jar*'s publication.

The only student who seemed to connect with the book was Maureen. She stared at him, chin leaned into palm, while he read passages from the book. After one class, she marveled over how "deep" the book was, with "real feelings," and how Esther Greenwood's nervous breakdown moved her to tears. "Sometimes I can relate to her," she said.

"We all feel a little crazy sometimes," Rob responded. "Some of us more than others. But we're not inherently crazy. We're just reacting to a crazy world."

One eye remaining shut, Rob arrived at the parking lot behind his apartment building, finding a space in the back. He parked, grabbed his brown briefcase and stepped out of the car.

As Rob walked toward the entrance to the front lobby, he noticed a man standing nearby. He was short, with a face lost behind glasses and a heavy brown beard. He appeared to be waiting for someone to come out—or arrive. Rob didn't give him another thought, until—

The man said, "Excuse me, are you Rob Carus?"

Rob stopped with his hand on the lobby door. His first thought was: *Collection agency*. He was still struggling with debt after the lawsuit. He was slowly catching up . . . but certainly there were some unhappy campers out there.

"That's me," Rob responded with a heavy sigh. The headache pulsed like a heartbeat. He forced both eyes to stay open.

The stranger said, "My name is Trey Wright. I'm familiar with your case against Richard Shepherd, and I want to talk with you about it."

Rob gave him an uneasy look. "Are you a reporter?"

"No," said the man. "You could say I represent citizens who are the victims of gross injustice."

"You're a lawyer? Listen, we already tried a civil case . . ."

"I'm not an attorney. Attorneys aren't the answer."

Rob allowed a small smile. "Tell me about it."

The man made his pitch then in a direct, businesslike tone. "I want to discuss an alternative for extracting damages. Are you interested in hearing more?"

"I don't know. I suppose so. What are you talking about, exactly?"

The man fixed Rob with a serious, unblinking gaze. "It's best that we go somewhere and talk, in private."

"You can't tell me here on the sidewalk?" said Rob.

Behind them, a woman approached and entered the building. Wright waited until she was inside and replied, "I'm afraid it would not be in our best interests."

What is this? wondered Rob. He looked Trey Wright

over. He really didn't want to invite this stranger into his apartment . . . but his curiosity was getting the best of him and he wanted to hear more.

"There's a bar down the road, two blocks south of here," said Rob. "It's called Halftime. Let me drop off my schoolwork, change out of my sportscoat, and I'll meet you there in, say, fifteen minutes."

"Fifteen minutes." The man immediately looked at his watch.

"Give or take a few," said Rob.

Then the stranger showed emotion for the first time. He smiled. "Good. See you there."

Rob was not a regular at Halftime, but he wasn't a complete stranger, either. It was a squat building with thin windows and a giant, black, antiquated satellite dish perched on the roof's edge like a pterodactyl. Inside, the patrons were a loose mix of blue collar guys and gals unwinding after work, Northwestern students strayed from campus, and old-timers within shuffling distance of nearby apartment complexes.

Rob entered and tasted smoke and stale air. He adjusted to the dim light and found Wright in the farthest possible corner, his hand wrapped around a drink. Rob circled past the billiard table and slid into the chair across from him.

"What are you having?" Wright asked.

Rob glanced at the neon brands decorating the back wall and picked green. "Beck's."

Wright waved over a woman in a white apron, her hair in a frazzled bun.

"A Beck's and another Scotch on the rocks," he told her.

She departed and he told Rob, "Don't worry, I got it."

"Thanks," said Rob. "So . . . what's this all about? Why are you stalking me?" He smiled to indicate he was joking, but Wright nodded seriously, pulling at his beard.

"I saw you on television," responded Wright. "After you lost the civil case, they showed you outside the Daley Center. You lunged at Richard Shepherd and had to be held back. You were shouting at him."

"Yes," groaned Rob. "I'm very embarrassed about that."

"You don't need to be," said Wright quickly. "Your rage was genuine and justified."

"I was infuriated out of my mind," said Rob. "All that had happened, all the stress leading up to that point, I basically lost my head. I had lost my fiancée . . . and Shepherd had this smug, arrogant smile . . . I can't describe it. I snapped, basically. I guess it did make for good TV."

"I followed your case in the newspapers, too," said Wright. "From the first report of the hit-and-run, all the way through the trial coverage. I was right there with you. I was on your side."

"Thanks," said Rob. "A lot of people have come up and said how they supported me and how I got screwed. But in the end, it doesn't add up to a whole lot. I've got the world's greatest collection of sympathy cards, but Beth is still dead, and Richard Shepherd is still a free man, running around town in the Range Rover he used to ram into us."

"I take it you're still angry," said Wright.

"Yes. I thought it would go away over time, but it doesn't. If anything, it builds."

"The anger you felt at that moment when you lunged at Shepherd . . . do you still feel that? That fire, does it still burn?"

"Yes," said Rob, matter-of-factly. "The fire still burns."

The drinks arrived. Rob waved away the glass and took the bottle. Wright consumed a swallow of Scotch.

"I know your story. Now let me tell you mine," said Wright. "Because there are some strong parallels I think you would appreciate. We have both endured tragedy followed by injustice."

Wright looked down, focused and studied, as if reading words off the tabletop. "Two years ago, my father was murdered outside a Chicago nightclub. It started as an argument with another patron inside the club. It continued outside, where the other person became violent. They attacked my father with a brick. They took the brick and hit my father in the head repeatedly, shattering his skull. He later died."

Wright looked up from the table and locked eyes with Rob. "My father's killer said the attack was self-defense. Nonsense. My father could yell and argue with the best of them, but he never hit anyone, ever. He had no record of violence. It was murder, pure and simple. We pressed criminal charges, and the whole thing went to court. I thought we'd get justice . . ."

Wright went silent for a moment. Rob heard the *click-clack* of billiard balls, murmuring chatter, a sports talk show on TV. He could sense what was coming.

"There was no justice," said Wright. There was a hard look in his eyes, behind the lenses of his glasses. "We got fucked over. There was a witness who lied under oath, and it was accepted as eyewitness testimony. They spun a story where my dad attacked first, that my dad was some kind of blood-thirsty animal who put the defendant's life in jeopardy. It was a joke. Never mind that my dad was twice the age of his attacker. Never mind that my dad had no history of assault. Never mind that my dad was unarmed, that he had arthritis and could barely make a fist.

"All it takes is a clever attorney, some lies and manipulation, a clueless jury, and the next thing you know, a murderer goes free. A criminal escapes. It's not the first time, and it's not the last time. There is something seriously wrong with our so-called advanced society when this type of thing is allowed to happen, time and time again."

Rob found himself nodding. In many ways, Wright's story was no different from his own. He felt oddly soothed that he was not alone . . . and freshly angered over the futility of it all.

"After the trial ended, I felt like you did," said Wright. "I wanted to attack somebody. I looked at that killer in that courtroom, and I was looking into the face of Satan. My father had been viciously and savagely beaten until he was barely recognizable. At his wake, his face looked like someone else. All I wanted was justice, but the system failed me. There wasn't a thing I could do about it."

Wright took a drink of Scotch, exhaled loudly, and said, "I wanted that killer destroyed. I thought about it every hour of every day. But I couldn't act. Everybody knew how vengeful I was—the cops, everybody. The story was in the papers. If anything happened to my father's killer, I would be the number one suspect. My reward for extracting justice and protecting society would be spending the rest of my life in jail."

Wright gave Rob a long look then and asked, "Do you ever fantasize about killing Richard Shepherd?"

Rob nodded. "Sure. I mean, I imagine it. I wouldn't—I couldn't ever actually do it."

"And why is that?"

Rob chuckled uneasily. "For one thing, I could never get away with it. Everyone would know it was me. The guy's got a restraining order on me. I'd feel good for about five minutes but then it's like you said—I would go straight to jail, and then I might as well be dead, too."

Wright nodded. Then he asked, "But if you knew a way to get the justice Beth deserves, without any trail leading back to you, without any danger of arrest, would you pursue it?"

Rob said, "Yes. Sure." He thought Wright's question was purely hypothetical. But Wright responded with a thoughtful nod and long stare. He sat up. He ordered them another round of drinks.

After the drinks arrived, Trey Wright told Rob Carus about "The Circle."

"You are not the only person I have spoken to. I have been meeting with other people with stories just like ours. They are victims from the Chicago area, from the inner city and the suburbs. The common denominator is that we have lost a loved one and faced a breakdown of justice. Some of these tragedies date back several years. Some made news, some did not. But none of them have been resolved. I am pulling us together to create a collective force. An exclusive group. I call it The Circle. We have but one goal. To eliminate our enemies, while protecting ourselves from prosecution. Rob, I want you to join The Circle. However, before you answer me, I need to make one thing very clear. If you choose to join, you cannot discuss our activities or share this information with anyone. This is an underground society. We are bound to one another by total and absolute secrecy."

Rob felt consumed by fear and curiosity. A cold sweat tickled his scalp. Wright was dead serious. His eyes were intense. He was opening a doorway to some kind of possible resolution. It was a light in the darkness. But at what cost?

"How will this circle . . . society . . . thing . . . work?"

"I am not at liberty to discuss that here. Rest assured, the 'how' will come later. Right now, I need to know if you are accepting of the concept."

"What will happen to our enemies?"

"They will be gone."

"What do you mean, exactly, by gone."

"Again, that is not a conversation for today. If you are coming on board, there will have to be an element of trust."

Rob's head was swimming. "Then I can't . . . say anything definite. I can't accept."

"That is your right." Trey sighed and pushed away his drink. "So you're out? You're okay with the way things are today?"

"No. I'm not okay. I'm not out. I'm just . . ."

"You need time to think about it?"

"Yes. Can I have . . . ?"

"One week," said Wright.

Rob nodded. "I should know in a week. I just have so many thoughts and emotions riding on this. You can understand?"

"I can understand," said Wright. "It is a complex decision. Not everyone takes me up on this offer. In fact, many people don't make it this far into the conversation. I have good instincts, and I weed out the weaklings early on. But you—my gut says I can trust you, Rob. That's why I have extended this offer. You are one of the chosen."

Rob simply nodded. He noticed he was gripping the side of the table tightly.

Wright stood up. "I will call you in one week."

"You need my phone number?"

"No. I have your number."

Wright left the bar and did not look back.

Rob stayed to finish his drink. The decision already weighed him down. Throughout the bar, there was the criss-cross of banal chatter about sports, women, billiards, lousy jobs. Meanwhile, anchored alone in a corner of the room, Rob Carus contemplated murder.

For the first few days, Rob settled on rejecting Trey Wright's offer. The Circle was ambiguous. It sounded dangerous. It was against the law. And what exactly would it accomplish? It wouldn't bring Beth back. The damage had been done. Would The Circle really establish any justice for Beth Lawter? Or would it merely be vengeance for Rob Carus?

He weighed the moral implications. He tried to be analytical. But then the emotions started to get in the way and it was a brand new ballgame.

"Hey look, it's our old friend asshole!" cried out Hank in the teachers lounge one morning. He showed Rob the business section of the *Chicago Tribune*.

Sure enough, there was a photo of Richard Shepherd's smarmy face, walking out of a courtroom with bulging files under his arm, conversing with the CEO of one of Chicago's public utilities.

The CEO was embroiled in scandal, under federal investigation for allegedly defrauding customers of millions of dollars through shell games on the balance sheet. The law firm of Shepherd, Sundern and Hirsch was defending him.

Everyone seemed to agree that the CEO was guilty. And the general consensus was that he would be acquitted after a long and drawn out trial that would cost the taxpayers more millions.

However, it wasn't so much Richard Shepherd's choice of clientele that fueled Rob's ire. Instead, it was his face.

Somehow the photo triggered flashbacks of Shepherd's arrogant expression when Rob confronted him in the lobby of his building . . . and Shepherd's smug smile in the courtroom when he beat the wrongful death rap. Rob could clearly imagine that same arrogant and smug face behind the wheel of the Range Rover when Beth was struck and killed.

The face of a man who knew he could get away with anything he wanted without any consequences. Someone who felt he owned the world.

The *Tribune* photo drove Rob closer to the edge. A few days later, he was prodded again.

On a Tuesday afternoon, after class, driving home from the high school, he had the car radio on. A song leapt out of the speakers that tore his heart apart.

It was the song from the engagement day at North Avenue Beach. The cheery piece of bubblegum pop that caused Beth to laugh and dance on the sand. The same song that had tormented him at the restaurant during his date with Ericka.

The music brought back such an overload of emotions that he had to snap it off, kill the radio, essentially killing off the presence of Beth, too, sending him into blinding tears and mass confusion. He pulled to the side of the road and screamed profanity into the windshield.

The next day, when Trey Wright called, Rob only needed to tell him two words: "I'm in."

Wright promised Rob he would be back in touch and hung up.

Six

Justin Hoyt sat in his favorite chair, a chair big enough to accommodate his huge frame and soft enough to sink into comfortably for the entirety of two college football games. His den was layered in the oak shelves and cabinets he had installed himself many years ago to hold the memories. Neatly aligned around the room, there were trophies, plaques, team pictures, game balls, and dramatic framed stills of his glory days with the Redskins, Cardinals, and Bears.

The most prominent space in the room, however, was devoted to Tommy. Propped on a wide, centered shelf space with plenty of breathing room, sat a color shot of Tommy in his green and black high school football uniform. It was from his sophomore year, and he was all smiles and muscle and good looks and focus, before the drugs seeped in and rotted him with slow motion decay.

Often these days, when Hoyt watched football on his thirty-six-inch television, his eyes would move to the portrait of his lost son, and he would merge the two worlds.

Tommy would be in college now. Big 10. He would be playing football. Most likely, he would be a star player. There would already be a buzz about this wonderful, amazing talent. NFL prospect. But he would have to graduate first, get his degree. That was for sure.

Another thing was for sure: Tommy would not be a fullback like his dad. Once upon a time, the fullback was the backbone of the running game, but now it was a dying position. Most fullbacks had essentially been reduced to blockers with occasional charity catches. As football evolved, Hoyt was having a harder time identifying with any of the players on the field.

It was another cold disconnection from the past.

Today, as Hoyt watched Michigan trounce Ohio State, he was saddened to realize how passionless he had become about football. Occasionally there was mild excitement over a play, or a genuine interest in the outcome, but more often it was blank indifference. And as he viewed closeups of fans and players, he kept catching glimpses of young, healthy college kids. It haunted him. *Tommy should be right there with the rest of them.*

Every now and then he would even see some boy who looked like Tommy. Same kind of strong face, bold eyes, square jaw.

Frequently, Hoyt's mind tormented him with the searing accusation *you could have saved him. It's your fault he's not with those kids right now, inside that stadium, having the time of his life.*

It was a notion that tore him apart many nights. Most horrible was the recurring dream where he was standing in a corner of Tommy's bedroom, watching the drug dealer scum inject his son with the fatal dose. Tommy was reluctant, but the dealer continued anyway, slapping the forearm, finding a vein, and pressing the needle deep into the flesh.

In the dream, Hoyt would try to scream for them to stop. But nothing would come out. They could not hear him. Hoyt would try to rush the bed to intercept the deadly dosage, but something always held him back—it was as if his feet were stuck in mud, or there were invisible blockers, and he couldn't gain yardage . . . and could only watch in horror as the injection continued. Then Tommy's eyes would roll back, white, and the drug dealer scum would *laugh*.

"We'll be right back!" On the wide-screen television, the score read Michigan 27, Ohio State 3. A commercial for car insurance came on. Hoyt heard Sandy shutting the front door. A moment later, she entered the den while sifting through a pile of mail.

"You've got something," she said, pulling out a padded, legal-sized manila envelope. She walked over and handed it to him.

"Retired ten years and you're still getting pictures to sign," she mused.

"Yup, then they sell 'em on eBay for three bucks," responded Hoyt, and it made her chuckle. Sandy left the room with the rest of the mail.

Hoyt looked at the package. Then he felt a small jolt and blinked.

The return address was nothing more than a drawing of a circle.

And in that moment, Hoyt knew exactly what it was.

Two days earlier, Trey Wright had alerted him by phone: "It's time."

"I'm ready," Hoyt had responded.

"You will receive a package at your home in a few days. Do not allow anyone else to open it. Do not tell anybody its contents. The package will include a map and directions. It is the where. It will not include the when. That I will tell you now. Please listen carefully. Are you ready?"

"Yes."

"December 10. Twelve midnight. Come alone. Don't be late. Don't park within one hundred feet of the destination. Do you have that?"

"Yes."

"The Circle is closed, and we are ready to begin. You will be there?"

"Damn right," said Hoyt.

The Michigan-Ohio State game returned, but it was a faraway noise. Hoyt continued to stare at the package. He listened for Sandy. She was in the other room, probably returning to her needlepoint. Needlepoint was her way of keeping busy, channeling the nervous energy into something productive. It was part of her therapy.

Hoyt's therapy was in the package in his hands. He went to a desk drawer, found scissors, and cut open the top of the envelope. He slid three items out.

The first was a map printed off one of those Internet map services. He saw O'Hare International Airport and thought, What the heck?, but then realized the destination was someplace near the airport, adjacent to the tollway, a motel. Traveler's Inn.

The second item was a slip of paper with only a few printed words:

DO NOT BE LATE.
ROOM 16.
KNOCK ON DOOR, WEARING ANONYMASK.

The third item was the anonymask. It was a thin, leathery black face mask with two holes for eyes, an indent for the nose, and a strap to hold it in place. It looked like something for a costume ball.

This is fruity, thought Hoyt, staring at it. It reminded him of that shrill musical Sandy dragged him to for their anniversary years ago . . . *The Phantom of the Opera* . . . the longest three and a half hours of his life.

Hoyt heard Sandy's footsteps approaching and quickly shoved the items back into the envelope.

"Autograph seeker?" she asked casually.

"Yup," said Hoyt.

"You want some lunch? I was going to fix something."

"A toasted cheese would be nice," said Hoyt.

"Saturday afternoon: college football and toasted cheese," she said with a smile. "How could I forget. And a ginger ale."

"Thanks, hon," said Hoyt. "You're the best." After

she left the room, Hoyt hid the package under some old *Sports Illustrateds* in a cabinet.

On December 10, he told her.

Not any specifics. And he was relieved to discover she didn't even want to know. She was supportive and understanding. Her loyalty was a rock. It was pure Sandy, and he loved her to death for it.

"I have to go out tonight, and I won't be back until very late," he told her. "It's for Tommy. I can't tell you anything more than that. But it's a good thing, I promise. You just need to trust me, Sandy."

She merely nodded. Tears welled up in her eyes. "All right, hon," she said. "Do what you have to do. Just tell me you'll be safe."

"I'll be fine. I promise."

He hugged her tight in his big arms. He rested his chin on her head. They swayed.

"I love you, girl," said Hoyt.

"I love you, big guy," she told him.

Hoyt pulled back gently and kissed her on the forehead.

Then he left the house.

Seven

The sky was black, squeezing out sleet that smacked against the windshield of Rob's Nissan. The tires hissed through wet, shiny streets. The wipers engaged in their rhythmic dance.

Rob made a left turn into the parking lot of JoJo's, a twenty-four-hour restaurant brightly lit to reveal perhaps two dozen people inside. He parked away from the other vehicles in a far corner, facing the road. He shut off his lights, killed the engine.

And he sat in the darkness.

It was midnight. Across the street, a pink neon sign on a post tried to announce Traveler's Inn, but enough letters had burned out to create a puzzle worthy of *Wheel of Fortune.* A smaller neon sign below said VACANCY.

Just beyond the motel, Rob could see a steady stream of cars and trucks streaking across a stretch of Highway 294. The lanes were elevated, winding through the thicket of hotels and motels that crowded the outskirts of the airport.

Traveler's Inn, or rather Traelr nn, appeared to be an overnight stop for the very budget conscious. It had two stacked rows of small units, each consisting of an exterior door with a number and a single large window framed by heavy curtains. The second floor was identical to the first, except for a long white railing. Paint peeled indifferently. The whole thing looked very 1950s.

Rob studied the building, watching it blur through his wet windshield as the sleet continued. He felt uneasy. The directions he had received in the mail were on the seat next to him, along with the black face mask.

He checked his watch. Now it was four minutes after twelve. He was late. But he felt afraid to move. He contemplated starting up the car, leaving the lot, returning to his apartment, and forgetting the whole thing.

Sorry, Trey, I chickened out.

Suddenly Rob was hit in the face with light. He immediately sunk in his seat. A vehicle had turned into JoJo's parking lot. It was heading in Rob's direction.

Why come back here? thought Rob. There was plenty of parking closer to the restaurant. But the realization quickly hit:

It's probably a member of The Circle.

Rob peeked. A blue pick-up truck pulled into a nearby parking space. Inside, Rob could see an enormous shadow.

The car door opened and the enormous shadow became an enormous man. He looked like a big, aging wrestler, with a buzz cut, broad shoulders, a thick neck, and bulging arms.

Rob slumped further out of view as the big man walked past his car. When Rob took another peek, the man was crossing the street toward the motel. Rob saw that he wore cowboy boots.

He looks like a badass, thought Rob.

It was almost ten after twelve.

At that moment, Rob decided to follow him. Most likely, the man was headed to the same destination, Room 16. Maybe Rob could get a glimpse, or a clue, of what was going to happen next.

Rob opened his car door and stepped out. He placed the black anonymask in his coat pocket. He quietly shut and locked the door.

Rob waited for a few cars to pass, then crossed the road. Just beyond the motel, he could hear the steady rumble and whine of vehicles on Highway 294.

Stepping into the motel lot, Rob stayed out of view, moving behind parked cars. The vehicles all looked old and tired, with dents, rust, and abandoned designs. Rob stopped behind a battered Gremlin with a black plastic trash bag covering a broken window.

He could see the big man in cowboy boots approaching the walkway that lined the front of the motel. The man hesitated, looked at a door number, then continued down the string of units. After passing several doors, he found the one he was looking for. He stopped and straightened.

The room was lit, a curtain covering the window, with movement and blurred shadows inside.

The big man stood there for a moment.

Rob remained perfectly still.

The big man fumbled with something. He brought his hands to his face.

For a split second, the big man glanced back at the parking lot. His face was covered in black. He was reduced to eyes, a mouth, and a chin. He now wore the mask.

Rob stayed frozen behind the Gremlin. Sleet landed in his hair, on his cheeks. The big man turned back toward the door. He knocked, loud and firm. It echoed into the parking lot.

After a few seconds, the door opened halfway. Rob heard a brief murmur of dialogue. He couldn't see inside the room.

The big man entered. The door shut.

There was nothing more to see.

Rob knew he had precisely two paths from which to choose. Back to his car. Or forward into Room 16.

He turned toward his car, which sat dark and alone across the street. Near the restaurant, he saw a young couple sharing one umbrella. They were approaching the eatery's entrance, huddled, cuddled, romantic.

Beth. Do it for Beth.

Rob stepped forward, eyes locked on the motel room door that had admitted the large man. As Rob walked, he took out the black face mask. His heartbeat began to accelerate. A gust of wind blew more freezing rain at him.

Rob approached Room 16.

He looked around and saw nobody. Just occasional

cars on the road nearby, and the steady hum of movement and lights from the highway above.

Rob placed the mask on his face, pulling the elastic band over his head and just above his ears. The mask was soft, covering most of his face above the upper lip. He adjusted the eyeholes. They permitted him to see straight ahead, but his peripheral vision was gone.

Rob knocked on the door, hard enough to startle himself. He was afraid of entering the room, but also afraid of standing outside with the goofy mask on. He imagined he looked like a cartoon robber, or a trick or treater, or—

The door opened halfway.

It was Trey Wright. He didn't smile. He looked impatient. He ushered Rob inside. "Come in, come in."

Rob stepped into the motel room and Trey quickly shut the door behind him. There was the thud of a bolt, the clink of a chain.

Looking through the eye holes, Rob had to turn his head from side to side to get a good look at his surroundings.

A group of people in black masks stared back at him, all eyes and mouth, expressionless. Some stood, some sat on the bed, some sat in folding chairs. Nobody was talking.

The room was bland, peach-colored. A simple piece of abstract artwork hung on the wall. The curtain was closed, gray and heavy. For a moment, the curtain lit up from headlights in the parking lot.

Rob stepped forward cautiously. He found a place

to stand, his back to the wall. Some others moved slightly to make room.

Rob caught a glimpse of his reflection in a mirror, features erased, hair askew from the weather.

Trey Wright moved away from the door and stood by an old television on a stand. He was the only person in the room without a mask.

"That's everybody," he said. "The Circle is complete. We can get started."

In a sweeping motion, Wright gestured to the people staring back at him. "There are exactly ten of you. You are the chosen. You come from the city, the suburbs, from near and from far. Some of you traveled fifty, sixty miles to get here. You took a gamble on a vague proposition from a stranger. Without a whole lot of information, aside from a shared objective, you agreed to be here tonight. You also agreed to absolute and total secrecy."

Wright approached the nearest individual. "Your identities are hidden. We will not exchange names or addresses or histories. But one thing, I hope, is apparent." He took the individual's hand and lifted it. The hand was masculine, black. "We represent all ages, genders, and ethnic groups. We are diverse because injustice and suffering touches everyone. No one is immune. Gathered here tonight, we have a businessman, a gas station attendant, a housewife, a retiree, a school teacher, a hairdresser, a machine shop supervisor, a former athlete, and many other walks of life. We are good people. We are decent people. And we have all been *wronged.*"

He let go of the black hand. He took hold of the next hand. Feminine, with nail polish and rings.

"We are The Circle. The Circle is family. We are brothers and sisters, united by tragedy, abandoned by justice. Justice stolen from us by corruption . . . by stupidity . . . by carelessness . . . or by a simple lack of financial means. Law enforcement and the courts have failed the people in this room. The police and the lawyers and the penal system have failed at their most basic duty. Where is the order? Black becomes white, white is black, and all that is right or wrong goes gray. That, my friends, is anarchy.

"When anarchy ensues, it's every man, every woman for himself, for herself. Yes, it's ugly. But there becomes no alternative."

Wright took the next hand. Bony, wrapped in veins and age spots. "You are good people, and your hearts ache. While no two human experiences are the same, we understand one another in a way that others, outside this room, do not. We have buried loved ones. We have been consumed by grief. We have something broken inside that must be fixed before we can go on with our lives." Still holding the bony hand, he took hold of the next hand—Rob's.

Rob felt a surge of fear. He remained very still. He knew his hand was slimy with sweat. Wright gripped it hard.

"I am going to cite some stories without naming names. I want you to be assured that your brothers and sisters in this room feel your pain. They know where you're coming from. They are bonded with you. They share the relentless pursuit to set things right again."

Wright dropped Rob's hand and the other person's hand. He stepped back and looked over the collective group. Then he began reciting his examples in a dramatic voice, punching out words for emphasis like a television announcer. His eyes grew fierce.

"A fifteen-year-old boy speaks out against the street gang that has turned his community into a war zone. He does the right thing, working with police to implicate the gang members in recent shootings that have wounded innocent children. His courage is heroic. On a Tuesday afternoon, coming home from school, he is shot and killed by the gang's leader. The victim's brother is unable to get the police to press charges against the gang leader due to a 'lack of evidence,' because witnesses and those in the know are too frightened to come forward. Where is the justice?

"A lovely young woman is viciously beaten and left for dead in a ravine by her ex-husband. She undergoes multiple surgeries just to survive. Her face is so badly damaged that she is scarred for life, losing an eye, plagued with daily migraine headaches. She loses her job, her home, her savings. The ex-husband spends six months in jail. He is now a free man who continues to taunt her. Where is the justice?

"A star high-school athlete is lured away from his wholesome life into a world of heroin and cocaine addiction by a drug pusher. At a party, the drug pusher delivers a fatal injection into the boy's veins while he is too high to resist. The boy, an only son, dies. Today, the drug pusher continues to peddle his poison to children, thumbing his nose at outraged parents. Where is the justice?

"An honest man decides he must part ways with a business partner who has been engaged in fraudulent and unethical conduct. He releases the partner from the company. The partner goes crazy, gets drunk one night and lights the man's house on fire. The man's wife is killed and his two daughters receive serious burns that will require years of physical therapy. The Bomb and Arson Squad know that the fire is deliberate, but cannot link the man's business partner to the crime, due to a sloppy investigation with numerous procedural errors. The killer continues to go free. The man's young daughters cry *every day* because their attacker has received no punishment. Where is the justice?

"A church-going citizen who serves his community in numerous ways sends his thirteen-year-old girl to a Michigan summer camp. At the camp, a camp counselor sexually molests the child. Afterwards, the girl is so grief-stricken that she commits suicide. The police do not prosecute the child molester, blaming the girl for ruining the investigation by slitting her wrists. Where is the justice?"

When Wright got to the next story, his forehead was spotted with perspiration, nostrils flared. He glanced at Rob—but just for a moment. "A young man loses the love of his life to a malicious hit-and-run driver who manipulates the legal system to get off scot-free. The young woman's neck is broken, and it is a deliberate act of murderous road rage. Yet the hit-and-run driver doesn't even get a speeding ticket. Again . . . where is the justice?"

He let the question hang in the stale air and it was met with silence.

"There are more stories in this room, but you get the picture," said Wright. "However, I would like to tell you one more experience. It is my own. I am one of you. That is why I feel so strongly about our cause."

Wright moved across the room, looking down at the carpet. His face tightened with pain. Finally, he turned back to the group.

His "announcer" voice was gone, replaced now by something softer, more thin and hesitant.

"My dad was murdered," said Wright. "He was in a Chicago nightclub and got in an argument with somebody. Well, that argument escalated into a fight. And that somebody turned out to be a cold-blooded killer. In a back alley, my father was attacked, struck in the head by a brick. My father never so much as laid a hand on anybody. He was ambushed. His skull was crushed. The killer is free today because defense attorneys managed to convince a jury that sixteen blows to the head with a brick, against a defenseless old man, was an act of self-defense."

Wright's lip trembled and Rob could tell he was fighting back tears.

"The time has finally come," said Wright, "to receive the justice our loved ones deserve. We must relieve the grief. We must honor the victims. We must restore balance to the scales of justice."

Wright wiped his eyes. Then he looked out at the group and a smile moved across his face.

"And now, the reason you are gathered here tonight. The master plan. The correction we have all been waiting for."

Wright walked up to a masked individual with thinning brown hair, a felt shirt, and blue jeans. He took the individual's hand. He also took the hand of a short, stocky masked female with flowing red hair. Then he joined their hands. He backed up and addressed the group.

"We will randomly assign our enemies to one another. Each of you will commit one act of vengeance, on behalf of another. You will terminate one life that does not deserve to breathe the air and walk the soil of God's green earth. None of you will know your target or have any reason to be suspected of your target's termination. At the same time, you will not know the identity of your own enemy's executioner. Even if someone caved in, they would not be able to identify the guilty party. Furthermore, no one in this room would be able to expose the plot without implicating themselves."

Rob felt fear. He moved his head, trying to catch a glimpse of the reactions of those around him.

"It is a foolproof scheme," said Wright proudly. "Think about it. A murder exchange among total strangers. No money is transferred, no written agreement, no names, no tangible evidence to make a connection. We become each other's saviors and protectors."

"Wait," said a voice. It was the red-haired woman. She let go of the hand of the man with the thinning brown hair. "Let me get this straight. You are asking us to . . ."

"Kill," said Wright.

The room became very quiet.

"Yes. That is the bottom line," said Wright. "But if we carry out the plan with precision, with intelligence, I am absolutely certain we can—"

"I'm all for it," interrupted a man with a gravelly voice. "Just tell me when, where, and who."

"Let's not get ahead of ourselves," said Wright. "All in due time."

"I'll do it," said a woman near Rob.

"You want us to murder a total stranger?" asked an older, cracking voice belonging to a male.

"How—" said another male voice.

"What if we get caught? I don't know how to—" said the older male.

"Whoa, whoa, wait," said Wright holding up his hand. "You will receive guidance. But it will come later. Not here. Not in a group setting. We will meet one-on-one. I will supply the weapons and instruction to enable each of you to commit your deeds swiftly and without detection. I am committed to making this work and keeping you safe. Work with me and nothing bad will happen to you. Only your enemies will be punished."

"I can't do this," said the older man. "I-I-I can't. I'm sorry, but I can't."

"Understood," said Wright. "That is why I am giving all of you, right now, one last chance to opt out. If you feel you cannot carry through with your responsibility, you are free to go, given that you never discuss this conversation with anyone, ever. And I'm confident you will oblige, because no one wants to go against the collective force that is The Circle."

The older man headed for the door. Some people moved to allow him a path.

"I-I'm sorry," said the man. "I'm going home. I'll forget this ever happened."

"That's right," said Wright. "It never happened."

As the older man walked out of the motel room, he tore off his mask and dropped it to the carpet. It landed face up, eye holes staring into the ceiling.

"Is there anyone else who wants to forfeit their opportunity for revenge?" asked Wright. "I do mean it, when I say this is your last chance."

The red-haired woman stepped forward. "I'm sorry," she said. It sounded like she was crying. "I'm so sorry."

After she was gone, Wright sighed. "Anyone else?"

"Damned cowards," said the man with the gravelly voice.

"It is their right," said Wright. "We still have eight. Eight is a good, round number."

"I have to tell you, I am scared to death," spoke up the man with the thinning brown hair and felt shirt. "I've never ever contemplated something like this before."

"We're all scared," said Wright. "But don't let the fear influence your decision. Your decision should be dictated by your desire to deliver justice. How many of you can sleep at night, knowing that the destroyer of your happiness is out there, *right now*, living it up, laughing at you, free and without consequence? I know I can't. I can't sleep. But when my father's killer is gone, I will sleep like a baby."

"What if we get caught?" asked the black man.

"Won't happen," said Wright. "That is the art of collaboration. You could not do this to your own enemies. You *would* get caught. Together, however, we are invincible. Think of the passion and focus we all bring to the table. We are stronger than those who brought us harm."

There was a long silence.

"I'm in," said the man with the thinning brown hair.

Rob had been staring at the door. His heart pounded. Two people had left, so surely he could make his move. The entire crazy thing could end for him now. Six, seven, maybe eight steps and he would be outdoors, back in the drizzle, heading for his car to return to his apartment.

Two words, "I'm out," and a few steps to break loose.

But he couldn't do it.

His feet were locked down.

And it wasn't necessarily fear. It was a flow of excitement in his veins: *Beth's killer will die and nothing will connect me to his death.* Richard Shepherd would be wiped off the face of the earth, the most beautiful thing he could imagine.

The price to pay: disposing of someone else's evil.

But could he take out another human being? He wasn't a violent man. He didn't even know how to behave violently. The actual act would certainly require

Wright's guidance, instruction, and reassurances that getting caught or hurt was not an option.

And who would his victim be?

From the heartbreaking stories he had heard tonight, Rob knew that there were other Richard Shepherds out there. Ruthless, deadly, and sick bastards who deserved to be erased from society, but had escaped their rightful punishment from an imperfect system. Killing one of them would just be killing another Richard Shepherd, without the danger of a logical connection between killer and victim.

"Anyone else?" said Wright. "Last call . . ."

Rob stared at the door.

He did not move. His mind raced furiously. *Should I? Maybe I should? Or—?*

"Good." Wright clapped his hands together. "The Circle is closed."

I'm in.

"We will now each take an oath," said Wright. "It is your pledge to The Circle. First, I want you to shut your eyes. Please. Everyone."

Rob shut his eyes.

"Now do this," said Wright. "Put a picture in your mind of your loved one who suffered at the hands of evil. I want you to see their face. I want you to look into their eyes."

In Rob's mind, Beth appeared, remarkably clear. Her eyes sparkled. Her smile encouraged him.

Wright said, "Now, one at a time, when I touch your hand, you will recite an oath. Not to me, but to your loved ones. Don't let go of that image. You will state loud and clear: *'I will restore justice and peace in your honor.'* "

A moment passed, and Wright must have touched a hand, because one of the male voices said, "I will restore justice and peace in your honor."

And one by one, each member spoke the line. Every voice sounded emotional, weary, broken by the unresolved crimes that still haunted them.

When Wright grazed the back of Rob's hand, Rob told Beth, "I will restore justice and peace in your honor." It felt good.

The final member of The Circle to recite the oath broke down in tears. He had a Southern accent. Rob opened his eyes. It was the towering man he had watched enter the motel room. The big man with snakeskin cowboy boots and a buzz-cut. Wright hugged him.

"I'm sorry," said the big Southerner. "I just get emotional."

"As you should," said Wright. "It's okay."

Wright stood back. Then he grinned ear to ear. "Welcome! You are The Circle. This is our first and last gathering. After tonight, you will only deal with me, one-on-one. Sometime in the next six months, you will hear from me, we will meet, and you will receive your assignment. Until then, just go on living your life, but feel a little stronger in the knowledge that justice will be served. We are going to fulfill each other's dreams."

Wright dismissed The Circle, one member at a time, in five-minute intervals, to allow each person a head start to leave the room, take off their mask, and disperse without being seen. Rob was one of the first to depart. He hurried into the blackness of the night. The fresh air felt good. The sleet had stopped. He crossed an empty road, removing the mask from his face. The crowd inside JoJo's had dwindled to about a dozen.

Rob climbed into his Nissan. As he started the engine, he saw the towering Southerner in the motel lot, approaching the road, making his way toward his blue pick-up truck. Rob quickly backed up his car. He departed from the lot. He passed the big man in the street. The man did not look at him and appeared deep in thought.

Rob drove all the way home with the black face mask upright in the passenger seat, eyes holes staring back at him, vacant.

Eight

Rage's head was spinning. A lot of shit was going down.

The Royal-Ts were tripping major league. Four nights back, Jitters lit up Big Talk and real fast the whole gang was bumping titties and jumping sets. Inside twenty-four hours, Jitters got smoked through the window of his crib by one of his own homies, a mad dog nicknamed ZigZag after the spastic scar across his face. ZigZag popped a cap in Jitters's dome while the fool was kicking it with a 32-ouncer, the Home Shopping Channel, and a bitch's head rolling in his lap, bobbing for apples.

A Royal-T Posse was hastily declared, but it was a pitiful spinoff of wankstas and baby Gs, and every banger from Austin to Cicero Avenue was already moving in on the Royal-Ts' turf, flying their colors and tagging every surface. The hood was under siege.

It was going to get messed up on the West Side, but Rage was cool. As he walked his hood, he stood tall because he knew the outcome: Killa Crew would take hold of more street, do more business, and reap the fruits. The rest of the motherfuckers would get beaten down.

Rage and his homeboys would show no mercy, leaving a trail of shells, dead punks, and dropped flags in their wake. People who pledged allegiance to the wrong color would feel pain and attend services. His taggers would spray the streets, combining Killa Crew's graffiti signature with the symbols of their rivals turned upside down and submissive.

It was a good time to get juiced. Two of his original Gs were back, freshly gated out after spending a bullet in state prison. They were hungry to return to the fold. They had pent-up hostilities to unleash on the pretenders who fucked with them. Rage was on his way to meet with them and two other hardcore members in the Killa Crew's new headquarters, an abandoned RV behind a junkyard on Chicago Avenue. Edgar, the junkyard owner, knew better than to complain or ask questions. He had a wife and kids.

It was two P.M., the sun was smeared in the sky, and the cold was bitter harsh, even for March. Rage moved under the el tracks and into a cramped alley with tall chain link fences, overflowing Dumpsters, and some damned pitbull terrier that wouldn't shut its yap.

Rage was strapped. He had a pistol in his waistband, a double deuce with the serial number scratched away. He could shut up the dog in an eye blink, but he had more important uses for these bullets. Like protecting himself from ambush.

Rage knew he was a prized target and particularly

vulnerable right now, without bookends at his side. There had been attempts on his life more than once. They were usually just a nuisance and never very smooth. They always ended with some fool in pain, usually cryin' and screamin' for his mama.

Just two weeks ago, a punk from The Viperz pulled out a 9, waved it in Rage's face, and said some shit. That was enough to warrant payback. One of Rage's boys later caught up with the fool, chased him with a machete, and gave him a second butt crack.

Rage had been watching his own back ever since he was twelve and left on his own. His deadbeat dad went to the pen for "criminal sexual misconduct" and his fried old lady gave up on the whole family thing and plain disappeared. Rage learned to fend for himself real quick. He had naturally fast instincts, big pride, and no hesitation to do what had to be done. He put snitches and cranks into graves. People don't dis you when they're in the dirt.

Word spread, and Rage attracted a lot of believers. They were loyal, they were family, and they protected him with their lives. Soldiers had fallen to cover his ass. They were the true brothers.

Rage walked out of the alley with eyes roaming the street. It was an area of two flats, his hood, but trouble traveled everywhere these days.

There was no suspense about his affiliation. He was proud. He was decked out in the Killa Crew maroon colors under his black, oversized, hooded sweatshirt. His shoelaces were maroon, shoe tongue out. His baggy pants hung low, cuffs rolled high. He wore a big crescent moon on a chain, baseball bill to the left, earring stud on the left. The front of his shirt was tucked behind his belt buckle, so everyone could read the letters. RAGE.

And, for the ladies, there was some ink on his chest and left of his navel, little billboards to remind them of the sponsor as they traveled south.

He was a Killa Crew member until the day he died. That was the sum up. If anybody had a problem with that, bring it on. They would become another casualty of the revolution.

A vehicle turned on the street down by the traffic light, heading his way. Rage watched, ready to move.

Chrysler LeBaron, cracked windshield.

It was cool. It was Mad Hatter.

Hatter drove past, and they exchanged signals.

As a reflex, Rage checked every vehicle on his streets. The one he was most concerned about was a PT Cruiser with tinted windows, owned by an asshole who called himself Caponey, of all things, and always wore a blue bandana around his head. Caponey had issued an R.I.P. on Rage's ass, which was fucked. Caponey thought he was hot shit because he ruled part of a housing complex for the aged and retarded. He was Big Boss of the Toothless while Rage ruled the Ruthless. Still, Caponey was a wicked recruiter, hustling kids as young as ten, and a B.G. could bust a cap as swift as any other motherfucker.

Rage continued east on the sidewalk and another car turned onto the street. He didn't recognize this one. Rage slowed his pace and locked his eyes on the vehicle.

A late '80s Buick Regal, cream-colored with rust. Who was driving this ghetto sled?

The Buick moved slowly, in little spurts. Not a good sign. Rage brought his hand toward his pistol. He identified quick cover, porches and shrubs, and a getaway path between two cribs.

The Buick rolled toward the curb, toward Rage.

Bold motherfucker, thought Rage.

There appeared to be one person in the car, a fat shadow behind the wheel. The windows on the passenger side began descending with an electronic hum.

Rage hid his hand under his black sweatshirt, gripping his gun. His pants were loose and baggy, the weapon would slide out fast and easy. He would fire at the melon head if he dared make a wrong move.

"Excuse me, sir," said the driver in a thin voice.

Rage could see him clearly now. *A peckerwood . . .*

The driver was a fat, balding, slobby white dude with ugly glasses and a scared, confused face.

This oughta be good.

Rage stepped toward the car. He removed his hand from the gun.

"You got a problem?" said Rage, keeping his face angry and hard.

The dork struggled for words. He was obviously nervous.

"I think I took a wrong turn somewhere," said Peckerwood. "Can you help me find Western Avenue?"

Rage almost laughed. "Aw, shit . . ." *I could use a G-ride. I'd jack this bucket, if it wasn't such a piece of shit. Probably smells like his fat ass.*

Rage bent his knees and peered in the window at the man. Rage could see beads of sweat between the stray hairs wrapped across the man's fat pink forehead.

"You're way off," Rage said. "This ain't your hood."

"I know, I'm sorry to impose. I'm trying to get to my Uncle Martin's apartment. I'm late for his birthday party."

"Jeezus," muttered Rage. "Okay, you wanna go back the way you came from, back the other direction. You know where Lake Street is?"

"What street?" said the driver, cupping a hand to his ear.

Rage groaned and leaned in closer. "Read my lips, fool. LAKE Street."

At that moment, the driver lifted a gun and fired it into Rage's face.

Trey Wright sipped a root beer float. He was seated at a red leather booth in the back of the Happy Platter, a brightly lit diner on Chicago's northwest side. A Britney Spears song played, and three booths away, giggling teenage girls sang the lyrics to one another, making exaggerated hand gestures, as if they were on stage somewhere. Trey watched and smiled. Crazy kids . . .

The front entrance opened, allowing for a momentary blast of outdoor traffic, and Raymond Brown, a young African-American stepped inside. He immediately searched the surroundings and found Wright. He approached the booth and slid across from him.

There were tears in Raymond's eyes.

"Thank you," he said.

Wright pulled the Carnival straw out of his mouth. "Don't thank me," he said. "It was The Circle. The Circle has begun its rotation."

"My baby brother is looking down at us and he is smiling." Raymond sat back in the booth. His eyes were tired, but his grin was broad and energized. "I can't express how big this feels. Vincent wanted to protect his neighborhood. This would have made him so happy. He did not die in vain."

"No," said Wright. "He did not die in vain. Now he is fulfilled. You are whole again. The leader of the Killa Crew has been erased from your community. He has been taken out. The gang has been decapitated."

Raymond nodded, lips pursed, tears returning. For seven months, he had been wracked in pain by the knowledge that his younger brother's killer roamed the streets, unavenged, gaining power, and creating more horror and loss.

Raymond's little brother had died on an autumn afternoon on his way home from school, the victim of a bullet to the back of the head. The word on the street was that Rage, the leader of the Killa Crew, had personally performed the hit. In an instant, fifteen-year-old Vincent was taken away forever. Vincent's crime? Trying to protect others from harm.

Vincent and Raymond had grown up together in a good, strong family. They never had any need for the bogus "family" of a gang. Their parents were good, solid people who shielded them from gangbangers and filled their days with positive, enriching activities.

Vincent was a gentle boy who created amazing illustrations in a sketchbook and always obeyed curfew and did his homework. He brushed off the overtures from more than one gang. He just wasn't interested. In the eyes of the gangbangers, that was his first mistake.

But the real ride to hell began at a Labor Day barbecue, attended by half the neighborhood, which, unfortunately, included gang members, drawing a tragic assault.

The barbecue was ambushed by masked men wielding AK-47 automatic weapons. They walked as they shot, without fear. They were the Killa Crew. One of them was Rage—Vincent had said he just knew.

Their intended targets were mixed with bystanders, and a lot of people got tagged. The police later estimated that the barbecue was sprayed with thirty-four rounds.

Some gangbangers died.

Some innocent people died.

Vincent's six-year-old sister got grazed by a bullet.

Vincent's best friend, Jaime, was shot in the back. His spinal injuries put him in a wheelchair. He was told he would never be able to walk again.

But in the aftermath, no one would talk about the culprits. Everyone was terrified. The police had a difficult time getting any witnesses to cooperate.

So Vincent stepped forward. He just knew it was the right thing to do. He told Officer Jenkins everything he knew about the Killa Crew, and their leader, a vicious thug named Rage.

Vincent had known Rage, a.k.a. Luther, ever since grade school, when Luther would beat up Raymond to establish his dominance in the pecking order by publicly bullying classmates.

Vincent helped the cops. But the cops didn't help Vincent. Rage was arrested and later released when his involvement in the barbecue massacre "couldn't be substantiated."

Six days later, Vincent was dead, face down in a pool of his own blood, his school binder snapped open on the sidewalk beside him, his papers scattered, carried into the street and bushes by the wind.

Vincent was buried in his favorite sports jersey, wearing the personalized knit hat his mother had made for him, with two of his favorite drawings nestled under his clasped hands.

It had been a horrible, extended nightmare for Vincent's family. But now the pain had reached some closure with the funeral of Rage, a.k.a. Luther, a.k.a. Vincent Brown's killer.

Raymond felt bricks fall off his shoulders. It felt so good and clean.

"The Circle has served your brother well," Wright told Raymond. "A loop in your life has been closed. Now it is time for you to serve another. You, too, will send someone away who is bringing down society. Now you can be a hero. That is why I called you here today."

Raymond nodded. "I understand. I am here to serve The Circle."

Wright reached down and picked up a medium-sized, padded envelope, several inches thick, that had been resting on the seat next to him. It was securely sealed. Nothing was written on the front. Wright placed it on the table in front of Raymond.

Raymond took it, moved it around in his hands for a moment, then started to open it.

"Don't," said Wright. "Take it home. Open it in private."

Raymond looked at Wright. "What is it?"

"Each member of The Circle receives one. It is the bridge between you and justice. On the handle, there is the engraving of a circle."

"A—a gun?" Raymond tried to control his nervousness, but the stutter was unavoidable.

Wright didn't respond. He reached down again and this time brought up a flat, 9×12 manila envelope. He handed it to Raymond.

Raymond put the first package in his lap. He stared at the envelope a moment before taking it. He looked at Wright.

"Go ahead," said Wright. "You can open this one."

Raymond unclasped the top of the envelope and lifted the lip. He slowly slid out the contents.

There were two pieces of paper.

The first one was a page torn out of a slick, tabloid-size magazine, *Chicago Law and Review*. There was a large color photo that accompanied an article about a law firm. The photo was a head shot of a distinguished, gray-haired attorney.

The caption beneath identified the man as Richard Shepherd.

The second item was a sheet of white paper with some information printed on it. A home address, an office address, and specific times marking arrival and departure.

Wright glanced around to make sure that the other

diners in the restaurant were far enough and preoccupied with their own conversations.

Then he began to provide verbal instructions. The basic information needed to find and surprise the man in the photo, commit the necessary deed, and make a clean getaway.

Wright did all the talking. Raymond listened in deep concentration, nodding.

When Wright was done, he asked, "Any questions?"

Raymond said, "No."

"You understand your mission?"

"Yes, I do."

"You will keep the justice in rotation?"

"I will."

"Good luck," said Wright. He left money on the table for his root beer float, plus tip, and exited the Happy Platter.

Nine

Richard Shepherd looked at himself in the full-length mirror next to the marble sink counter and thought, Damn I look good.

He could hear Stephanie, his wife, humming in her bathroom on the other side of the master bedroom suite. A happy, chirping bird. He thought about how lucky she was to have him, this house, their life together. She was a fine woman: refined, obedient, loyal to a fault, and committed to keeping her looks in check through exercise and surgery. She had never quite lost the charming, slight Southern Belle music in her voice, even though she had been in the Midwest for twenty plus years. She played the good wife in private and in public, well aware that it was the best way to keep her prize. Otherwise, *kaput*, *vamoosed*, like the grumpy, bitter ex-wives of so many of Richard's uppercrust colleagues who traded away the sag of seniority for perky youth, sometimes several times over. He appreciated the look of apprehension in Stephanie's eyes when another peer showed up at a banquet or fundraiser with a twentysomething tart in tow. It kept her well-behaved.

Stephanie not only had the great fortune of landing one of the most powerful attorneys in the state, she was also married to a man of impeccable taste. The evidence, Your Honor, filled every room of the sprawling colonial home they shared, from the enviable European art collection on the walls to the carefully chosen English antique furniture that Stephanie's grubby little nephews and nieces were not allowed to touch. (They were restricted to a children's playroom in the furnished basement—not a bad banishment, given the arcade game collection.)

Today, Richard Shepherd wore his dapper, custom-tailored, steel-colored Kiton wool suit from Naples, one of the great prizes in his magnificent wardrobe. He loved the loose and supple feel, lightweight construction, and styling. It turned the heads of the fashion conscious. All the partners and associates in his law practice gravitated toward quality handmade suits with exclusive fabrics—it was the firm's "uniform." You could spot one of the boys from Shepherd, Sundern and Hirsch a block away. Perhaps other, lesser firms had been beset by casual days and inferior ragstock off the rack. But not Shepherd's team. They studied swatch books and bragged about the numerous fittings and months it took to achieve the perfect fit from the perfect imported suit. They argued Milanese vs. Roman style vs. English elegance. They made field trips to the legendary Savile Row in London, tailors to royalty since the early 1800s. They were excited by 12.9-micron, Super 210 wool from a rare breed of sheep, spun delicately on special looms in the English countryside. They enthused over French shoes made by hand by craftsmen with their own tannery to ensure the proper aging of the leather. They showed off handmade, seven-fold silk ties with historic English patterns, individually numbered like works of art. They compared notes on the finest 200-count Egyptian shirt cottons and ruminated on the necessity of single-needled construction so the seams didn't pucker. They snickered at the lackadaisical wardrobe indifference of other firms that wondered why they couldn't impress the really big clients. Hell, simply the wrong wristwatch could doom landing a lucrative account.

Shepherd understood the importance of looking good, dressing smart, and feeling confident, especially in the legal world. Perception was crucial, and image fed perception.

There was a reason he was tops in his game.

His Kiton suit used fine silk thread exported from England to Italy and required twenty-five hours of labor and nearly four dozen tailors, split into teams. There was the buttonhole team, the pocket team, the sleeve team, and so on. Each suit required thousands of hand stitches and numerous hand pressings, using heavy vintage irons and local spring water. Shepherd knew all this because he had visited the Kiton factory personally with one of his partners just last year.

Shepherd was currently awaiting shipment of the latest Kiton innovation: a lightweight sport coat crafted from a blend of silk, linen, and pineapple husk.

Maybe he would have it in time for the Highland Park Flower and Garden Gala. He reminded himself to call Oxford Clothes and apply some additional pressure on the delivery date.

Shepherd added the finishing touch to his day's attire—gold oval cufflinks—and met up with Stephanie in the master bedroom.

"How do I look?"

"You look stunning," she said. Right answer.

"I am a stun gun," he replied.

"Dressed to kill." She brushed the back of her hand against a smooth suit sleeve.

He instinctively pulled back.

"Hey, I'm not going to wrinkle it," she smiled.

He checked his Rolex. "I better get moving. I'm meeting with my troops at eight to go over our battle plan for Jeffy's."

"Well, I hope you shut them all down," said Stephanie, a stern look in her baby blues. "That waitress we had that one time was so rude . . ."

"They're sad clowns, and they're going down," said Shepherd. He kissed Stephanie on the forehead.

It tasted like makeup and he grimaced. He pulled out his handkerchief and wiped the brown crap off his lips.

"Sorry, hon," said Stephanie. She squeezed out a smile.

"Gotta go," he muttered. He made a half wave, turned and headed for the staircase.

Time to go kick Jeffy's ass.

Jeffy's was a chain of nine local restaurants. Shepherd's firm was developing a class-action lawsuit against the entire enterprise based on the chain's egregious conduct and reckless indifference to public safety.

The lawsuit was being filed on behalf of duped Chicago-area vegetarians from Waukegan to South Holland over the past year who had unwittingly consumed animal products in Jeffy's Garden Burger.

The facts: Jeffy's Garden Burger was served with guacamole that contained gelatin as a thickening agent. This gelatin was a byproduct of pig skin, boiled to release the collagen from the animal tissues. Thousands, perhaps tens of thousands of vegetarians had been sold Garden Burgers on false merits.

The facts: Devoted vegetarians were lied to, deceived, and became devastated, traumatized, and physically ill. Large numbers of these vegetarians had lost sleep, required medical attention, and been forced to seek psychiatric counseling.

The facts: Jeffy's management disputed the allegations until scientific analysis proved them wrong. Therefore, Jeffy's was guilty of misleading the public and causing undue physical and emotional harm.

Naturally, the owners of Jeffy's had done their best to boo-hoo in the media that they were being abused by a "frivolous lawsuit" and that they were victims of a "predatory plaintiff's attorney" seeking to "extort money" due to a "minor infraction."

They pleaded ignorance to the whole guacamole-gelatin animal tissue thing. *Sorry, but your callous stupidity is not an adequate defense.*

They played the ethnic card. They played the "You'll drive a small business bankrupt" card.

They also refused to acknowledge the only reasonable resolution: settle the thing out of court and bypass the entire ugly ordeal. Pay up or perish.

For some unfathomable reason, Jeffy's was opting to perish.

So be it. Get an ass-kicking in court. Not a wise choice, but these were not wise men. They were bumbling immigrants without street smarts, bush leaguers unfamiliar with the rules of major league ball.

They had only one chance in hell: their legal team.

The Jeffy's people had hired one of the other top firms in the city: Balazs, Graham and Schwalb.

BG&S had the misconception that they owned the town, that *they* were the Windy City's legal powerhouse. They were a tough gang, certainly, but vulnerable. They knew how to fire off some lethal rounds, but their shotgun approach didn't always hit the target, and they had been blown away before.

The whole Jeffy's thing was a sexy story for the media, but an even more interesting case for the legal world because of its precedent-setting nature.

If Jeffy's was guilty, it might be time for some hardcore analysis of McDonald's, Wendy's, Arby's, Denny's, and the rest of them. What kind of false promises were being made to the nation's vegetarians? Did those companies even know the content of their product? Maybe it was time to get Ronald McDonald and the rest of them to cough up some serious dough.

Shit, even the marshmallows on Rocky Road ice cream at the local parlor could be called into play. Does the pimply fifteen-year-old ice cream scooper in the paper hat know he's serving up animal byproduct? Is he prepared to warn his vegetarian customers? Or is the entire enterprise indifferent as long as they get their consumers' cash?

"I could lose everything I worked to achieve for twenty years, all because of an accident," moped a well-rehearsed Ernie Muni to the TV cameras just one week ago. Ernie was the bushy-eyebrowed owner of Jeffy's, the son of poor immigrants who blah-de-blah . . . "I survived two recessions and the fast food chains just to come to this?"

Well, yes. Sorry pal, but you fucked up. Maybe you can peddle mislabeled food to the public in your country, but here in the good ol' U.S. of A. we have a little thing called truth in advertising.

Read up on it sometime, maybe you'll learn something. Indifference is not a defense.

If found guilty, Muni would have to pay his victims punitive damages, lost wages, medical costs, and pain and suffering to the tune of twenty million dollars.

It would take a lot of hamburger sales to pay that invoice.

So why wouldn't Muni surrender and settle for a far less amount?

The answer: his counsel's advice.

Balazs, Graham and Schwalb wanted to rumble.

So Jeffy's would crumble in the crossfire. A casualty of war.

Bring it on.

Shepherd stepped out of his home and breathed in a lungful of fresh air. The sun was on its way up, and it was going to be a nice day with an invigorating chill. He strayed off the walkway and stepped onto his manicured lawn, looking for *The Wall Street Journal.*

Ordinarily, it was just two, maybe three steps from the brick walkway, flat on the grass.

But today it was oddly missing from the usual spot. He searched his vast lawn.

What the hell?

Then he saw it . . . a glimpse of the blue plastic wrap . . . on the sidewalk in front of his house.

That made no sense. It also angered him. Now he would have to walk across the grass in his Mantellassi shoes.

He headed for *The WSJ*, grumbling.

Did the paperboy have a broken arm?

Was it some lazy substitute paperboy?

Who just drops the paper at the curb?

He made a mental note to put an entry into his Palm Pilot: call and complain.

Stupid nuisance. It's the story of my life. Call and complain. If you added up all the time I spend fixing these types of problems, and billed it, it would add up to . . .

Richard Shepherd reached the sidewalk, bent over with a grunt and grasped his paper.

He heard a car slowly approaching, moving down the street, but didn't even give it a glance.

Shepherd turned back toward the house. He began fishing in his pocket for the keys to his Range Rover. Then he heard a shout behind him.

"Hey, Shepherd!"

Shepherd stopped and turned. What kind of rude neighbor—?

Shepherd wasn't even fully facing the street when

the first shot rang out. It sounded like a firecracker, an abrupt *crack.* Shepherd caught a glimpse of the car—an old, lime-green Chevy Nova—and a black man inside—and Shepherd's confusion was immediately replaced by pain.

A fire burning in his side.

A hole in his Kiton suit!

It took a second shot for Shepherd to realize that it was a bullethole and that the driver of the vehicle stopped in front of his house was shooting him.

Shepherd tried to run, but more shots rang out, and his limbs stopped cooperating.

Shepherd fell to the grass and felt horrible stinging in his abdomen, his thigh . . .

—*CRACK*—

Then worst of all, in his back, searing pain reaching like branches all over his body, and Shepherd doubled up, started screaming, who was doing this and why, what was going on, it didn't make any sense . . .

"Help!" he shouted, but it was alarmingly thin and feeble.

Shepherd saw his Range Rover parked in the driveway up ahead. It loomed like a big silver sanctuary.

If he could only get to it . . . get inside . . . lock the doors . . . grab his Nokia car phone . . . he would be safe . . .

Shepherd grabbed at the grass. He tried to pull himself forward, but it was very difficult, and he only managed to advance about three feet when the dirt kicked up in front of him and sprayed his eyes—

—another shot—

Shepherd heard a strange noise in his ears then, a

distinct sound he had not heard in twenty, thirty, maybe forty years . . . his own sobbing.

He screamed out a final plea to his unknown attacker.

Another bullet hit—this time exploding in his ass.

Shepherd twisted and rolled and wound up on his back. The sun shined on his face, insanely warm and inviting.

The next shot put out the lights.

Rob Carus was teaching his fourth period composition students about transitive and intransitive verbs when the knock sounded at his classroom door. He could see Hank's face in the glass. Hank had an unnaturally urgent look. He motioned for Rob to come out.

Hank didn't ordinarily just show up and disrupt his classes, so Rob knew it must be something important. He told his students to create ten sentences—five with transitive verbs, five without—and promised he'd be right back.

He joined Hank in the hallway and shut the door behind him.

"What's wrong?" asked Rob.

"Richard Shepherd is dead."

Rob nearly stumbled backward into the door. "Holy shit."

"It's bigger than holy shit, buddy," said Hank. "The guy was shot to death in front of his house. It happened this morning. I heard it on the radio in the teachers' lounge. They don't know who did it."

"Oh my God," was all Rob could say. Images flashed

in front of him. Trey Wright. The motel room. The Circle.

"I guess there are a lot of people out there who hate him," said Hank. "You're not the only one."

"No," said Rob quickly. "I'm sure he has a lot of enemies. Tons of them."

Hank cracked a grin. "Unless *you* shot him."

Rob forced a chuckle. "Yeah, right."

"I mean, this is like your wildest dream come true, isn't it? That mad bastard is gunned down. You couldn't script it any better."

"I know, I know," Rob said, dazed, his head swimming. He wasn't feeling good about this. There was no joy, just terror.

"Hey, cheer up," said Hank, gently pushing on his shoulder. "You're looking like Richard Shepherd was your best friend. He's the world's biggest asshole. You can celebrate this. It's okay."

"I will celebrate," said Rob, but it sounded hollow. "I'm just . . . I guess I'm blown away."

"I think you should have a party."

"No, Jesus," snapped Rob. "A man is dead. Knock it off."

Hank studied Rob. "I feel like you're pissed off at me for telling you that you won the lottery. Believe me, when this sinks in, you'll want to party."

"I don't know. I have to get back to my class. I need to think about this, it's too . . . crazy."

Rob started to feel faint. His scalp felt prickly.

"All right," said Hank. "You'll come around. This is party material."

Rob returned to his class, shaken and wobbly. The students were busy drafting their sentences. A few looked up. They didn't seem to sense his overwhelming feeling of dread.

Rob dropped into his chair and let out a big sigh. That caused more faces to look up.

"It's nothing," said Rob. "Return to your work."

Even as he stared at them, the students quickly faded away. All he could see was Shepherd getting shot to death, falling to the ground in front of his house.

Several months had passed since the meeting of The Circle. The late night at the motel room had quickly become a surreal memory, like a weird dream. He had actually gotten used to the thought that the whole thing had become a half-baked, failed scheme . . . an exercise of chest-thumping that derailed when it became time for action.

But no. The Circle was for real.

And Beth's murderer was dead.

Rob couldn't enjoy the moment. It had nothing to do with sympathy for Shepherd, and everything to do with massive fear for himself:

I'm going to get arrested. Somehow they're going to trace it all back to me. Why did I agree to this? I need psychiatric help. This is absurd and horrible. Oh my God, what do I do?

Two hours later, Rob was in the school library with his seventh period English Honors class. They were researching their topics for a midsemester essay, and he was moving from student to student to help out with finding reference materials, as needed.

Rob was sitting down with Jessica Spring, who was researching the history of paper-making, when he saw the other faces in the room, one by one, turn toward the library entrance.

Rob moved in his chair to see what they were focused on and saw two policemen accompanied by Adrienne Archer, the principal. Her eyes searched the room for him.

Rob didn't move. He didn't offer himself up, but he knew what was coming.

Adrienne saw him. She said something to the police, then left the officers at the entrance to walk over to Rob.

"Robert, the police would like to talk with you," she whispered. "They have some questions . . ."

"Sure," said Rob, trying to remain calm. "I think I know what it's about. It's okay."

Rob stood up and smiled weakly at Jessica. "Sorry about this. It's just a . . . thing. I'll be back."

Rob stepped into the hall, and the police detectives cordially introduced themselves. Detectives Justie and Stinson. They asked Adrienne for a private place to talk, and she offered her office.

The detectives interviewed Rob for forty minutes. Rob kept a tight lid on his panic; so tight that he felt he might throw up at any minute.

They asked about his morning. When did he leave his apartment and come to school? Did he stop anywhere on the way? Who saw him first at the school? Names, approximate times.

It was then that Rob realized he had an air-tight alibi. At the time of Shepherd's shooting, he was already at the high school, getting an early start, grading papers, preparing his lesson plan. At least a dozen people, faculty and students, had seen him.

I'm in the clear.

They asked some general questions about the "accident" with Shepherd's SUV, the civil trial, and the encounter between Rob and Shepherd at Shepherd's downtown office.

Rob heard himself telling the cops that he wasn't going to shed any tears for Shepherd and that he would always believe him to be guilty. "But I wouldn't wish this on anybody," he said. "It's terrible."

His words felt hollow at that moment, and he hoped the detectives couldn't tell.

That night, Rob watched all the coverage on the news, absorbed every detail.

Dead at the scene. Discovered by his wife, who heard the shots, but did not see the car or the shooter.

No witnesses. No suspects. No motives.

One of the television reporters suggested that perhaps it was connected to the current lawsuit against the Jeffy's chain of restaurants.

"Sources say the police are investigating possible ties between the restaurant ownership and local organized crime. The police say it is too early to speculate."

On Saturday, Detectives Justie and Stinson met with Rob again, this time in his apartment. They asked a lot of questions and tried to snoop around without being obvious.

Rob knew he had nothing in his apartment to incriminate him.

"You certainly had public sentiment supporting

you in your court case," said Justie. "Are you aware of anyone who made death threats, even facetiously, on your behalf?"

"Not death threats, no," said Rob.

"Have you met up with anyone else who also had issues with Shepherd, who offered their own stories, their own desires to 'get back' at Shepherd?" asked Stinson.

"No, I can't say that I have," said Rob.

Justie asked, "Are you familiar with the Jeffy's case?"

"A little bit, from the newspaper."

"Do you know anyone associated with the restaurant or the pending court case?"

"No," said Rob. "I ate there once. Does that count?"

When the detectives left, concluding their second lengthy interview with him, Rob felt his first pangs of happiness. The police were done. They had gleaned no useful or incriminating information from him.

They were not even treating him like a suspect.

They seemed more interested in the Jeffy's people.

They appeared to know absolutely nothing about The Circle. And why would they?

Rob realized he was off the hook, and it filled him with something like joy. Now he could truly derive satisfaction from Shepherd's death. No, something better than satisfaction. Exuberance. Hank was right: It was time to party. The initial shock and horror was melting away.

An enormous weight, no doubt lifted by a crane, was being removed from his shoulders. And it felt great.

Late one night, Rob had his party. He returned alone to North Avenue Beach. He sat down on the spot in the sand where he had proposed to Beth and she danced to the goofy song on the radio. He popped open a bottle of champagne and lifted it to the stars that blinked in the heavens.

"We got vengeance, baby," he said, tears in his eyes, and he drank.

Closure. A horrific story had now reached its final chapter. The conflict had come to a resolution. Good had triumphed over evil.

The end, thought Rob to himself. It's over.

Now we can shut the book.

Ten

Spring swept across the Midwest like a cleansing breeze. The skies regained their color. Moods lifted with each sunrise. The students at ETHS shed their coats, exposed some arm and leg, and hung out in energized groups on the school lawn, finally freed from cold weather captivity.

Rob felt renewed. His footsteps felt lighter. He no longer had the dragging sensation that gravity was trying to suck him into the ground. His students noticed his changed attitude. Word spread that "Old Mr. Carus" had returned, and he was teasing with them again, smiling for real, and grading on a more generous curve.

Rob had also broken out of his cycle of assigning grim and nihilistic literature. He was now tossing them "fun" classics like Mark Twain's *A Connecticut Yankee in King Arthur's Court*. He overheard a sarcastic student remark, "Hey, a book that doesn't make me want to slit my wrists."

When his twenty-ninth birthday arrived, Rob expected at least a temporary return to melancholy, but temperatures soared, his desktop filled with cards, and somehow he felt like part of the human race again. Life was moving on, and he was still on board.

Maureen surprised him in class with a plate of chocolate chip cookies, wrapped tightly in cellophane. "Happy Birthday, Mr. Carus," she said sweetly. When he asked how she knew, she shrugged, tilted her oval face and smiled at him. "You always said to be diligent with research," she said with a sly expression that was a 10 on the cute-o-meter.

Maureen received a wary look from some of the other students who probably considered this bribery for grades, but he knew it wasn't. She was already an "A" student. She was just a good kid, period.

He took the cookies, the cards and the good feelings back to his apartment. He ate a cookie, then another, then half the plate and ruined his appetite for dinner. Sitting on the sofa, he debated whether he felt lonely, then debated whether to reach for *Utne* magazine or *TV Guide*. He finally decided what he really needed was some fresh reading material. That would be his birthday present to himself. A shopping spree at the Evanston Barnes and Noble. Why not? Charge it to the card, write it off to impulsive splurging.

At the bookstore, he allowed himself one book from five different sections—literature, science fiction/fantasy, sports, film, and history—plus one magazine. An hour and a half later, after he had browsed everything from Asimov to Zen Buddhism, he made his final selections and headed home.

As Rob stepped through his front door, he heard

the phone ringing. He quickly put down his bag of books and hurried to grab the call before the answering machine kicked in. He figured it was probably his mother and stepdad, and they were going to sing "Happy Birthday" to him, like they did each year, corny, but sweet . . .

It wasn't happy birthday.

"Hello, Robert," said the calm male voice on the other end. "This is Trey Wright."

Rob felt his heart skip a beat.

"It is time for us to meet," said Wright. "We have an appointment . . . Hello?"

"Yes, I hear you," said Rob.

"Good. Let me give you the arrangements. Ready?"

"Yes. Go ahead."

"We're going to meet at 10:30 tomorrow morning."

"Ten-thirty?"

"That's right."

"No—I can't," said Rob. "I have to teach."

"Get a substitute," responded Wright.

Wright's tone indicated there was no wiggle room for negotiation.

"All right," Rob said. "Where are we meeting?"

"The food court at the Hawthorne Mall. Do you know where that is?"

"Yes. That's pretty far from where I live . . ."

Wright asked, "You'd be more comfortable someplace where people might recognize you?"

"Point taken. Should I bring anything?"

"Just an eagerness to learn."

"All right."

"What's the matter, Robert?" asked Wright. "I

thought you'd be in better spirits. Aren't you happy now?"

"I'm happy. I'm very happy. I'm just . . . you know, nervous."

"Say no more. I understand. But don't be nervous. Everything will work out. Believe in it."

"I know."

"Your turn has come. This is a big moment."

After the call ended, Rob remained standing by the phone, staring at it. Panic had him grounded.

Oh my God. What have I gotten myself into?

Suddenly the phone rang and he nearly jumped through the roof. He snatched the receiver, stuttering like a fool, "H-h-hello?"

And then his mother and stepfather proceeded to sing Happy Birthday.

The next morning, Rob called the high school and feigned a scratchy throat and cough. "I better stay in. I don't want to get the kids sick," he said. They agreed with his decision and began the hunt for a substitute.

Rob arrived at the mall fifteen minutes early and wandered its length, trying to burn off nervous energy. The place was gradually filling with a weekday crowd of beleaguered moms, hyper kids, and slow-motion seniors.

At 10:30, he approached the food court. All the expected fast-food options lined the walls, with a large seating area of white chairs and tables in the center. Rob's eyes bounced from table to table . . .

. . . and then he saw Trey Wright by himself near Taco Bell, surrounded by empty seats. Wright was eating a pink frozen yogurt with sprinkles. A large Carson Pirie Scott shopping bag rested close to him, touching his leg. He looked as innocuous and forgettable as any other drab morning mall patron.

Rob felt fear, dread, and the urge to spin around and hustle out of there.

Instead, he walked over to the table.

Without looking up, Wright said, "Welcome. Have a seat." He scraped a final spoonful from the bottom of his cup.

Rob sat down.

Wright's eyes rose to meet Rob's gaze.

"Are you ready to shine?" Wright asked.

Rob hesitated. Shine? Wright was staring, eager for a reply. So Rob blended a shrug with a nod. It was weak.

"I know, I know," said Wright. "But you'll feel good when it's over. Trust me. You'll shine because you'll have accomplished something positive and useful in your life. You'll make a difference. Society will benefit. Look around you. These sorry souls. How many people, really, can say they've made the world a better place? They get knocked around by life. They accept the lumps. They don't push back when they get a raw deal. That, my friend, is why the bullies and crooks rule the system. Because John and Jane Doe are resigned to being helpless. Passive. Weak. It's a universal mindset. They're scared into their turtle shells. But it's all perception. We are stronger than that. We can fix what's broken. We can right what's wrong. We have untapped strength and powers. It's a fantastic feeling when you find that strength and let it come alive. Robert, I want you to feel it in your heart and mind, all the way down to your bones. Because you will need it for your mission."

Wright reached down and took the handles of the large Carson Pirie Scott shopping bag. He slid the bag across the floor to Rob.

Rob looked inside and could see a plain-looking, medium-sized package and a large flat envelope.

"Your target lives and works in Barrington, Illinois," said Wright.

Rob listened, perspiring. A trembling moved up his legs, into his chest and arms.

"This person lives alone in a large Tudor manor, middle of the block, set back from the street, an expansive lawn, trees, lots of cover," continued Wright. "This person owns a small retail shop in downtown Barrington. Home by seven o'clock, most nights. Asleep by eleven. Up at five-thirty, leaves the house at seven. No one else living in the house, no dogs. Here's my recommendation. Ready?"

Rob nodded.

"Behind the shop, there's a narrow alleyway with a high fence. This individual parks the car in the alleyway and enters the store from the rear to set up and open shop. In the early hours, there shouldn't be anyone else around. It is a good, isolated location to conduct the shooting."

The word "shooting" pierced Rob like a dagger.

Wright could see the fear on his face and grew stern. "Robert, I want you to remember the elation you felt when you heard that your enemy was dead. The feeling of justice. Resolve. Peace. It is time for you to create that for someone else who has been wronged. It is your duty. It is your debt. We must keep The Circle in motion. Tell me you understand."

"I understand," said Rob.

"Inside the brown package is a loaded, double-action, semi-automatic pistol. It's a point-and-shoot. You don't need to cock the hammer. It does everything for you. You have eight shots in the round."

"I've never fired a . . ." Rob stopped short of completing the sentence.

A tubby, hairy man with a tray of breakfast burritos walked past.

This is absurd, thought Rob.

"Your anonymity will be your greatest asset," declared Wright. "It allows you to get close. Aim for the head and chest, and squeeze the trigger hard. Be prepared for the recoil. Stay balanced. Basically, don't miss, and don't stop shooting until your target is dead."

Rob tried to picture all this, and failed.

"Scout out your location in advance," continued Wright. "Find a place to corner your victim. Establish a clean getaway route. Be prepared to get as far away as quickly as possible. Just be smart. No witnesses. No security cameras. Planning and patience is everything. Remember, you control the moment."

Rob felt nauseated. "Who is my target?" he asked softly.

Wright smiled and gestured to the Carson's bag. "Take out the flat envelope. Open it."

Rob reached down and retrieved the unmarked manila envelope. He unclasped it and could see two items inside. He pulled them out.

The top sheet was a piece of plain white paper with a name, home address and business address printed on it.

The name was Shannon Mayer.

Stunned, Rob lifted the sheet to see what was underneath.

A black and white still photograph, like a headshot from a modeling agency. Shannon Mayer stared back at him . . . young, smiling, vibrant, and absolutely beautiful. Her eyes were warm and inviting, and waves of dark hair rolled alongside prominent cheekbones and perfect skin.

"She's . . . a she," said Rob.

"Now you know everything you need to know," said Wright.

Eleven

Where do I hide this gun?

Rob circled the interior of his small apartment several times, carrying the padded, brown mailing bag. He had taken the gun out only once, very carefully, curtains drawn, to look at. Now he wanted it out of sight entirely, someplace safe and inconspicuous. He had already tucked Shannon Mayer's photo and addresses inside the large Magritte art book on his coffee table, somewhere between the final stages of his career and the index.

Initially, he considered placing the bag with the gun on the top shelf in his small coat closet, behind the winter hat, scarves and ear muffins. But there wasn't a whole lot of room up there. It kept peeking through. Then he thought about the little cabinet in his bathroom, under some towels, but no, what if a visitor discovered it there? He briefly considered fitting the gun inside one of his large pots or saucepans under the kitchen sink, but nixed that idea, too. Under the mattress in his bedroom made him uneasy—the thing was loaded, what if he rolled over in the middle of the night and set it off?

Under the sofa? No. On the bookshelf behind some books? No. In the trunk of his Nissan wedged next to the spare? No.

He finally settled on a drawer of his bedroom dresser, under T-shirts, socks and underwear. On the one hand, it was silly to mingle a deadly weapon with his boxers and BVDs. But it also made some sense—it was the one place where a visitor probably wouldn't stumble on it. Why would anyone be rummaging through his socks and underwear?

Wright had encouraged him to throw the gun into the lake or a river after committing the deed, to dispose of the only evidence. It actually created an incentive for Rob to hurry up and blast his target. Then he could get this damn gun out of his home and close the book on all this madness.

Even after slipping the gun out of sight, it stayed vivid in Rob's mind. He kept seeing the circle engraving on the handle. He couldn't look at his bedroom dresser without thinking of the sleek black murder tool that rested inside. The dresser seemed to take on the presence of a live being. Buried inside, a lethal weapon waited, prepared to spring into action and create mayhem, like a coiled rattlesnake.

Early on a Sunday morning, Rob drove thirty miles northwest of his apartment to the community of Barrington. He wanted to get a flavor of the neighborhood and atmosphere. He wanted to see his target's house and shop. He did not bring the gun. This was research only.

Although he knew about Barrington, he couldn't remember having ever visited before. He was surprised to find a small city nestled within a broad, lush countryside. On the outskirts, there were farms, horse-riding trails, and miles of open green space. Unlike the North Shore of Chicago, there wasn't a manic attempt to squeeze housing into every available acre.

Downtown Barrington had a historic feel with Victorian-style lampposts, brick walkways, pedestrian benches, and a genuine Main Street. There were small specialty shops and family restaurants gracefully blending into the traditional, turn-of-the-century architecture. The center of downtown even had a gazebo plaza.

The ambience was quaint and relaxed. It was early, and the community was just starting to rise. He didn't see too many people out.

Using a street map he pulled off the Internet, Rob found Shannon Mayer's shop, Charms. Charms was comfortably snuggled in a red brick building between a florist and a small art gallery. The pink awning promised GIFTS, IMPORTS & TREASURES.

Everything was closed. He was able to pull up his car to the curb, parallel to the storefront. There was a large window stylishly decorated to display all sorts of pricey paraphernalia: elaborate, regal candlesticks; handcarved chess sets; ribboned baskets filled with colorful bath soaps; upscale birdhouses; fancy wine racks; and picture frames.

Rob heard a car coming. He looked into the rear-view mirror and saw a police vehicle headed in his direction. Rob's entire body exploded with instant panic.

The police car passed him, its driver staring straight ahead.

Whew, that was a close one, thought Rob, followed by: *A close what? I'm not doing anything wrong. I'm just sitting here!*

He decided to leave anyway.

He grabbed one of his map printouts from the Internet and headed for Shannon Mayer's house.

She lived in a residential area with large lawns and plenty of space between houses. Her neighborhood looked fairly wealthy, the houses were lavish and well-maintained. On the outside they retained their old-world charm, while on the inside they no doubt contained all the latest twenty-first century comforts and amenities.

Shannon Mayer's address was 621 Alta. He found it and rolled to a slow stop.

He remained there just long enough to get a good look . . . but not long enough to start arousing suspicion.

Wright had told him she lived by herself. Yet she had a home that probably could fit a family of five. It was a renovated Tudor-style home with exposed wood timber framing and patterned stone work. The roof was steeply pitched, with overlapping gables and tall, narrow windows. The yard was tastefully fenced in, with immaculately manicured landscaping.

Overall, the property had a medieval flavor. Fit for

a king, thought Rob. And I live in a crud apartment with thin walls and cookie-cutter banality.

Down the street, he saw a kid on a Razor scooter coming his way. Rob tossed the car into drive and left the neighborhood.

He went home, flipped open the Magritte book and took out her photo.

Everytime he looked at it, he felt stingers.

She's gorgeous. What the hell?

Well, beauty could be evil, right? Shepherd wasn't ugly. Who said the woman had to look like Kathy Bates in *Misery*?

Still, there was something disarming about the way she smiled in the picture. She was youthful, she looked friendly. Her eyes were brown. They looked kind.

Where was this picture taken? It looked like some kind of professional, soft-focus studio portrait. Was she a model or an actress?

And what was her crime?

He needed to know more. He wasn't supposed to know more. But just ambushing someone from a photograph . . .

On Institute Day, he got out of school early and decided to return to Charms.

The gameplan: He would simply walk inside, blend in with the other customers, browse like any other nobody, check the place out, and maybe get a good look at Shannon Mayer, see her interact with a customer, hear her voice, watch her mannerisms, get a better sense of what this woman was all about.

Again, no gun. Just research.

Rob drove into downtown Barrington and found street parking. He walked down the block to Charms. There was a chalkboard propped out front on an easel. It read: *Bargains for your gardens! Go cuckoo for our clocks!* in happy, multi-colored lettering.

I'm already cuckoo, thought Rob, and he pushed through the door quickly, before he could reconsider the visit.

A little bell chimed.

There were no other customers in the store.

"Hello there! Can I help you find something?" said Shannon Mayer cheerfully.

She stood next to a display of birdbaths.

She was beautiful and youthful and happy.

Just like the photo, except now there was an entire figure, very feminine, medium build, with an olive blouse, black skirt, pink thighs, black boots.

Rob did his best to appear nonchalant while hammers pounded inside his chest.

"I'm just looking," he said.

"For anything particular?"

She's already suspicious! said a voice in his head.

That's idiotic, why would she be suspicious? said a competing voice.

Answer her question! screamed both voices.

"A gift," he said.

"Great." She finished positioning a small, handwritten card on a sculpted, stone birdbath. *Invite your winged friends to flock around the water cooler*, it said, above an exorbitant price.

Cute writing, he thought.

"Is it for someone special? Your wife?"

"I don't have a wife," he said with a forced chuckle. "It's for my mother. Her birthday is coming up."

Her birthday was last month! said the panicky voice in his head.

How the hell is she going to know that? responded the rational voice.

"Birthday gift for your mother . . ." said Shannon, turning and glancing through the store. "What type of things does she like?"

"I don't know," he said weakly. "She likes knick-knacky things."

"Knick-knacky," she repeated back at him.

Oops. Did I just insult her store?

"Nice knick-knacky things," he offered, and she just nodded, eyes searching, and he knew he wasn't giving her much to go on.

As she was turned away from him, he had a chance to really look her over. Her hair was beautiful, thick and layered in that way that some people are just born with. Her outfit fit snugly and confirmed to the curious that the curves were in all the right places.

The boots he liked.

Snap out of it, he told himself.

"What kind of price range were you thinking?" she asked.

He shrugged.

"Something that says I love you without breaking the bank," he responded.

She laughed, a sweet, genuine laugh. "I like that," she said. Then, "Let's have a look around."

He never wanted this much attention. It was all wrong.

Where are the other customers? I should have come on a Saturday!

She spent the next fifteen minutes showing him different areas of the shop, engaging in pleasant, jokey chatter. The store was filled with sweet odors—incense, soaps, and candles—spread by ceiling fans. Drifting, synthesized new-age music played from small speakers on the wall. She was very talkative and he responded with interest and questions. They looked at Chinese watercolor paintings of flowers, backgammon sets, elephant bookends, curio cabinets, trinket boxes, elegant teapots, table lamps with beaded shades, handsome leather photo albums, and stylish letter openers. He hit his head on some dangling windchimes and made a dumb joke about hearing a ringing in his ears, but she laughed.

"For his mother," he wound up buying a five-inch-tall porcelain puppy figurine, sad-eyed with floppy ears and a real chain collar. His mother loved little dogs but couldn't have one because of her new husband's allergies.

"This shouldn't make him sneeze," said Shannon. "And you don't have to walk or feed him. Plus he doesn't bark."

"Perfect. Say, do you have any porcelain kids?"

She laughed, loud. "No porcelain kids. No real kids, either." It almost sounded like a come-on. Or was he overreaching?

After buying the puppy, he continued to linger, and they continued to talk, mostly about her store and some of the new items she was expecting, and before he knew it, he had bought more merchandise: a hand-carved, painted soapstone coaster set from Kenya and artsy wine bottle stoppers. His wallet was drained dry.

When he left her shop, he realized that their conversation had become so engaging that he actually forgot he was destined to kill her.

Google was no help.

Back at his apartment, seated in front of his PC, he entered "Shannon Mayer" in the search engine and called up a whole bunch of Shannon Mayers, but none of them seemed to be her, except for one. Her name appeared in an online article about Halloween decorations with a quote from her about pottery jack-o-lanterns and a reference to her store.

When he Googled her store, there were various references in listings and directories. He found a mention of Charms's sponsorship of a children's art exhibit at the local library, plus a few other innocuous mentions that offered no clues.

Curiosity engulfed him. He had to know more about her. But he couldn't ask around. He couldn't engage others on his behalf. He was on his own.

Who does she hang out with? he wanted to know. *What does she do outside of the gift shop? Where does her life intersect with something horrible? She's so carefree and pleasant on the outside. Where is the layer of evil?*

On a Saturday, he returned to downtown Barrington. This time, he parked a good distance from Charms and walked. But he did not go inside the shop. He circled behind it. He scouted the back alley, the area Trey Wright recommended for a swift and efficient assassination.

Aim for the head and chest, Wright had instructed. Make sure it is done right. You only get one chance.

The alley was empty, save for trash bins, some crates, and a few parked cars. The ground was an uneven stretch of gravel, weeds and potholes. There was a high fence that walled off the alley from a nearby residential area. The alley was certainly out of view and uninviting, but the backs of these stores had doors, and someone could pop out at anytime . . .

I can't get caught. Getting caught is not an option.

A white BMW sat behind Charms. Shannon Mayer's car. The distance between the car and the rear entrance of her store was roughly twenty-five feet.

Rob shuddered and left the alley.

Charms closed at five on Saturdays. Rob sat in his car, parked on the street that fed the entrance to the alley. The BMW stayed in his view.

At 5:20, he saw Shannon exit the rear of the store alone. She wore a jean jacket and jeans, ankles exposed above her white tennis shoes. Her hair was pulled into a ponytail. She was far enough that she did not see him watching from his car.

She didn't even look his way. She approached the driver's side of the BMW, unlocked and opened the door, and slipped inside.

When the BMW pulled out of the alley and onto the street, it turned past Rob's Nissan. Rob waited a moment. Then he put on his sunglasses, a baseball cap, and followed.

What does beautiful, single Shannon Mayer do on a Saturday night? Whom does she hang out with?

He kept his eyes locked on the BMW, remaining a few car lengths behind. She didn't go far.

After five blocks, she pulled into a small strip mall consisting of a bank, a furniture store, Starbucks, and a Chinese restaurant. She parked, and he parked one row back.

Shannon walked into the Chinese restaurant, Beijing Station. Getting carry out?

Rob sat there, and when fifteen minutes had passed with no exit, his question was answered. She was eating inside. So whom did she meet?

Maybe somebody diabolical and the two of them were plotting their next . . . whatever.

Rob knew he was going to have to check it out. It didn't make sense to follow her here and then not get the information he was seeking. He had his sunglasses, his baseball cap.

He was just one shop customer from last week, one of . . . hundreds? Dozens? In any case, she wouldn't recognize him. He was just going to walk in, grab a carry-out menu, take a quick look, then boogie.

Rob climbed out of the Nissan. He stepped across the lot and up to the front entrance of Beijing Station. He hesitated.

One . . . two . . . three . . . go.

Rob pulled open the door and entered. He walked up to the counter, while his eyes strayed, searching for . . .

Shit, she was seated at a table right near the counter.

Eating. *Alone.*

"Hello—" said the hostess.

Rob grabbed a carryout menu from the holder on the counter and promptly spun around, heading back to the door. He left the restaurant.

She didn't see me.

He sat in his Nissan, somehow amazed that this beautiful young woman was eating in a restaurant by herself on a Saturday night.

Maybe her next destination would provide a clue.

When Shannon finally departed from the restaurant, he jammed his key into the ignition. When she started her car, he started his. He followed her out of the strip mall parking lot.

She drove about two miles to another area of retail stores on a main road not too far from downtown Barrington. She parked against the curb. He drove past her.

He pulled into a spot about fifty feet ahead, then immediately turned to look.

She was walking into one of the stores. He craned to see what it was, nearly climbing into the backseat for a better view.

A book store.

"Read All Over." One of the last of the independent bookstores . . . at least until Borders or Barnes and Noble rolled into town.

What was she doing there?

He sat for a while, before determining *screw it, I can check it out without being seen.*

He checked himself in the rear-view mirror. It was evening, the sunglasses were going to look silly, so he ditched them. But the baseball cap could stay.

Rob walked up to the bookstore. Like everything else in this town, it looked very charming and personable, something held over from a bygone era.

Through glass doors, he could see that the bookstore was actually busy, bustling with people.

Good. I'll blend in with the crowd.

He entered and walked around casually, checking out New Releases, Mystery and Thriller, and biking books, while glancing around for a Shannon Mayer sighting.

I wonder what kind of books she reads. And then he found himself admiring her all over again. *She's in a bookstore while most everybody else is at home watching crap on TV.*

He leisurely moved through the aisles of books, stopping on a regular basis to pick something off the shelf and flip through it—not all that different from his regular behavior.

After about ten minutes, he became concerned that he hadn't spotted Shannon. Did she leave the store and he missed it? Had she actually entered another store?

As he reached the back of the store, he stumbled on an open area where about a dozen people were seated, listening to an author give a talk.

The author, a fiftyish man with a salt-and-pepper mustache and eyebrows to match, wore a tweed sports jacket with patches at the elbows. He stood behind a table with a stack of books.

Ice and Shadow by Les Jacobson.

Hey, I know that author, thought Rob. He just won some big national award, I think it was the . . .

"Hello, there," said Jacobson, and it took a moment for Rob to realize that the author's attention was off his audience, and he was talking to Rob specifically.

"Huh?" said Rob.

"Please join us, have a seat," said Jacobson, gesturing to an empty chair.

"Oh, I—"

The people in the audience started turning to look at Rob. "We have plenty of seats," said Jacobson.

Stop drawing attention to me!

"We're just getting started," Jacobson said. "Don't worry. I don't bite."

"Okay," smiled Rob, moving sideways, quickly slipping into a seat in the middle row. "Sure."

"Great," said Jacobson. "As I was saying, *Ice and Shadow* is my fifth novel. It's about a young woman who returns to her childhood home in Minnesota to rediscover herself after cancer takes her husband, and her daughter leaves to study abroad . . ."

Rob half-listened, waiting for his opportunity to slip out of the chair and return between the bookshelves.

". . . she gets a job in the movie theater where as a youth she dreamed about being an actress . . . one of the other employees is an ex-con . . ."

"Psst."

". . . they strike up a friendship, and then one afternoon, they make love during a matinee in the back row of the darkened theater . . ."

"Psssst!"

Rob turned around. Who was *psst*ing?

Shannon sat behind him and made a small wave.

Rob did not smile inside, but managed to force a grin.

"You like Jacobson, too?" she asked.

Rob nodded.

"One of my favorite writers."

"He's good," agreed Rob, trying to return his attention to the author.

"He's great," said Shannon. She had several hardbacks in her lap. "I'm going to get him to autograph these."

Rob nodded and looked at Jacobson. He wanted to bolt.

"I'm going to read you a passage," said Jacobson. "It's the nervous-breakdown scene."

After the author finished his reading, he signed books at the table.

Rob saw his chance to scoot out.

But Shannon blocked him.

"How did your mother like the basset hound?"

"She loves it," he replied. "She really . . . can't stop talking about it."

"Wonderful," said Shannon. "So have you read *Ice and Shadow*?"

"I've been meaning to . . ." said Rob. "I read the review in *The Tribune* book section."

"Oh yes, they raved about it." Then she tilted her head and chuckled. "You know, I don't think I ever formally introduced myself at the store. I'm Shannon Mayer."

She stuck out her hand. He shook it and, without

time to come up with a better lie, replied, "Hi, I'm—Hank."

"Hi, Hank."

Somehow, in the bright bookstore lights, Shannon looked even more radiant than the last time, even though she was dressed down. Her complexion was flawless. She wore lip gloss, smiled wide, with round cheekbones . . . and that insanely inviting warmth.

She urged the conversation forward, and he opened up, complied. She was genuinely interested in talking to him. She cracked up at his dumb jokes, she looked at him like . . . he was engaging. Attractive, even.

"Wait here one second," said Shannon. "I need to get my books signed, then I want to ask you a question."

"Sure," said Rob.

He stood there, and she walked over to the table and chatted for a moment with Jacobson as he signed her books.

Rob felt nauseated. Hunger, terror, confusion, shock . . . all blended into one big upset stomach.

Shannon came back with her books. Except now she had two copies of *Ice and Shadow*.

She handed one to him.

"I got an extra. For you. I had him sign it to you."

Rob was floored. "Thanks. Really, you didn't have to . . ."

"You *have* to read it. Then we'll compare notes."

Compare what?

"Listen," she said. "I hope I'm not being too forward. It's in my nature. But, if you're not attached, I'd like to ask you to dinner next week."

Rob went silent. His brain stopped for a second.

Gridlock. Finally he blurted: "Dinner? I don't know." He chuckled nervously. "I mean, you know, I just, I'm sort of . . ."

She thumped a finger against his chest playfully. "Don't play hard to get, that will only make me more aggressive."

He shrugged. He looked into her gentle eyes. That smile. He was buckled. "Of course. Sure."

"Red or white?"

"Excuse me?"

"Wine."

"Red?" he responded, but it sounded more like a question. The question mark was really meant for *What the hell am I doing?*

"I want to have you over," she said. "I'm a good cook. *Really.* Don't make that face. I read a lot of fiction, but I also have this monster collection of cookbooks. I have some things I want to try out. Oh, don't worry, Hank, I'm not going to experiment with you. If it goes bad and I burn everything up, we'll order out for pizza."

Les Jacobson passed them on his way out. He waved cheerfully. "Enjoy the books, kids."

Rob looked at him wearily.

Yeah, thanks, Les. Thanks a ton.

Twelve

Throughout the next week, Rob tried to find Trey Wright. But he had no way to contact him—no phone number, no address, nothing. He could not find a "Trey Wright" listed anywhere in the Chicago area. His encounters with Wright felt like a weird dream, yet now he was stuck in a frightful reality.

He had agreed to shoot someone, fueled by his own mad obsession to see Shepherd go down. Now Shepherd was gone, eliminated, and the rage that had blocked Rob's rational thinking was conveniently absent.

I'm not a violent man, yet now I must shoot this attractive, sweet young woman and I don't know why. Excuse the cliché, but what's my motivation?

What was Shannon Mayer's crime? Why did she deserve the death penalty? Who did she destroy?

It haunted him each day.

And very quickly, it was date night.

Rob realized that, in a way, she had made things

easier for him. She had invited him inside her home, where he could commit the deed without witnesses. The body wouldn't be found for hours, maybe days. It was an improvement over the public alley behind her store. Aside from the mess in his head, the plan itself would be very clean:

Show up for the date. Wear a sports jacket, keep the gun hidden from view. Kill her in the first thirty minutes. Simply wait for the right opportunity . . . wait for her back to be turned . . . maybe while she's preparing the food . . . then lift the gun . . . point it at the base of her head . . . very close, can't miss . . . and fire.

Rob shuddered.

He got dressed in nice khaki slacks, a white cotton dress shirt, and a navy blazer. Not real hip, but he looked pretty good in it anyway. He kept the belt tight and practiced placing the gun in his waistband, grip protruding, hidden under the flap of his sports coat. The safety was on, so he wouldn't accidentally blow his balls off. He had researched the gun to death on the Internet (and promptly emptied the browser cache), so he was knowledgeable about how to use it.

He looked at himself in his bedroom mirror and could see no evidence of a gun under the clothing. Good.

From the dresser, the puppy figurine with the floppy ears watched with big, sad eyes. Rob turned it to the wall.

As the Saturday sun melted into the horizon, Rob

climbed into his Nissan and embarked on the journey to Barrington, but not before laboring over what CD to play in the car and almost forgetting the bottle of Cabernet. He placed the gun under his car seat and made sure to stay inside the speed limit.

Objective #1: Do not get caught.

His CD collection had not offered much in the way of the proper mood music—The Beach Boys and Paul Simon were just not going to cut it—but after some digging, he found Stravinsky's *The Rite of Spring* and Mussorgsky's *Night on Bald Mountain*.

He played them loud.

Think evil.

Think Shepherd.

I am killing someone else's Richard Shepherd.

It is a noble and necessary thing to do.

Rob parked down the street and around the corner from Shannon's house. It helped that he didn't know a soul in this town, and that the homes in this area were big, set back on deep lots, and reasonably isolated from one another. He didn't see another person.

No witnesses.

He slid the semi-automatic pistol behind his waistband and under the sportcoat flap. He grabbed the bottle of wine, took a deep breath, exhaled, then left the car.

He moved quickly—but not too quickly—toward her house.

621 Alta Drive.

He strolled up the elegant stone walkway and to the front door. The door was large, oak, with stylish trim.

He stared at the doorbell for a long moment. *Inside of one hour, you will be on your way home, deed done. Stay focused, and all of this will soon be behind you.*

He pressed the button and could hear a cheerful, melodic series of tones. Then he heard footsteps quickly coming toward him on a hardwood floor.

The door swung open and Rob faced the most beautiful woman in the world.

His heart pounded insanely. Going on a date with this stunner made him nervous enough without having to kill her.

"Hank!" she exclaimed, huge smile.

He almost glanced over his shoulder to look for Hank.

"Come in, come in," she said cheerfully. "You had no trouble finding the place?"

"Not at all," Rob said, entering a spacious, open foyer. He could see large, high-ceiling rooms in every direction, richly decorated in art and upscale furnishings, an energetic mix of contemporary and antique.

"You brought wine. That's so sweet, thank you," she said. She accepted it from him. She closed the front door behind him with a definitive *slam.*

"Come with me. Dinner is still a work-in-progress, but I have some hors d'oeuvres to hold us over."

He followed her into the kitchen.

"We're having filet mignon. I hope you're not a vegetarian. I was going to call, but I realized I don't have your number."

"I love filet mignon," he said, followed by "Wow."

It was a dream kitchen: tall wood cabinets with glass

panels, granite countertops with full marble back splashes, and top-of-the-line, stainless-steel appliances.

In the center of the room there was an island with seating under a ceiling rack of dangling pots and pans.

The kitchen flowed into an adjacent breakfast nook on one side and a deep pantry on the other. All this kitchen for one person? Who probably weighed 110 pounds?

She placed his wine bottle among about two dozen others in a large, wrought-iron rack embedded in a cabinet. "I hope you don't mind. I've already got some wine here that I picked just for tonight."

"Not at all," he said. "This is a beautiful home. You live alone?"

"Yes," she said, a bit of sadness in her voice.

"You must be your own best customer," he said, looking over a lineup of colored-glass spice jars in a hand-carved rack.

"I know where to get the best," she said. "It's my job." Then, "Want the dime tour?"

"Sure."

She took him around the first floor, but they did not go upstairs. Every room made his eyes pop: the living room with arched entries, pillars, stone fireplace, and suede sofas and chairs; the den with a grand, old writing desk on turned legs, full of cubbyholes and graced with fancy carvings; the handsome, cherry-accented library with built-in shelves and an admirable stock of first editions of quality literature; the relaxing family room with a home theater and a wall of French doors overlooking a garden patio; and finally, the formal dining room, chandelier dimmed, candles lit, and table set with linen cloth, fine china, and a fresh bouquet.

"I probably overdid it, but that's my nature. I don't mean to overwhelm you," she said, standing close to him. She smelled good.

"Thanks," he said. It was a slightly awkward thing to say, but he meant it.

She had done all this . . . for *him?*

He was glad he would never have to show her his pathetic little apartment. Or fess up to his glamorless teaching career. He just had to weave enough fiction to get him through this night.

"I'll go get our wine and the appetizers and we can have a seat in the living room," she said.

"I'll help you carry the appetizers."

"That would be great."

He followed her into the kitchen. She poured two glasses of wine, fuller than he expected, and he took the tray of carrots and artichoke dip.

As he lifted the tray, he felt movement in his pants.

The gun was slipping. Rob quickly placed the tray back and grabbed at the weapon before it could begin sliding down his leg. He adjusted the best he could—as quickly as he could—and she glanced at him, did a subtle double take.

Great, she thinks I'm playing with my crotch.

He reached back for the tray, acting cool, like nothing was wrong, and she turned back, and he followed her out of the kitchen.

Well, I just embarrassed myself big time in there, he thought. *Now I really have to kill her.*

It was a joke to himself, but he wasn't smiling.

He was petrified.

In the living room, a sleek black stereo played a circular piano composition, both haunting and elegant. He noticed the CD case: Philip Glass, *Glassworks.*

"I play it in my store all the time," she said, setting down the wineglasses on illustrated coasters on a table crowded with extravagant knick-knacks. Extravagant knick-knacks—was that an oxymoron?

Oxymoron . . . good vocabulary word for class.

His mind was running off in 200 directions, scattered by panic.

She cleaned more space, and he placed the tray on the table.

The gun started slipping again.

God damn it.

"Where's the . . ." he said, ending his sentence with an embarrassed smile.

"Bathroom," she caught on. "Sure. Through that door, a left and a right."

He moved quickly to avoid another crotch-grabbing scene.

Rob found the bathroom—also crammed with colorful clutter, decorated like one of her store displays—and closed the door behind him. He locked it.

Fifteen minutes into the date, and he was already frazzled into near hysteria.

A laughing ceramic frog holding out a bar of soap greeted him at the sink. *Screw you, frog!*

He had to get this over with. True, dinner smelled good, but he was just extending the agony, and it was time to shoot, watch her drop, and leave.

This whole absurd nightmare needed to end, or he was going to blow it for certain.

Rob eased the semi-automatic out of his pants. He gripped it and wrapped a finger around the trigger.

Bang bang, then bye-bye. Drive off into the night. Return to a normal life with normal pressures. Never come back to this town again.

Just shoot her.

He was really psyched to do it, too, but then he made a fatal error.

He glanced in the mirror.

And he saw how ridiculous and unnatural he looked.

A bookish high school English teacher with a gun.

It looked all wrong. It looked comical.

Six-foot-one of milquetoast and sensitivity with a deadly weapon on the end of one arm, like an abnormal growth.

I can't do this. But I have no choice.

He finally arrived on a simple solution: drink several glasses of wine first.

He was thinking too much and the wine would help with that.

Who said he had to kill before dinner?

Rob flushed the toilet, and under the noise of the churning water he snapped open the tall cabinet alongside the sink. He buried the gun deep under a rainbow assortment of bath towels.

I'll come back and get it later. This is going to happen. Just not right now.

Rob returned to the living room.

The Philip Glass music was speeding up, frenetic woodwinds and strings, still making circles. It made him dizzy. Nauseated.

Right. Blame the music.

Shannon sat on the sofa, biting into a carrot. He moved around the table to sit next to her.

As he sat, she smiled, while chewing, brown eyes warm, on him. He watched her mouth move, and it was sexy.

Rob nabbed his wineglass and took an extended sip.

He noticed her glass was already half empty, too.

He took a carrot and chewed slowly.

She finished chewing and asked a question. "What did you think of *Ice and Shadow*?"

He nodded, swallowed. "I haven't started it yet, but I'm looking forward to it." Actually, since it was already signed to Hank, he had toyed with the idea of giving it to Hank for his birthday.

"I really got into it," she said. "I don't want to ruin it for you, but, conceptually, it's about the way we never really live in the present, we're always pulled into the past. The past should be forgotten and buried. It holds us back."

"Sometimes there's just more clarity looking backward than forward," suggested Rob.

"And that's the trap," said Shannon. "We need to be more about our goals and potential, so we control our destiny. In *Ice and Shadow*, Ellen, the main character is confused about life, so she goes back to her childhood home to find comfort, like returning to the womb, but she finds that it's not her salvation. It won't solve her struggle. In fact, her problems all stem from seeds planted in her past. She needs to cut loose and be reborn."

"Yes. Starting a new chapter in your life instead of rereading the old ones," Rob said. That was actually how he had tried to approach life post-Beth. Like his life was a narrative that must move forward. Sometimes it worked; sometimes it didn't, and he lost his place.

"And the prose . . ." said Shannon. "Jacobson has a way with words that makes you really feel the characters come to life. It's so rich and eloquent."

Rob smiled then. "I'm just amazed to meet someone else my own age who can appreciate good writing. Today, everything is movies, TV and the Internet. And computer games. Who has time for books?"

"It's a shame," she said. She reached for more wine. As she turned away, he took full advantage of the moment to scan and admire her comprehensive beauty. She wore a black blouse with a white collar opened to show her collarbone. Her pants were charcoal and hugged her hips. She wore pointy black dress shoes with a dramatic spike.

Her facial features were perfectly sculptured and balanced with a dash of drama—a long, sloping nose with a slight upturn. She wore lip gloss and a little blush. She had thin, dark eyebrows that gave accent to her expressions, often lifting to open up her face, in sync with her frequent smiles.

"So tell me about yourself," she said. "I don't even know what you do."

"I teach . . ." he said too quickly, foolishly, and he

had to immediately amend the truth with a lie "... college history."

"College history?"

"History at college."

She laughed. "I know what you mean. What college?"

"Northwestern University."

"Wow. Northwestern," she said. Then, "Shoot, I better go check on dinner."

"Do you need help?" he offered.

"No. I've go it under control."

She left, and he emptied his wineglass.

Dinner went well. Too well.

He really liked her. She scored 100 and earned extra credit. Personality was an "A." Looks? Well, can you go any higher than "A+++"?

He would have been more comfortable with a flunkee.

It was eating him up inside, so he continued to drink wine. So did she, and they were well into their second bottle before dinner was half finished.

The filet mignon was magnificent, generously seasoned and sharing the plate with roasted baby red potatoes and sautéed spinach. The feast was preceded by a fabulous, wet Caesar salad, served on chilled plates, dusted with Parmesan cheese and a couple of anchovies. It was the best meal he had consumed in months, maybe years.

Dessert, promised Shannon, would be a grand finale.

She was right. Chocolate mousse. Served with sweetened whipped cream and grated chocolate.

"Chocolate makes me crazy," she said, rolling her eyes with exaggeration.

"Me, too," he replied, reaching for more wine.

Their conversation flowed with an unexpected ease for two strangers, and he had to carefully sidestep his personal details and steer the talk into unrevealing areas. Their mutual interest in the arts helped. As did their loose, humorous banter.

All through dinner, a voice inside his skull firmly reminded him to go ahead and have fun, but when dessert was finished, it was time to take care of business.

Now he was staring into an empty, stemmed glass of chocolate mousse. The sight sent a shudder rippling throughout his body.

Well, maybe there's one more spoonful, if I scraped . . .

Shannon stood. "I'm going to move the dishes into the kitchen."

Rob started to rise, offering, "I'll help," but she waved him down: "No, no. You sit. It'll just take a sec. I'm just going to move them off the table."

She left for the kitchen with an armful of plates.

Rob sat in his chair for a few seconds, then stood up again. "I'm going to use the little boy's room," he said. It sounded dorky. Extremely dorky for a killer.

Rob finished the rest of his wine.

He went into the bathroom, closed the door and locked it.

The frog laughed at him. He didn't care.

Rob flushed the toilet and snapped open the cabinet door. He reached into the shelf of towels for the gun.

It wasn't there.

Rob stumbled back several steps. Holy—! Where the—? What the—?

He saw his own petrified expression in the mirror. He paced the interior of the bathroom in a quick circle, mind racing, and returned to the cabinet.

Then he noticed another shelf below, also stocked with an assortment of towels. He gently reached in . . . felt the lump . . . dug out the gun.

This time, he did not look at himself in the mirror. He placed all attention on the gun.

He could hear the clatter of dishes in the kitchen, flatware dropping into the sink.

How am I going to do this?

Deep breath, deep breath.

Imagine she is Shepherd. Yes, that was it. That was truly the only way he could draw from the well of hatred that must still be inside him. *Her death equals Richard Shepherd's demise.* That was the whole concept of The Circle. The genius. It was substitution.

He would be shooting Shannon Mayer, but really he was blowing away Richard Shepherd, Beth's murderer.

Whoever killed Shepherd must have done it the same way. Shepherd's killer was envisioning his or her own enemy because, most likely, he or she had no beef with Shepherd. He probably looked like a kindly older gentleman to them. Shepherd's killer probably felt all the guilt and confusion Rob now felt.

Think: substitution.

Beth's killer. In that kitchen right now.

Go! Now!

He unlocked the bathroom door and emerged.

He gripped the gun, finger on the trigger. He

stepped through the corridor and into the kitchen.

Get close, raise it, fire it.

But she wasn't in the kitchen.

"Hank?" he heard her call out.

He turned, brought the gun up, looked around, but she was in another room.

"Hank, I'm in the living room," she said.

Rob heard the voice of Shannon Mayer, sweet and beautiful Shannon Mayer, not Richard Shepherd, no matter how hard he tried to fool himself.

"Okay," he responded, probably several beats late.

He saw the second bottle of wine open on the kitchen counter, still one-third full. He grabbed it by the neck and chugged it dry, still holding the semi-automatic in his other hand.

He put the empty bottle down, hoped the wine would help, but it didn't. It just didn't.

"Hank, are you lost?" she said, and she laughed, cheerful and warm, and he could picture her sitting there, amused, sexy, eager to talk more about art or books or her shop or . . .

"Hank? Are you okay?"

Great, now I'm arousing suspicion.

Rob quickly shoved the gun into his pants, behind the waistband, off to one side, the grip hidden by the flap of his sports coat.

He strolled into the living room. "I was just admiring . . ." he started. Then he stopped.

The living room lights had been dimmed considerably.

"Are we going to play hide and seek?" he joked in a weak voice.

She giggled, seated on the sofa, shoes off, feet tucked under her. "Could be."

She had changed the music on the stereo to something slick and sexy. It sounded like Bryan Ferry. *Oh shit, Roxy Music, Avalon. I made out to that sophomore year in college.*

"Are you going to leave me alone in the dark?" she asked, lifting her wineglass to her lips. "Hey, where's your drink?"

"I'm okay," he said, and he was anything but.

He walked over, trying not to bang into anything in the dark, carefully avoiding the ottoman and a pedestal table showcasing crystal.

He sat on the sofa next to her, but not near her.

She moved closer. "Why are you waaaay over there?" Her voice was soft and slurred.

He shrugged, smiled, and felt the gun press against his stomach as he adjusted his position.

"I'm really glad I met you," she said. He saw her brown eyes lock on his.

"I'm glad I met you," he responded in a voice way too formal.

Her hair was thrown forward, dropped in front of her shoulders. There was a hint of mischief in her smirk.

He saw her coming and could not, could not, could not move away.

She pressed her lips against his mouth. His mouth didn't react at first, because he was distracted by the fireworks in his brain, but it felt extremely nice, and she smelled so good that he began to answer the kiss with a warm reception.

Things were happening fast. Bryan Ferry crooned. Shannon Mayer's hand explored, moving across his chest, swirling, while the kiss continued on a course of its own. Rob put his hand against her hair, cupped it gently, and moved his lower half to closer proximity. She moved in closer, too, and the kiss kept gaining momentum, and her fingers kept moving, enjoying a tour of his body, his chest, his thigh, his—

—gun?

He realized she had brushed past his gun and he immediately jumped, pulled away, bolted upright.

He couldn't tell from her bewildered look if she had felt something suspicious, been startled by a misinterpretation, or was simply reacting to his jump.

"I have to go," said Rob. He moved off the couch and made sure the sports jacket covered both lumps.

"Go?" she said.

"I have to grade a bunch of grammar tests," he said. "I almost forgot, they're due t—"

"For a history class?"

"It's grammar history," he said, perhaps his most moronic lie to date, but she seemed more attuned to his abrupt termination of the intimacy.

"I hope I didn't—" she started.

"Oh no, it's not you. You are great. Dinner was fantastic. Everything was fantastic. This has been an evening I will always remember." And that was no lie. And with that, he started for the door.

She quickly followed.

"Hank . . ."

"Thanks for everything, Shannon. I had a really

nice time." He continued to express his gratitude, even while fleeing.

He opened the front door, stepped through, then spun around for one more goodbye.

Her face had a new expression he had not seen before. Hurt.

"I'm sorry," said Rob.

"I don't understand." She made a small shrug, a desperate smile. "Were we hitting it off?"

"Yes," said Rob firmly.

"Then—"

"It's the timing," said Rob.

"Will I see you again?" she asked. Backlit. Beautiful. Those eyes.

"Yes," said Rob, but there was uncertainty in his voice.

"Yes?" she prodded for a better intonation.

"I promise," he said, more affirmative.

Shannon relaxed a little. She looked Rob over, and then asked him, coyly, "Cross your heart and hope to die?"

Thirteen

Bill Wilk was a fat rich kid. Chubby cheeks, bosoms, and an attitude. He liked to anchor the corner seat in a back row and not contribute. He was not stupid, and his grades were good. But he was lazy. At sixteen, he had the assured presence of someone whose future was already neatly assembled before him. He openly bragged that one day he would inherit his father's soap company—a soap with a muscular brand name and legacy that had been woven into the fabric of popular culture.

The soap brought great wealth to several generations of the Wilk family and showed no signs of letting up. Up-and-coming competitors were quickly gobbled up and swallowed into the empire. Wall Street loved them.

Bill and his parents lived in a mansion on Lake Michigan with a private stretch of beach that rivaled some of the public beaches. Bill and his parents also went on frequent exotic vacations: European getaways, African safaris, excursions on a private yacht in the Caribbean, whatever took their fancy.

Often, Bill's chair in class would go empty for several days, or a week or two, preceded by a formal, typed letter from his parents explaining the necessity for Bill's travel. The letter did not ask for permission, it was simply for "informational purposes." Rob didn't know how the other teachers dealt with the abrupt absences, but he had grown accustomed to letting them slide. The kid was probably learning more seeing the world than he would get from textbooks and classroom exercises.

Then, over the course of time, Bill Wilk's trips became a good thing. Two years earlier, during a warm stretch of spring, Bill and his parents took off for Alaska, and Rob had used this knowledge to further his courtship of Beth. He had been desperately searching for someplace private and romantic for a special evening and hit upon a thought, first in sarcastic bemusement, but then with increasing consideration.

Go to the Wilks' beach. What the hell, they're not home.

The Wilks' mansion sat near a curve in Sheridan Road with a small parcel of public beach not far off. If you followed the right path, and stayed in the shadows, you could spill out onto their beach, isolated and undisturbed, listening to the waves, huddled under the moon.

It was a beautiful setting. Rob and Beth made several trips to the Wilks' beach, timed with Bill's vacations. They always had a great time in the dark, usually splitting a bottle of wine, never encountering another soul.

No witnesses except for the face of the moon.

Now, two years later, Rob came to class and saw Bill's empty chair and held the letter that had been deposited into his teacher's mailbox.

The Wilks had left for Madrid.

Rob phoned Shannon at her shop from a pay phone outside a pharmacy. He didn't want a phone record to identify his apartment.

"Charms."

"Shannon, it's Hank."

"Hank!" She greeted him cheerfully. "How are you? What's going on?"

"Listen, I wanted to apologize for leaving so abruptly the other night . . ."

"Don't worry about it," she said. "Please, I know I can get—"

"No, it's not that," he said. "It's just . . ." Just what? "Anyway, let's get together again. What do you say? I'd really like to see you."

"I'd love to," she responded. Then he heard her tell a customer: "I'll be with you in a moment. I have to take this call."

"You fixed such a wonderful dinner on Saturday," said Rob. "Now it's my turn to do something special for you. Does Friday night work?"

"Yes, Friday works great."

"I've got an idea for a really cool date night, but I want to keep the details a secret."

"Ooh, a secret," she cooed. "Mysterious. I like it."

"Why don't you come out my way this time."

"Sure."

"I've got a full day at the university. That's the only hitch. Maybe we could meet on campus around six-thirty? I can give you directions."

"Sure, I can meet you. Northwestern's such a beautiful campus. I haven't been there in ages."

He gave her directions to a parking lot behind Pick-Staiger Hall. "Wear comfortable clothes," he told her. "That's my only hint."

"I can't wait," she told him. "I love surprises."

After the call ended, Rob went home and began planning Friday night's fatal finale.

Saturday night at her home had been a failure. He had not committed the necessary act, and as a result, things had dragged out. A big problem. He was becoming less anonymous, and the situation was becoming more dangerous.

On Friday he could not chicken out. No matter how pretty and spunky and nice she became, he had to get this hellish deed over with.

This was the final step in bringing closure to Beth's murder, regardless of how disconnected it felt. The Wilks' beach was a perfect opportunity. Rob and Shannon would be hidden by darkness, muffled by crashing waves, away from witnesses. He would bring a picnic basket filled with good food, good wine, and a false padded bottom—under which he would hide the semi-automatic with the engraving of The Circle.

Rob tried very, very hard to convince himself that

Shannon deserved her fate . . . just like Shepherd. She needed to be disposed of. Justice must be served.

True, it was a vague and uncertain justice. He was leaning heavily on trust. Trusting The Circle. Trusting Trey Wright. Shannon Mayer had been identified for execution for an unspeakable crime. Perhaps it was best that Rob didn't know the details.

The scene played out in his mind like a movie clip: He saw himself pointing something out to her in the water, perhaps an imaginary boat. Shannon would turn her back to him. He would fire a shot, point-blank, to the back of her head. He would drag her body into the water to accelerate the decomposition process. Then he would get the hell out of there. He would throw away his shoes in the Dumpster behind a fast-food restaurant far away so that no one could ever match them to the prints in the sand.

Then go home, lay low.

And forget.

Don't read about it in the papers. Don't watch it in the news.

Because it never happened. He told himself: You will convince yourself it never happened. Cleanse the mind. Because that is the only way you will ever regain your sanity.

He would commit the unspeakable, then imagine himself breaking out of a long and strange dream, ready to enter reality again.

Rob was staring again at Bill Wilk's empty chair when Maureen stepped into his view.

Well, sort of Maureen. She had undergone some

kind of transformation. Her hair had been dyed deep black, frazzled into an unmanageable perm. Her outfit was black, including a short skirt. Her fingernails were black. Her legs were . . .

Stop it. He forced his eyes to cancel their roaming.

She was telling him about her new website.

"I want you to check it out and tell me what you think. It just went live," she said. "It's called Elusive Intent. I posted my poems and stories and other stuff. It's kind of a meeting place for other girls like me who want to read my stuff or chat about, you know, death, sex, religion, politics, whatever. I wrote some CD reviews, too. You'd really like the design. I used this template I found. It's really gothic, like H.P. Lovecraft."

Rob responded, "You look . . . different."

"I *feel* different," she said. "I got rid of my stupid kid clothes. That's not who I am. I'm blossoming. I'm blossoming into a black flower." She giggled at the notion.

"So you're growing up," he said.

"In seventeen months, do you know how old I'll be?" she asked him.

He shrugged.

Her eyes seared him with heat. "Eighteen!"

Rob felt dizzy.

Eighteen. Stop telling me this. Stop dressing this way. I have enough pressure without . . .

"Do you know who's really cool?" she said then.

Another shrug. "I don't know . . ."

Then she named a legendary Hollywood actor known for his quirky roles and intensity. At first, it was just meaningless chatter, but then she made a point of mentioning: "He's like, fifty-eight, but he's got a girlfriend who's nineteen. And they are so in love. They don't let the age thing get in the way at all. Isn't that the coolest?"

New subject, please. "I'll have to check out your website," he told her.

"Yes, and there's a link where you can e-mail me. Oh, please e-mail me. That would be so cool. Elusiveintent-dot-com. Some of the poems and stories you've seen, but there are new ones, too."

When Maureen finally left the room, Rob's eyes watched, and in the stupid goth get-up she somehow looked alluring and exotic, with the good curves accented. He had a moment's fantasy of something raunchy taking place on his teacher's desk, papers scattering like flower petals in the wind, followed by insane guilt, and he had to go into the restroom and splash water on his face to rinse away the madness.

As Rob was coming out of the teachers' washroom, a hand struck the back of his shoulder with a loud smack. Rob jumped, spun around, eyes wild.

It was Hank: one of his aggressively friendly claps on the back. "How you doing, buddy? Jesus, I didn't mean to scare you."

"Don't do that," said Rob sternly. "I mean it. I don't like it."

"Sure, okay," said Hank. "Didn't mean to piss you off, just saying hi."

Rob walked away, and he heard Hank mutter, "Lighten up."

* * *

Rob stood against his car in the Northwestern parking lot and Shannon pulled in, exactly on time, in her BMW. She grinned and waved behind the sunset glare on the windshield. She parked next to his Nissan, sleek elegance alongside dusty drab.

She stepped out of her car and into the dying daylight, tall and beautiful. The wind blew and lifted her hair. She wore jeans, a short white top that revealed her tummy, a studded belt, jean jacket, and penny loafers. She had a small wrapped package in her hand. She came up and hugged him. She smelled nice. Her hair touched his face for a moment.

She pulled back and thumped the package against his chest.

"Open it. It's for you."

He handled it. "Feels like a book."

"Maybe."

He glanced around. No other people, but that could change at any moment. He really wanted to minimize the chances of anyone seeing them together.

He tore open the package. Another Les Jacobson book.

Rob read the title: "*The Reluctant Soldier.*"

"It was written ten years ago, but it's really timely in today's political environment," she said. "It's about this young army recruit who gets pulled into another country's civil war. It's South America, but it's allegorical. He's under orders, but they aren't aligned with his heart, and it's all about the conflict between his sense of duty and inner feelings. When do your personal values override authority? Who do you trust and where is your true obligation? It really got me thinking about the people serving our leaders and the moral dilemmas they must face."

"It does sound interesting," he said. "Thank you. I'm sure it's a great book. I like his writing."

She addressed him playfully. "So now, what's my surprise?"

"A picnic." Rob smiled.

"I love picnics."

"At our own private beach."

"Really?"

"Actually, it's a beach belonging to the family of one of my students at the high— at the college." She didn't seem to notice his fumble, and he kept going. "Are you up for being a little sneaky?"

"Meaning we don't have permission to use this beach?"

"Meaning nobody will be there for us to ask permission. They're on vacation."

"Sure," she said. "I can be naughty."

"Me, too."

They climbed into his car and he drove off campus into an area of extravagant residential properties on the lakefront. They parked several blocks away from the Wilk residence. Most of the homes were buried deep inside large estates, without views to and from the street. Rob got the picnic basket out of the trunk. As they began their walk, Shannon took his hand.

It surprised him, but he didn't let go.

After two blocks, she giggled, "Your hand is sweaty."

"I'm nervous," he admitted, although for reasons she would never know.

"Nervous?" she said. "What's the worst that could happen? Somebody chases us away? This will be fun. Like being teenagers again."

The daylight gave up and evening took over. As they made their way onto a narrow path between high bushes, the footing became guesswork. She pulled closer.

"I should have brought a flashlight," Rob said, although he had intentionally left it behind.

"It's really dark," she said. They zigged and zagged without a visible destination, and then in a heartbeat, the path ended and a wide, empty beach greeted them.

The waves rolled in and lapped at the wet sand. The moon created slivers of light on the water. A wooden staircase led from the beach up a steep bluff and into darkness, presumably the path to the Wilks' mansion.

It was secluded and calm. Rob didn't even see any boats. It was still a few weeks before Memorial Day. Warm enough to enjoy the beach, but too cold for swimming and boating.

"This is beautiful," Shannon whispered.

"That's why I chose it," Rob said. "You can't beat this."

"You've been here before?" she asked.

"Once or twice."

They found a spot on the sand. She kicked off her shoes. Her toenails were painted scarlet. He spread out a blanket in the dark.

"Do you have a candle?" she asked.

"Oops," he said. "Forgot that, too."

"The moonlight's more romantic anyway," she remarked.

He brought out the food and plates and arranged the meal on the blanket: gourmet cheeses, fruit salad, sandwiches on rye, and two large fudge brownies. All purchased a short time ago from his grocer's deli.

As he was setting up, a small white piece of paper fell out of one of the sacks. The wind swept it away, toward the tangled brush in the bluff.

His credit card receipt.

"Shit!" he said aloud, jumping up to retrieve it.

He lost sight of it and panic seized him.

In a flash, he could see a scene the next day where homicide detectives scoured the beach, and one of them cried out, "Hey look! The killer left us a receipt! How convenient!"

"Are you okay, Hank?" asked Shannon.

"Yeah . . . I just don't want . . . That was my credit card receipt." He ran off toward the bluff.

He didn't see it anywhere. He didn't even know where to look.

"I wouldn't worry about it," she called after him. "Come back and eat."

Now he really wished he had a flashlight. He started to swear internally.

"C'mon, Hank . . ."

"Just a minute . . ."

"Do you have any mustard in here?"

Rob turned and saw Shannon reach into the picnic basket, starting to dig around.

Oh shit, the gun.

"Mustard! Yes! Wait! Hold on!" He spun from the bluff and bounded toward her.

He grabbed the basket, and she jumped back. "Whoa. Relax," she said. "If you don't have any, that's cool."

He found the mustard packets and handed them over. He moved the basket to the far end of the blanket, as far from her as possible.

He looked back toward the bluff. He saw something white flutter.

The receipt!

He jumped back up and left the blanket.

He chased the fluttering receipt, stumbling in circles through the sand, tracking it like a butterfly, until he finally had it in his grasp. He crumpled it and shoved it in his pocket.

When he returned to the blanket, Shannon had poured him a glass of wine.

"Here, I think you need this."

Rob burst out with a laugh.

"Yes. Yes, I do," he said.

She poured herself a glass and they made a toast.

"To a romantic evening on the beach," she said, looking into his eyes, lips curved in a smile. "Thank you, Hank. This is so sweet and wonderful and creative."

"Even if we are trespassing."

"Hey, makes it interesting. I like a little danger." They drank.

Rob and Shannon engaged in an easy, flowing conversation, accompanied by the steady rhythm of the rolling waves. They were compatible conversationalists. They traded humorous quips. As he consumed more wine, Rob decided to try to probe gently about her background. What did she do before Charms? Did she have any family in the area? Had she been in any lengthy relationships? Maybe somewhere, somehow, she would serve up a clue to justify her fate.

Now it became Shannon's turn to tense up. As he tossed out the questions, she became elusive about her past. She sidestepped his inquires, offered nothing further than what he already knew, information about her shop and some hobbies and interests. He learned a great deal about her past year or two. And absolutely nothing about her life before that. She was almost cagey about it.

The moon was becoming obscured by clouds, rendering the beach darker.

"I don't feel like I'm getting a sense of your history," Rob finally told her, pointblank.

"That's how I feel," she responded.

"Pardon?"

"I don't feel like I really know about your background. I mean, I know you're a history professor at Northwestern, but aside from that, I don't really know who you are. You haven't exactly been forthcoming, either. It's a two-way street, you know."

"My life story isn't very interesting," he said.

"Neither is mine," she said.

There was a moment of uncomfortable tension. He broke it with humor. "Well, I guess I could tell you about my fifteen years in state prison for bank robbery, but I prefer to think of those years as my lost episodes."

She laughed. "Right. A bank robber. You."

"Actually, it was murder."

"Murder. Even funnier." She laughed harder.

There was something in her playful tone then, her eyes, that made him think of Beth. Maybe it was the tricks played by shadows, or the familiar beach setting where he had brought Beth for intense and romantic interludes. But it was a glowing vibe that had not been present in his soul since the night Beth died.

Rob felt overwhelmed by confusion.

The setting was not supporting him. It was stirring up deep feelings. He was filling with warmth, not heartless cold. The mood was all wrong for what he had to do.

He couldn't help being distracted by Shannon's beauty and radiant personality, it was impossible to avoid.

They continued to exchange jokey banter and share good feelings, and it was all wrong, so wrong. Then, all of a sudden, without warning, they were kissing—

—and he was deeply shocked—

—to realize that he had initiated the kiss.

She pressed into him and he brought his hands forward, moving one into her hair, the other against her back, gently pulling her tighter.

"Hey!"

They jolted apart. A white spot bobbed in the distance. Someone on the beach walked toward them with a flashlight.

"Oh shit," said Rob and Shannon in unison.

It appeared to be a scrawny old man in a windbreaker and baseball cap.

"You kids don't belong here! This beach is private property."

Thinking as one, Rob and Shannon jumped to their feet. Rob shoved the food items into the basket. Shannon grabbed the blanket and her shoes.

They ran away. The old man waved the flashlight, causing the beam to dance all over the sand.

"If you come back, I'm calling the police!" cried the old man. "These beaches are private."

Rob and Shannon made a graceless escape, kicking crookedly through the sand, stopping a few times to pick up paper plates and other items that spilled out of the picnic basket. They ran through the beachfronts of several properties, finally moving completely out of view of the old man.

They collapsed on the sand. Shannon giggled. It was contagious, and Rob joined in. Then they both exploded into all-out laughter.

"Youse kids get off my property!" Rob said in a shakey voice that mimicked the old man.

"This here is private beach!" Shannon chimed in.

They were both on their backs, panting, on the sand. Rob reached, took her hand, and turned toward her. She met him halfway, and they resumed kissing, more passionate than before, hearts thumping from the run, already sweaty, already accelerated.

He reached under her white top. She stopped him and took it off. He opened his jeans and began tugging them down. She did the same.

In a matter of minutes, Rob and Shannon were making love between the sand and the moonlight.

* * *

The next morning, as a pink dawn struggled to break across the sky, Rob sat in his car, parked at a bridge overlooking the Skokie Lagoons in Winnetka.

He waited until he was certain no cars were approaching from either side, and then he climbed out. He stepped to the rail and looked down into the swirling, murky waters below.

The dark lagoon hypnotized him for a moment. He reflected on the evening he had just spent with Shannon. He couldn't wait until his next date with her. And the next one after that. And all the others, ad infinitum.

Eyes still focused on the swampy waters, he recognized a peace and warmth inside him that he hadn't felt since Beth was alive. It was extraordinary. He was finally starting to feel whole. He never thought he would feel this good again, ever, in his life.

Shannon was healing him. She was his savior. The missing piece. The world was turning again. Time no longer stood still at that horrible night with the SUV.

Rob checked one more time for cars. Then he produced the semi-automatic pistol with The Circle's engraving on the grip. He gave it a final look.

Then he chucked it into the water and watched it sink from sight.

Fourteen

Why would anybody want this woman dead?

The question still haunted him, and he had no answers. Shannon Mayer was sweet, funny, educated, engaging, and, yes, sexy as hell. He simply couldn't connect her to some hideous crime, no matter how hard he stretched his imagination. There was no way she could deserve a death sentence. Somewhere, somehow, The Circle had garbled information, made a mistake, latched on to the wrong person.

Shannon Mayer was perfect. She was everything. Rob didn't relate easily with women. Beth had been an exception. But now lightning had struck twice, a true miracle.

No one had made him feel this way before, except Beth. None of the women before Beth. None of the dates after Beth—those desperate set-ups by Hank that only deepened his depression.

No, this was the real deal.

At the high school, Rob moved through his days in a daze. Roughly ten percent of his focus was on the setting and classwork before him. The rest filled with images and thoughts related to Shannon, their date on the beach, her voice, her face, the high-cheekboned smile, expressive eyes, the dates to come, the opportunities to touch her all over again . . .

In the teacher's lounge, Hank watched Rob stare into space and told him, "Buddy, either you're high, or you're in love."

Rob looked at Hank, mulled it over for a few beats, then replied, "I'm high."

For their next date, Rob went for goofy. There had been the formal dinner at her house and the romantic night on the beach. Now it was time for a new tone and texture to mix it up and keep the relationship energized.

So he took her to glow-in-the-dark miniature golf.

It was a new place, conveniently located halfway between their homes. The indoor, eighteen-hole course snaked through a Day-Glo jungle under black lights. Pockets of people moved amid a psychedelic parade of purple dinosaurs, pink boulders, yellow sharks, and green elephants. As Rob's eyes adjusted, he realized the jungle was swarming with swooning teens on dates—kids with raging hormones who had broken past puberty but not yet achieved drinking age.

The golf balls radiated with an electric sheen as they zinged through the dark wild. Heavy techno music pounded out of heaving speakers.

"An acid trip without the acid," exclaimed Shannon giddily.

Rob took her by the hand to a garden of neon flowers sprouting impossible colors and kissed her. She reciprocated so eagerly that he had to break it off before they become entertainment for the rest of the crowd.

Rob and Shannon played the cartoony course with a playful competitive spirit, stepping through the surreal props and obstacles, dipping in and out of strange rooms and compartments. As they reached the final hole, Rob added up their scores and announced, "Hey, we're tied. This is it."

"How about a friendly wager?" she asked him.

"Sure. Drinks?"

"No." She pulled him near and whispered into his ear. "The winner gets to be on top tonight."

Rob nodded. He teed up. He fired his ball into the darkness. Then he turned, dropped his club, and shrugged.

"Oops. Your turn."

After golf, Rob took Shannon for drinks at a nearby tavern shaped like a small house. Inside, blue- and white-collar workers mingled in a dim, smoke-filled haze. If the mini-golf place was Mars, the tavern was definitely back on Earth.

"So how come you keep taking me to dark, secluded places?" she teased him. "The beach, glow-in-the-dark golf, now this. Do bright lights hurt your eyes?"

"No." He chuckled.

"Are you married? Are you having an affair?"

"Nope and nope."

"Are you hiding from anyone?"

"Just my parole officer."

That earned a laugh. Next, she asked him about Les Jacobson's soldier book, which he had started to read. It carried the conversation for a while, but then an unsettled feeling began to surface from deep inside. The drinks had rumbled things loose.

"I really like you, Shannon," he blurted, no context, but a necessary lead-in.

"I 'like' you," she responded in a tone that seemed to tease his understatement.

"What I mean is . . ." He realized he should have rehearsed this better in his head, but what the hell, here goes.

"I have a confession to make."

"You *are* married?" She became genuinely alarmed.

"No, no, no. Not married. Never been married. And not gay. We can strike those two from the table."

She was looking at him very seriously now, no sense of playfulness in her eyes, and it made him nervous.

"What do you mean, a confession?" she asked.

"I told you I was a professor at Northwestern," said Rob. "That's not exactly true. I don't know why I said that. I guess I did it to impress you. I *am* a teacher. But it's high school. I'm a high school English teacher. It's still—"

She broke out in a grin. "*That's* your big confession?"

He nodded.

"Hank," she said. "I'm not a snob. I think it's great and noble and wonderful that you teach, whether it's high school or Ivy League, that doesn't matter. It's funny that you thought I would even care."

"There's one other thing . . ." he said. "You called me Hank . . ."

"It's really Henry?"

He broke out in a laugh. "Yes! No . . . Sort of. Hank is my . . . middle name. My actual name is Rob. I told you Hank, well, to keep a little distance. I didn't know where this was going. I know it sounds weird. But I don't want to keep a distance anymore. I want you to call me Rob."

She gave him a long look. "Okay, Rob. Hank. Rob Hank. Are there any more confessions?"

He looked down at his hands, then back into her brown eyes.

"Yes, just one," he said.

"Shoot."

The irony of her reply startled him.

"Let's hear it," she said.

He spoke slowly. "Part of the reason I created a little bit of an exaggerated identity . . . It's been very hard for me to get intimate with anyone. A while back, I was engaged to this girl, and now she's gone. I don't need to go into the details, but it devastated me for a long time. I've had a hard time dating—meeting my expectations, my dates' expectations . . . I've been reluctant to get close."

She asked him, "Are you still reluctant?"

"No, Shannon." He smiled, and it was genuine. "Not at all. That's the good thing. You've changed all that. I feel like I've made it over the hump. I'm different now. I feel healed. And that's because of you."

She reached across the table and took his hand.

"You poor guy," she said. She squeezed his hand.

"Thank you for understanding."

"Thank you for being so forthcoming."

"Better late than never, I suppose."

New drinks arrived, and Rob wasted no time breathing in more alcohol.

Shannon had grown quiet. The vibe at the table remained serious, candid. Rob knew that this was his chance.

It was time for Shannon to reveal more about herself.

"I told you more about me," said Rob. "Now, I'd like to know more about you."

She raised her eyebrows. "Okay—what's to tell?"

"I don't know. Your past. Your background."

"I'm afraid I don't have any interesting stories. I have my shop. I live in Barrington. I'm a single gal enjoying life . . ."

"So who are your friends?"

She laughed a bit nervously. "What, you want names?"

"I don't know."

"Okay. Dana, Tracey, Nick . . ."

Rob frowned. She was mocking him.

"What about enemies?" he asked.

Her eyes hardened. "Enemies?"

"Sure. Everyone has their friends and enemies."

"What are you talking about?"

"It's a question."

"It's a stupid question, Rob, Hank, whoever you are."

Her tone struck him like a slap. It was a sharpness

he had never heard from her before. An edge. The warmth that ordinarily filled her face had quickly drained.

"I revealed more about me," he said carefully. "Now I would just like you to do the same. I know you, but I don't really *know* you."

"Then that's your problem, because I have told you everything you need to know about me."

"You've opened up?"

"Yes, I have opened up to you. Damn it, that night on the beach, making love, how much more opened up do you want?"

"I'm not talking about sex."

"Tell me what you're looking for."

"I mean—it's not—I guess it's hard to—"

"*Spit it out.* I really want to know."

The fierceness was freaking him out. The familiar Shannon was gone, replaced by another person, and he was frightened by this person. But he couldn't back off. He had opened this door and it couldn't shut yet.

"Do you have something in your past that you're not telling me about?"

"Why are you so suspicious all of a sudden?"

"I'm not suspicious."

"Bullshit you are."

"I'm just asking . . ."

"And I'm just telling: lay off. Why don't you trust me all of a sudden? What did I do? I don't like this conversation."

"I want to know more about your past."

"What is this obsession with my past?" she shouted.

People at other tables were turning, looking for the source of the raised voice.

"It's not an obsession," he said quietly.

Her tone remained raised. "Why don't you trust me? This hurts. It really does."

Rob gambled then. He laid out a zinger, the exact thought in his head at the moment. "The way you're reacting right now implies that maybe you do have something to hide."

Shannon snapped. Her face turned pink with fury. The eyes flared with intensity.

"Stop provoking me! This conversation is stupid, and *it's over.*"

She sprung out of her chair, pulling her purse, and stormed toward the exit.

Rob stood. "Shannon, wait . . ."

She pushed past two startled women and slammed through the door leading outside.

Rob ran after her.

He found her in the gravel parking lot, stopped near the hood of a car, slumped, her hand over her eyes.

His footsteps crunched as he approached. She turned and looked at him.

"Why don't you like me anymore?" she asked.

"That's not it, not at all."

"You don't understand . . ." she said.

"You're right, I don't understand."

"I'm in love with you."

That stopped him cold. He felt a hundred emotions, swimming, lost, until he heard himself declare: "I think I love you, too."

She reached out and hugged him. He held on, and it felt right and good.

"I'm sorry," he said.

"Don't be sorry," she said. She sniffled. "I have a temper. You got to see it tonight."

"It's not so bad."

"I don't want to frighten you away."

"You didn't." He brushed hair from her face. "Nothing scares me."

They climbed into his car, drove to her house, and went into the bedroom, hands clasped all the way. As he began unbuttoning his shirt, she slapped his fingers into retreat and yanked the shirt open, sending buttons bouncing to the hardwood floor. "You're taking too long," she told him.

She brought him between silk sheets and purred, "I want to devour you."

The next morning, he awoke from her touch as she took his wrist and guided his hand to her chest, resting it over her beating heart, wordless.

More dates followed.

Each encounter compounded his feelings of deep joy and spiritual healing. His soul became lighter. Initially, Rob was shocked that he had returned to this place, a sensational happiness that had been deflated the day Beth died.

But now it was back with a vengeance. And it no longer felt foreign or strange. It just felt good.

At ETHS, Hank continued to sense change in Rob. Rob had a new energy and vigor. He smiled a lot.

"Yep, either you're high or in love," Hank reiterated in the teachers lounge one morning.

This time, Rob confessed. "Well, I'm not high, so you can draw your own conclusions."

Hank threw up his hands and exclaimed, "Way to go, buddy. Welcome back to the human race."

One day, after a late afternoon of grading papers, Rob changed into shorts and a T-shirt and slipped inside the gymnasium to shoot some hoops. A few years back, it was a regular habit, a reward at the end of the day. Now he was trying to get back into the groove, burn off some energy, get some exercise, and fantasize about helping the Bulls beat the Knicks in Game 7 of the NBA Finals. The gym was empty, surrounded by empty bleachers. The basketball made powerful echoes as Rob dribbled up and down the court.

He dodged phantom players, scored at the buzzer, worked up a good sweat, and felt younger than his age. He landed a satisfying number of shots at the beginning, but gradually lost his accuracy, and finally sent himself to the showers.

As Rob returned to his street clothes, Tony the janitor stuck his head in the locker room and reminded him to shut off the lights and close up on his way out.

The sky was a wall of gray when Rob stepped into the teachers' parking lot. The sun had sunk out of sight, and the students and remaining faculty had all departed. The usual schoolyard commotion and noise had been replaced with an unnatural silence.

As Rob made his way toward his car, he saw a figure standing in the shadows. The figure stepped forward, and it was Trey Wright.

Wright stood between Rob and his car. "Hey," he said.

Rob slowed to a stop. "Hi."

They studied one another for a moment.

"It's been several weeks," said Wright. "And I wanted to know if everything is okay."

Rob nodded slowly. "Sure."

Wright's eyes continued to study him. "Problems?"

"No."

Wright glanced around, checked his surroundings, and then said, "Okay, let's cut the bullshit."

Rob nodded, sighed. "Okay, listen," he said, keeping his tone lowered. "I don't think she's a monster. I think there has been some mistake."

Wright promptly shook his head. "No. The Circle does not make mistakes."

"This isn't just some hunch," said Rob. "I've gotten to know her. I've spent some time with her."

Wright's eyes widened. "Spent some time?"

"It started as an accident. I was just doing research. But the more I've learned about her and talked with her, the more I think that somebody, somewhere made a mistake or provided misleading information."

"That's not the case," said Wright firmly. "You think I don't screen these things? You can't question the integrity of The Circle."

"I have gotten to know her. I have spent a lot of time with her."

"That wasn't in your instructions!"

"I'm very close to her now. As close as you can get. I have no reason to believe—"

"No, no, *no*," said Wright, spitting out the words. "This is all wrong. You are being suckered, my friend. She's got you by the balls. That is a very bad position to be in, trust me."

"She's a good person inside."

Wright made a small, sad laugh. "You have been seduced by her beauty. You're not thinking straight. You have to get beyond the tits and ass. You are placing yourself in a very dangerous place."

"How?"

Wright pressed his lips shut. He said nothing.

"Exactly," said Rob. "That is the information I'm going with."

"You took an oath," said Wright. "No one has ever broken the oath."

"You misled me."

"I did nothing of the kind, Robert."

"Then tell me why she needs to die."

"I can't do that."

"That's nonsense. Of course you can."

"Look," said Wright sharply. "The person who killed Richard Shepherd did not know why. He did not know he was doing it on your behalf, under your orders. That was for *your* protection. That is the way it must be for everybody. The Circle is based on trust."

"Right. But you can't trust me with the information I need?"

"You do not need any information! You have all the information you need."

"Yeah, a name and address."

Wright jabbed a finger at Rob. "You don't understand the basic premise. This cannot work without total anonymity. That's the oath you took. If everyone knew everything, and one person got caught, everything would unravel, and *you* would go to jail along with everybody else. There cannot be a path that leads back to the source, do you understand me? *There must be total anonymity.*"

Rob said, "I still don't buy it."

Wright scowled into Rob's face. "You know what? I don't care. You have your marching orders. You will kill Shannon Mayer."

"It's not an option. I took your gun and I threw it in the river. No one is killing her. She's off the list."

"I trusted you," said Wright bitterly.

"And I trusted you," replied Rob. "But not anymore."

Wright gave Rob a long look. "You're making a huge mistake," he said. "So I suggest you listen up. I'm going to give you one last chance to reclaim your loyalty. You have one week to complete your obligation. One week from right now, this minute, to finish the job. I hope you will give this serious, deep thought, my friend. You have your deadline. You have your instructions. If you choose to betray The Circle . . ." Wright searched for the words, nearly panting with emotion. "If you betray me . . . then God help you."

Trey Wright turned and walked away, leaving Rob standing alone in the faculty parking lot.

Fifteen

"Welcome to my humble abode," said Rob, opening the door to his Evanston apartment. Shannon stepped inside.

"Not too messy for a bachelor's pad," she said.

"That's because I don't have a lot of stuff."

She walked over to one of the bookshelves that lined the living room walls. "Except for books."

"Books are my passion. I try to instill that passion in my students. Sometimes it works, and sometimes they just look at me like I'm from outer space."

She examined the selections on the shelves, occasionally nodding and smiling in recognition, or touching a spine. Her hair was tied back neatly, showcasing her flawless complexion.

"Would you like a glass of wine?" he asked, and she responded, "Absolutely."

He went into the kitchen and retrieved the bottle he had put in the refrigerator earlier. He was nervous. This was Shannon's first visit to his residence. Compared to her lavish home in Barrington, his apartment was cheap and plain. The rooms were tiny. The furnishings were dull. Of course, he didn't have his own boutique to tap into for décor.

Rob returned to the living room, carrying two glasses of white wine. Shannon was seated at the couch, flipping through the Magritte art book on his coffee table.

"I don't know about you," he said, "but after the day I've had, I could really use a glass of w—"

The Magritte book?

She was turning the pages, getting closer to the later years, where Rob had hidden the photo and instructions from Trey Wright.

"Let's have a toast." He stuck the glass of wine in her face, forcing her to pull back from the book. She took the wine, and he shut the book and slid it across the table. He held out his glass to her.

"A toast to . . ." His mind reeled for a quick improvisation. ". . . us."

She laughed slightly. "Okay . . ."

They tapped glasses gently.

He sipped and remained blocking her return to the book.

"I know the movie starts at seven, but we should probably get there early," he said. "It's getting really good reviews."

She looked up at him from the couch, locking eyes on him with a thin, mischievous smile. "That doesn't give us much time to play."

Rob's heart beat faster and excitement swelled elsewhere. She could do that to him with just a look.

"I think we have eight and a half minutes to spare," he said.

"We could be very productive in eight and a half minutes," she said, "but we're wasting time." She put the wine aside and moved toward him.

They missed the first ten minutes of the movie.

Rob didn't care. At the theater, he couldn't concentrate on the film anyway. He was looking forward to the sequel to their living room antics.

After the movie ended, he took Shannon's hand and they joined the shuffling throng that moved toward the exits. He couldn't help noticing the heads that turned—young males, mostly—stealing an eyeful of the dark-haired beauty in tight jeans and a slinky, sleeveless pink shirt.

He had been in their shoes before and knew their thoughts: *Who's the lucky schmuck?*

As they spilled out into the lobby, eyes adjusting to the lights, Rob caught a glance of a familiar face moving in the crowd. He almost said "Crap!" out loud.

It was Maureen.

He pulled Shannon in the other direction, making up an excuse about wanting to see the poster for an upcoming Johnny Depp movie, but there were too many people, they couldn't move fast enough . . .

. . . and Maureen stepped directly into their path.

Rob watched Maureen's expression go from recognition to shock to crumple.

"Hi, Maureen," he said cheerfully.

"Hi," she said, very softly.

He was still holding Shannon's hand. He saw Maureen's gaze move from their clasped hands up Shannon's arm, to Shannon's face and perfect features.

"Maureen, this is Shannon," said Rob. "Shannon, this is Maureen, one of my students."

Shannon smiled sweetly, and her tone was probably a tad patronizing, as if she were talking to a ten-year-old, not a sixteen-year-old. "Hello, Maureen. *Very* nice to meet you."

"Nice meeting you," said Maureen, shifting her glance to the carpet. "Well . . . bye."

As Maureen sidestepped them and departed, Rob caught a glimpse of tears in her eyes.

In the car, Rob told Shannon, "That student we met, she has a crush on me."

"She was acting a little strange," said Shannon.

"I don't know what to do," said Rob. "I don't encourage her, but I don't want to hurt her feelings. She's a nice kid, a good writer."

Shannon giggled then and started singing the Police song about an infatuated school girl.

Rob laughed. "Exactly."

They went for a late dinner at an Italian restaurant. The awkward encounter with Maureen weighed heavily on his mind. He had tried to keep his relationship with Shannon very private, even secretive. He hadn't introduced her to anyone, including Hank. The whole thing was just . . . too complicated.

And it was about to get worse.

In less than twenty-four hours, his deadline with Trey Wright would be up.

At dinner, Shannon could sense something was wrong. He was quiet.

He blamed it on Maureen's obsession with him. But it was much more worrisome than that.

As always, Shannon managed to ease his mind by overwhelming him with fantastic distraction. Back at his apartment, she returned her attention to his bookshelves and asked him to pick his favorite erotic passage for a private bedroom reading.

There were several candidates, but he quickly landed on an intense and arousing selection of text from his Oxford World's Classics edition of *Memoirs of a Woman of Pleasure*. It was an eighteenth-century novel by English novelist John Cleland, banned in the U.S. until the mid-1960s. It was extremely graphic in the most elegant prose.

Undressed and illuminated by flickering candlelight, she brought the words to life in a lively and sensual bedroom reading that sent his fears scattering.

" 'Taking advantage of my commodious posture, he made the storm fall where I scarce patiently expected, and where he was sure to lay it . . .' "

In his English Honors class, he assigned *Romeo and Juliet*, and the discussion turned to forbidden love. He asked the students to come up with examples of real and perceived romantic barriers, and received the expected results: economic status, religion, race.

"Age," said Maureen firmly.

"That's right," said Rob with equal firmness. "Would that be a real or perceived barrier?"

"Perceived."

"I would have to disagree," said Rob. "Because there are actual laws in our society."

"Juliet was thirteen," said Maureen.

"Society is different today."

"But love isn't," she responded. "Love doesn't change."

After class, he made a conscious effort to make a dash for the door, but the students, as always, were quicker than he was, and the ensuing logjam allowed Maureen to approach him.

"Did you like the movie?" she asked, and he knew that wasn't her real question.

"The acting was pretty good. I thought the script was thin, they could have done more to flesh out—"

"Who was that girl?" asked Maureen. "I mean, is she like your girlfriend?"

Rob nodded, swallowed. "Yes."

"Her name is Shannon?"

Rob felt a sweat breaking out. "Yes."

"Shannon who?"

"Why does her last name matter?"

"How did you meet her?"

"Not here," he replied, a bit curt, and he immediately felt bad, but she was so damn *nosey* . . .

"Do you love her?" Maureen asked, and her voice hit bumps, her face sagged.

"Yes," said Rob plainly. "Yes, I do."

And with that, the Q&A session ended, and Maureen left.

At the end of the day, Rob returned to his apartment. A clock was ticking in his head. Pressure was mounting. Because he knew that his deadline was looming. It was almost exactly one week after his encounter with Trey Wright in the teachers' parking lot of Evanston Township High.

Sure enough, the call came in at the precise minute the ultimatum had been delivered seven days earlier.

Rob picked up the call.

The voice on the other end simply said, "So?"

"I'm not going to do it," said Rob.

"Are you absolutely certain?" asked Wright.

"Nobody is going to harm this woman."

Wright sighed. He didn't sound mad. Just saddened. "You failed me, Rob. I had so much faith in you. But you double-crossed me, and you double-crossed everyone else. You broke The Circle. The wheel of justice has stopped."

"I don't want you to call me ever again."

"Have you forgotten what The Circle has done for you? Obviously you have. You lied to us, Rob. All of us."

"Shannon is not who you think she is," said Rob, voice shaking. "Whoever gave you Shannon's name, they fabricated some terrible story. Maybe it's a jilted lover, I don't know, but they're lying. *They're* the liars."

Wright's voice took on a crisp, authoritative tone. "Robert Carus, you have been expelled from The Circle. You are through. This is your official dismissal. Someone else will have to take care of Shannon Mayer."

Rob felt a boiling rage rush to the surface. "If anyone touches her, I'll go to the police."

"And tell them what, exactly? That you're an accomplice to murder? That you solicited the shooting death of Richard Shepherd? You put me in jail and we're going to share the same cell, my friend."

"I don't care," responded Rob. "I will expose this entire scheme if you so much as lay a finger on her. *Do you understand me?"*

Rob heard nothing, followed by a *click*.

Sixteen

Rain punished the earth, shaping puddles, then rivers. A hard wind scattered twigs and leaves across roadways. Car headlamps punched through the unnaturally dark morning as low, dense clouds grumbled.

Set back from a busy intersection, inside the fluorescent storefront of a Dunkin' Donuts, Trey Wright sat at a small table, reading the newspaper and sipping coffee from a Styrofoam cup. He was the only customer, undeterred by the storm. A female clerk half-heartedly wiped counters while stealing glances at a Spanish-language soap opera playing on a snowy black-and-white TV.

A short, stocky man entered. His body was box-shaped, with an equally square head resting on top of angular shoulders. He had freckles, a grave face, and wore a black turtleneck. He shook the rain off his umbrella.

"May I help you, sir?" asked the clerk.

"No, thank you," said the man. He walked over to Trey Wright.

Wright recognized Hector Scrimm and smiled. He greeted Scrimm with "Praise the Lord."

"Praise the Lord," echoed Scrimm, seating himself.

Wright tapped his finger on the newspaper. He adopted an indignant tone. "I was just reading about these ignorant fools who want to eliminate capital punishment. They want taxpayers to pay for food, clothing, and shelter for these sinners. There are good people who can't even make ends meet for their own families, yet they are expected to forfeit their earnings toward criminal hotels, so these monsters can continue to breathe God's air and walk God's earth. I ask you, is that right?"

Scrimm frowned. He stated, "*Whoso sheddeth man's blood, by man shall his blood be shed: for in the image of God made he man.*"

"Yes, exactly," said Wright in quick agreement.

"Genesis 9:6," said Scrimm.

"Of course," said Wright.

Scrimm clasped his hands together, tightly. "The world has become a much different place than our Lord intended. I can't even read the papers or watch television anymore. It saddens me too much."

"That is why we're here," Wright said. "The Circle has a righteous duty. With our collective strength, we put on the armor of God and confront the wicked with decisiveness and finality."

"The sinners dangle over a great and fiery furnace," said Scrimm. "It is a bottomless cauldron. Society must not continue to rescue these sinners from their fate. It is wrong, and it invokes God's fury toward us all."

"Praise the Lord," said Wright. "That is why you are here today, Hector Scrimm. God has chosen this time for you. Are you prepared to serve?"

"Absolutely and without a doubt in my soul."

Wright placed the package containing the gun on the table. "The means have been chosen," he said.

Scrimm nodded. He picked up the package, felt its weight, and understood. He placed it in his lap.

"You have been empowered to deliver the sentence of the fallen," said Wright.

"*We beareth not the sword in vain, for we are ministers of God, revengers to execute wrath upon him that doeth evil,*" said Scrimm, noting, "Romans 13:1–4. New Testament."

"Ah, yes," said Wright, nodding.

Wright reached down to the seat next to him and brought up a flat manila envelope. He handed it to Scrimm. "This the subject of God's wrath."

Scrimm nodded, took the envelope.

"Open it," said Wright. "I want you to get a good look at the face of evil."

Scrimm unclasped the lip and slid out the contents. There was a color photograph clipped to a sheet of paper.

A photograph of Rob Carus.

The shot was of Carus walking to his car in the teachers' parking lot, unaware that his picture was being taken, strolling with his brown briefcase, expressionless.

Wright told Scrimm, "The sheet underneath contains his name, his residential address, and his place of occupation. He lives alone. He is a very wicked and dangerous man and he must be removed. Do it quickly, without haste, as you draw strength from the destruction of your own darkest demon. Hector, I ask you to recall the sinner known as Arnold Barnhardt."

When Wright referenced Barnhardt, Scrimm tensed up. Barnhardt was the Michigan camp counselor who molested Scrimm's teenage daughter two years ago, an ordeal that drove her to suicide. Scrimm's heart filled with fury just to recall Barnhardt's face. His fingers tightened their grip on his instructions.

Less than one week earlier, Barnhardt had been shot dead in his bed by an intruder in his East Lansing home. The local police suggested it was a burglary. There were several items stolen from the home to help create that misconception.

But Scrimm knew the truth and shared it with no one but God. The Circle had crushed another sinner, like the tire of a Mack truck rolling over a fallen man.

It was right and it was just.

Now Scrimm had his marching orders. He had been presented with a moral duty, a way to truly honor God. And he was elated to oblige.

Scrimm returned Rob Carus's photo and information inside the envelope.

"It is done," he said.

"God bless you," said Wright. "Let us pray."

Wright and Scrimm joined hands across the table, bowed their heads, and called on the Lord to provide the strength necessary to carry out His law.

Seventeen

On the way home from teaching, Rob stopped at the liquor store and bought a bottle of white wine for the following night's dinner date at Shannon's house. She was eager to cook him another extravagant, candlelit meal, and perhaps complete the intended storyline of their first dinner date, which had come to an abrupt and awkward end when Rob . . . chickened out.

But that was another Rob. A confused Rob. Now his confusion had been wiped away, replaced by, for lack of a less trite word, love.

Rob had offered to bring a side dish, but Shannon insisted nothing was needed, *just bring yourself*, so the compromise was a bottle of white Zinfandel.

Rob paid the store clerk, who slipped the bottle into a narrow paper bag and wished him a good day.

Rob wished him the same and headed out the door.

The wind hissed across the trees in rising and falling waves, but the rain from earlier in the day had halted, leaving shrinking puddles.

Rob drove to his apartment building and parked in

the back. He was tired, the kids today had been fairly hyper, and now he had to catch up on a backlog of uncorrected papers. It would be best to plow through as many as he could tonight, so tomorrow night could be guilt-free.

In the building lobby, Rob collected his mail, nestled it under his arm, and entered the elevator to ride to the second floor.

Too tired to take the stairs one flight up. How's that for pathetic? I need to start biking again, or I'm going to wind up with a gut like Hank's.

Rob walked the short corridor to his apartment. He unlocked the door and entered. He shut the door with his foot, dumped the mail on a small table, and dropped his briefcase to the floor. He started to head for the kitchen to place the wine in the refrigerator . . .

. . . but after four steps, he stopped.

The morning's *Chicago Tribune* was on the sofa where he had left it. But it was rustling, pages turning, as if being read by a ghost.

Rob's eyes moved from the couch to the sliding door of his balcony. The door was opened a crack, allowing a cool breeze into the room.

Fear pierced Rob's heart. Did he leave the sliding door open? Or had someone entered his apartment?

He didn't remember opening the balcony door that morning, although sometimes he did crack it if the air inside was stuffy and stale. But he always remembered to close it before leaving, especially if the sky threatened rain.

Damn it, I can't remember . . .

He cautiously circled the room. Nothing looked

disturbed. He looked down the short corridor that led to his kitchen and bedroom.

Rob slipped the paper bag off the wine bottle and let the bag drop to the floor.

He took a firm grip of the bottle by the neck.

"Hello?" he said.

Dead silence. Except for the rustling newspaper.

If somebody's hiding in here, are they really going to respond to "Hello"?

Rob walked slowly, noiseless footsteps, into the kitchen. He circled behind the counter . . . nobody crouched and hiding here. Nothing disturbed.

Check the bedroom.

Rob realized that his heart was pounding fast. His grip on the wine bottle became loosened by sweat.

He stepped to the bedroom door, which was closed halfway. He pressed his hand against it and pushed it open. It let out a long, dramatic *creak*.

The bedroom looked like it always did. Unmade bed. Clothes on a chair. Books on the nightstand.

Nobody could fit under the bed, so that was ruled out. The only other possible hiding place was the closet. Lots of room in there.

Rob slowly approached the closet door. The thought that somebody could be hiding in there, between his shirts and sports coats, freaked him out. Was Trey Wright so vindictive that he would break into his apartment and stand in his bedroom closet, waiting all day to pounce . . . ?

Rob wanted to turn and run.

Maybe I should call the police.

And tell them WHAT?

Rob stepped very close to the closet door, nearly placing his ear against it.

He listened.

Nothing.

If he was in here, wouldn't I hear something? A slight rustling? Breathing?

Rob raised the wine bottle in one hand and placed the other hand on the doorknob.

He yanked open the closet door.

In the split second that followed, Rob thought he saw a person standing there, and he jumped back with a gasp, dropping the wine bottle to the rug with a thud.

"Aah!"

But it was just one of his blue shirts staring back at him. Nobody inside the shirt.

"Oh God," said Rob softly. He kneeled and picked up the wine bottle. "This is nuts," he muttered.

Rob left the bedroom. He felt his muscles start to relax. *Is this my new fate? To live in constant fear and paranoia? Maybe I should move. I can't deal with this every day.*

Rob headed back toward the living room to close the balcony door. As he passed the bathroom, he caught something out of the corner of his eye.

Rob whirled just in time to see a thick, freckled man emerging from the bathroom, pointing a gun.

Rob let out a yell and slammed the wine bottle across the man's forehead. The contact created a loud, dull *thump!*

The man grunted and stumbled off balance for a moment, but didn't topple. He quickly thrust the barrel of the gun toward Rob, aiming into his face. With every ounce of strength in his body, Rob shattered the wine bottle against the side of the intruder's skull. The impact created an explosion of glass. The intruder fell to the floor. The gun dropped from his grasp.

Rob dove for the gun.

So did the intruder, sliding across the broken glass with a fierce and determined face. Rob collided with him, and their arms became entangled as they fought one another off. The man was wet and sticky from the wine, and stripes of blood crawled down his forehead. Rob struggled to climb over him, toward the gun, and received a hard punch to the stomach. He kicked furiously, pushed at the man's face with one hand and reached out with the other.

Rob's fingers brushed the barrel of the gun. The intruder began pulling himself on top of Rob, yanking his shirt, and Rob slid back a few inches, watching the gun grow farther away. Rob made a final, ferocious push to make another grab.

The intruder punched Rob across the jaw, dazing him for a moment, creating white flickers in his sight, and then Rob saw the intruder getting to his knees, gripping a chunk of broken glass.

Rob tried to scramble away, but the intruder clutched a hand against Rob's face, tightly covering his mouth and nose. The man aimed the pointed end of the glass toward Rob's throat.

Rob squirmed madly, threw a fist forward, and hit the man squarely in the chest. It knocked the wind out of him for a moment, and a moment was all Rob needed to slide another eighteen inches toward the gun.

Rob slapped a hand down on the weapon, wrapped his fingers around the lower part of the grip, and raised it fast, loosely.

"I will shoot!" screamed Rob before he had even worked a finger around the trigger, but it worked, because the man lunged backward, away from him.

Rob secured his grip on the gun, really did wrap a finger around the trigger, and pointed the weapon squarely between the attacker's eyes.

The attacker's eyes shut tight. He threw up his hands. "Don't shoot me!"

"Who are you? *What's your name?*" shouted Rob.

"Hector Scrimm. Don't shoot me. I have a wife. I have four children. Ages three to nine. Carol, Barbara, Kimberly, Wade Michaels . . ."

"I don't care. *Listen to me.*" Rob's words were unnaturally ferocious, almost like he was channeling another person, or releasing something primal from deep inside. "I will kill you . . . if you ever come back here. Do you understand?"

"Yes . . ." Scrimm still wouldn't open his eyes. "Please," he begged, terror reverberating in his voice.

"Say 'yes, I understand.' "

"Yes, I understand."

Rob continued to point the gun at Scrimm. The thought of killing this man who tried to kill him remained quite active.

Then tears rolled out of Scrimm's shut eyes.

"Carol, Barbara, Kimberly, Wade Michaels . . ." he said again.

Oh my God, thought Rob.

"Just get out of my apartment," said Rob.

Scrimm opened his eyes and nodded profusely. The two men rose slowly, cautiously, in unison. Rob kept the gun on Scrimm.

Scrimm turned and headed for the door.

"I'm serious," said Rob. "If I ever see you near me again . . ."

Scrimm disappeared behind a door slam.

Rob locked the door. Bolt and chain. Then he walked over to the balcony. After a minute, Rob saw Scrimm in the parking lot, scampering toward a Ford Taurus. The car's back window and bumper had stickers and decals that appeared religious. There was an image of a cross on one of them.

Scrimm climbed into his car and the car screeched out of the lot.

Rob stared down at the gun in his hand. It was identical to the gun Trey Wright had given him, right down to the engraving of a circle on the handle.

The Circle, thought Rob. Hector Scrimm must have been one of the people that night in the motel room, behind the masks. Rob tried hard to remember any identifying characteristics, but he had avoided looking at the others that night, not wanting to know.

But one thing was for certain: Trey Wright had ordered Hector Scrimm to kill Rob. Just like Wright had ordered Rob to kill Shannon.

People were being sent on blind, murderous missions. *God only knows what Trey Wright told this man about me . . .*

It was out of control.

Rob knew he had to keep the pistol. It would not

get tossed into the Skokie Lagoons. Now he needed to protect himself.

If anyone was expecting a mild-mannered English teacher, they had another thing coming.

Rob slept in spurts that night. He couldn't calm down. He couldn't quell the fear. His apartment was locked and secure. His lights were on. He brought the semi-automatic pistol into the bed with him, and no one was going to take it away.

Rob knew that his dangers were far from over. Trey Wright would not give up. The police were not an option. There was nowhere to turn.

The Circle had been turned against him, and Rob Carus was on his own.

Eighteen

The kids in the neighborhood, being smartasses, called him 3D or Triple D or DDD. As in "Hey, 3D, can you score me some bud?" or "Yo Triple D, I need to buy some X." The nicknames derived from the indisputable fact that he was Doug the Drug Dealer. Fortunately, they didn't know his last name, because then they really would have had a field day. He was Doug Decker.

If he preferred any of the monikers, perhaps it was 3D—like a 3D movie, trippy, with cool effects, rather than Triple D, which was a fat chick's bra size, or DDD, which just sounded dumb dumb dumb. Of course, if he voiced a preference, the brats would gravitate toward the ones he liked the least. That's the way they were.

But 3D got the last laugh on these snots. He got their money. He soaked up their spoiled little allowances. In exchange, they received marijuana, cocaine, heroin, ecstasy, mushrooms, whatever their hearts fancied. And they usually came back for more.

His greatest profit margin, actually, was pot. He had a great supplier who imported high-quality, active cannabis seeds from the Netherlands, grew the plants in a greenhouse, cut and dried the leaves, and sold the results to 3D for five bucks a gram. 3D simply added a 100 percent profit margin and hit the streets.

There were always buyers.

Of course, there were brushes with the law, and the continual risk of police sting operations. Every now and then, some parent or community leader would start screeching about teenage drug use, and he'd have to be extra careful. But he knew how to play the game. He could ride the waves.

The biggest hassles resulted when his product caused people to do stupid things, like wrap their car around a street lamp, or overdose. Specifically, there was the knuckleheaded son of that big, washed-up, hick football player who used to be on the Bears. The kid got hooked on H too fast, couldn't slow down, and croaked. There were people screaming for 3D's head for awhile. The police tried extra hard to nail him, but in the end, they couldn't because they were sloppy, plus he had covered his tracks well. You can't prosecute on hearsay. You gotta have evidence. The only true witness was a dead dude.

3D's customers these days were mostly regulars, mostly quite a few years younger than himself, students at one of the two area high schools. They bought a steady succession of small purchases, dime bags, so he never had a whole lot on him at any one time.

But then one night this middle-aged, scary-looking lady showed up wanting an entire ounce.

She approached him at his usual hangout, the alley behind the convenience store and videogame arcade, where teens gathered on weekends to skateboard, smoke, drink beer from paper sacks, and generally talk trash.

3D's first thought: Oh shit, it's someone's mom coming to chew me out.

Instead, the lady said she wanted to score.

Moments like this required very careful analytical skills. Because she could be an undercover cop. But something about her felt very genuine.

For one thing, she truly looked like some kind of addict. Her face was all wrinkly and haggard, with some weird scars, and one of her eyes had bad aim, looking in all the wrong directions. She moved slowly, as if her entire body ached with one big pain. Her teeth were gross, probably stained from a million cigarettes. Her voice was rough and cluttered.

She was asking for a big score. She was offering three hundred dollars for an ounce. She showed him the cash.

"I don't carry that much pot on me," he told her.

"I know," she said. "Get it and we can arrange to meet somewhere. People know me around here, so it's gotta be private, like the forest preserve. Okay, hon?"

3D studied her, then said, "How about you pay me half now, half on delivery."

"Done," said the lady, without hesitation. She forked over a wad of green bills.

He swiftly transferred them to his jacket pocket in one smooth move.

"Burris Woods," 3D said. "You know where that is?"

The lady nodded. "Sure."

"I'll meet you there tomorrow night at seven. At the picnic grove. If there are people there, we'll go someplace else."

"Fine. Great." And the woman left, walking slowly. She appeared to limp.

"Hey Triple D, that your girlfriend?" yelled one of the skateboard punks.

3D gave him the finger. "Remind me to spike your THC with PCP," he said, and the others chortled.

The next evening, 3D arrived at Burris Woods at dusk, and the picnic grove was empty. He brought an ounce of Mary Jane in a plastic, zip-lock bag, shoved deep into his windbreaker pocket. He surveyed the area and paced a bit, hanging near some thick brush. If he sniffed a bust in the works, he could strew the weed into the weeds.

Creepy lady showed up on time, alone.

"You got my stuff?" she asked. Her one eye was doing that weird thing again, staring off in another direction.

"What's with your eye?" he asked.

"It's a glass eye."

"Cool."

"Not cool."

"What happened?"

"My husband beat me and left me for dead," she said plainly. "My skull was fractured. My face required

72 stitches. I still get migraines, usually one a day."

"Shit," said 3D. "I'm sorry."

"Don't be. He's dead now."

"Excuse me?"

"So you got my stuff?"

"Yeah. Sure." 3D reached into his jacket pocket and produced the bulging bag of pot. "This should help you with your headaches. It's good stuff. I have a pipeline to the real deal, not like some of that Mexican crap that's going around . . ."

As 3D was talking, the woman reached into her purse. She did not bring out the remainder of the balance due.

She brought out a gun.

"Whoa!" said 3D. He dropped the bag of pot.

The woman pointed the gun directly at his head. 3D put his hands up.

"Okay, Okay," said 3D, alarmed. "I got you. We're cool."

The good eye stared at him. The spooky eye wandered away.

"Are you a cop?" asked 3D.

"No," replied the lady. "I'm afraid it's much worse than that."

He didn't have time to ponder the statement. She fired the gun.

3D felt his lower jaw explode.

3D meant to say: "Holy shit, lady!!" Instead, it came out *"Blaaaghh"* as his mouth erupted with blood, broken teeth, and chunks of gum and tongue.

Immediately, 3D turned and ran. After two steps,

the pain arrived like a thundering freight train, sending searing pain in a hundred directions. He ran into the woods, shoving past the branches and brush that crisscrossed before him.

CRACK!

He heard the next shot, but did not feel its impact—she missed. He had to get away fast, create distance. This crazy bitch wanted to kill him, and he had no fucking idea who or why . . .

CRACK!

She missed again. Her limp, the one eye, it was going to save him, it had to save him.

He continued deeper into the woods, crunching through leaves, dodging trees, plowing through brush and stumbling over roots. Branches appeared fast in his vision and slapped at his face, but he did not feel them.

3D brought a hand up to where his mouth should be and felt a river of blood and missing parts.

He started to whimper.

CRACK!

3D felt a scorching hole in his lower back and toppled, hard, to the blurry ground. Leafy green and dying sunlight filled his sight.

He screamed and screamed, legs kicking, thrashing, entangled in branches and leaves and madness.

He heard panting. The one-eyed crazy lady was gaining fast.

3D desperately tried to get back on his feet, almost started to rise, but then he saw her arrive, and she was almost on top of him—

CRACK! CRACK! CRACK!

* * *

Rob unlatched his brown teacher's briefcase, lifted the lid, and shifted some papers around to clear a space. Then he placed the semi-automatic pistol inside.

Rob shut the briefcase and latched it.

Time to go to school.

He was ready to defend himself, whenever and wherever. This target was going to shoot back. Unlike the others, this target knew what was coming. He knew about The Circle.

During the drive to Evanston Township High, Rob heard "Beth's song" on the radio. It startled his raw nerves more than ever. He had not thought about her in days. He had not even thought about Richard Shepherd. Now old emotions piled onto new emotions, scrambling his brain, making him crazy—

Rob frantically shut off the radio.

If Beth only knew what had transpired after her death. This spiraling madness . . .

Beth Lawter felt like another world now, another lifetime, a book that had given him great pleasure years ago but now sat fading on the self, remembered in vague, occasional scenes.

The realization rocked him with pain.

Rob pulled into his parking space at the high school and surveyed the area before climbing out.

He recognized the other teachers. He didn't see anything unusual. He was probably safe here.

Rob brought the briefcase with him into school.

He kept the briefcase near him at all times. In his classes, he couldn't help staring out the window, checking out every stranger who walked past or appeared to linger on the sidewalk.

Would a sniper's bullet take him out in front of the students? It was a horrible notion.

Finally, in his afternoon classes, Rob shut the curtains to stop the distraction.

"Hey, why are the windows closed?" complained Bill Wilk in his English Honors class.

"Shut up," said Rob.

He owed the class corrected essays. Rob cautiously placed the briefcase on his desk and flipped the lid up so that it blocked their view of the contents.

"Most of you did very well," he said. "A good job."

He carefully slid the papers out. Some of them were tucked under the gun. He shook them loose.

As he was doing this, Maureen stepped up to his desk. He didn't notice her until she was nearly at his side.

Rob jumped and slammed the briefcase shut.

Maureen gave him a funny look.

Had she seen?

"What?" said Rob, impatient. Then he apologized, and offered a less edgy tone. "I'm sorry . . . What is it, Maureen?"

"I need to leave early for yearbook committee. I have a note."

"I don't need to see it," said Rob. "Go ahead."

As she was leaving, she looked back at him over her shoulder. It was another odd look. He waited until she was out of the room, then opened the briefcase and retrieved the essays. He noticed the other students staring at him. They could sense his anxiety.

"I consider . . . your grades . . . very confidential," Rob explained to them. "I don't want anyone coming up and seeing your grades . . . so I shut my briefcase . . . I'm just protecting your privacy."

"Whatever," said Bill Wilk.

In his teacher's office, Rob took a phone call from Shannon.

"I am so excited about our date tonight," she said. "I'm cooking a killer meal. What time do you think you'll be here?"

"I'll head over as soon as school lets out. I should be there by five."

"Are you okay? You sound winded."

"No, I'm just, yes, I ran for the phone." In actuality, he had been out of breath all day from the panic that choked him.

"I love you," said Shannon.

"I love you, too."

"I love you, too," said Hank, entering the office.

After Rob hung up, he shot Hank a look.

"What?" said Hank. "I'm just funnin' with you. I think it's great that you've found your soul mate. I just want to know when you're going to introduce me to her. She's like a big secret. What's the story? Is she a transvestite or something?"

"Hank, not now," sighed Rob. The briefcase with the gun rested on the desk in front of him. It was at the very center of his mind. Hank was out of focus, a hundred miles away.

Hank just looked at Rob glumly and said, "You used to be fun." He left the office.

Rob looked out the window. A middle-aged man

with a black mustache paced small circles on the sidewalk. The man looked around, in all directions, waiting for someone to emerge. He wore a long coat. It looked downright suspicious.

Rob studied the man and ugly fears jumped into his head. *Who is stalking me? Does he have a gun*?

But then the man's teenage daughter walked up to him, said "Hi, Daddy!" and hugged him. They departed together from view.

Shannon greeted him at the door with a verbal menu of the evening's homecooked delights: "Fettuccine alfredo with chicken, broccoli with raisins and nuts, croissant dinner rolls, and a Greek salad. For dessert, apple pie and Haagen Dazs ice cream."

"Shit," responded Rob. "I forgot—I was supposed to bring the wine." He had forgotten to replace the bottle of wine he had shattered against the intruder's skull in his apartment. Not too hard to see how it slipped his mind . . .

"Don't worry, I have wine." She chuckled at his grave expression. "Come in and relax. We're almost ready. Do you want to start with a drink?"

He entered and stated, "Yep."

She sat him in her living room in a very comfortable chair. Relaxing music that sounded far eastern played on her stereo. She delivered a glass of wine.

"You sit right there and chill out a bit," she said. She wore a short red skirt that seemed to lengthen her legs, a white top with flowing sleeves, and her hair up in an elegant bun with just a few strands reaching down over her cheeks. She smelled like exotic soap. She kissed him, smiled and left the room. He began gulping wine.

After a few minutes, he realized the wine wasn't calming him down. He felt antsy. He looked around the room. He needed something to concentrate on, something to do.

He saw a large stack of magazines in a wicker holder by a chair near the fireplace. He put down his wineglass and walked over to see if he could find something of interest.

He sat in the chair, pulled out a thick pile of publications, and began to thumb through them. There were a lot of antique and fashion publications and catalogs, mostly periodicals related to her business, but also a few architecture and entertainment magazines. He found a few *New Yorkers,* including the annual fiction issue, and put them in his lap.

He was stuffing the rest of the magazines back into the wicker holder when something caught his eye that didn't look right.

It was a copy of *High Living* magazine from a few years back, older than the others, cover creased, a subscription copy.

The address label read SHANNON STROM.

Who is Shannon Strom?

The address was different, too, another town, Lake Forest.

Rob looked through the other magazines and found one other Shannon Strom address label, an issue of *Interior Home Design,* also from a few years ago.

"I can put on some other music if you're not into Kitaro," she called out from the kitchen.

"No, it's fine," said Rob. He hurried the magazines back into the holder. "I don't mind it."

Within ten minutes, dinner was ready.

Rob took his seat at the table, another feast of food and romance, with fresh flowers and candlelight.

"You spoil me," said Rob.

"It's payback," she smiled.

Dinner began well, with good chit-chat, insubstantial but pleasant, and Rob continued to guzzle wine. It loosened his inhibitions, a necessity because he needed to do something very soon that would be awkward, but deeply interesting and valuable.

Halfway into their Greek salads, Rob dropped the bomb.

"Who is Shannon Strom?" he asked her.

Shannon's eyes hardened in a flash. She shot him a piercing look from across the table.

"I beg your pardon?" she said slowly, measured.

"While I was sitting in the other room, I was flipping through your magazines, and I saw a couple with mailing labels that said Shannon Strom with some other address."

Shannon thought for a moment, then stabbed a fork into her salad. "I don't know, 'Hank.' It must be some sort of mistake, don't you think?"

Her tone chilled him. It was the same icy transformation he had witnessed in the bar after miniature golf. She was slipping into another, altogether harsher personality. He looked at his plate, but felt his appetite vanish as his stomach muscles knotted.

"Let's not play games," he said gently.

"I don't know what you're talking about," she said, chewing on lettuce.

"Shannon . . ."

She didn't respond, and he knew he couldn't just drop it. There was too much at stake. Way too much.

"Shannon," he said. "What are you hiding from me?"

She tossed her fork into her salad and it clanged against the edge of the dish. "*Hiding* from you? Nothing. Fine. What do you want to know? It's no big deal. I used to be married."

"Okay, well, you never told me that before."

"I never told you a lot of things. Why is it relevant?"

"I think it is," he said, tone growing firmer.

"Why?"

"Because I want to know everything about you. That's part of being in a relationship and getting close."

"I am *not* Shannon Strom," she said sharply. "I am Shannon Mayer. I was Shannon Strom for two years. I used to be married, and now I'm back to my maiden name. End of story."

"Okay." Rob nodded. A long silence passed. Then he said, "So tell me about your ex-husband."

"Oh Jesus Christ . . ."

"What's the big deal? This is not out of line. I think anybody in a relationship would want to know—"

"But it doesn't matter."

"I think it does."

"That's *your* problem then."

Rob was getting angry. "What have you got to hide? Why can't you tell me about this guy? What are all these secrets? You're not being fair to me. It's a simple question. Who did you marry, why did you divorce?"

"We didn't divorce."

"You didn't . . . divorce?"

"I have told you, several times, I'd rather not talk about it."

"I know, but—"

Shannon shot out of her chair. Her face was pink with rage. She grabbed her plate of salad, turned, and flung it hard against the wall, where it exploded with a bang, sending pieces of food and plate in every direction. She whirled back to face Rob and exclaimed: "He's *dead.*"

Rob, shocked, leaned away from the table not knowing what to do.

Shannon stomped over to him and stood over him, practically hyperventilating. Her face had lost all softness, becoming at once tight and hardened. "My husband died. It was a horrible, ugly accident. It is very painful for me to talk about. It brings back a lot of bad memories. I don't want to discuss it any further. This conversation is *over.*"

Shannon stormed out of the room.

Rob remained frozen in his chair. He saw a scar on the wall from where the plate had hit it. Salad was everywhere.

Rob heard Shannon sobbing in the other room.

He felt awful.

Something terrible and tragic had happened to her husband, and now he had ripped open a painful, unhealed wound. Rob heard the crying and felt a heavy stone in his gut. He got up from the table to go find her.

She was in the kitchen, hunched, her back to him, crying into her hands.

"Shannon . . . I'm so sorry . . ." he said.

She didn't respond, still crying.

He slowly approached. He touched her shoulder.

She jumped and spun around. Her face was soaked with tears, makeup running, the corners of her mouth pulled down.

Her arms came forward. They embraced. She shook. They held tight.

"I'm sorry . . . I never meant to do this to you," said Rob. "I swear, I didn't know."

"I know you didn't know," she said between gasps. "Don't be mad at me."

"I'm not."

When Shannon had gained some composure, she pulled back slightly, just enough to look into his eyes.

"I apologize for my behavior," she said, lips still trembling.

"I told you, it's fine," he said.

"I need to cope better . . ."

"The salad needed tossing anyway."

She let out a loud laugh then, a huge release of tension. "You're such a nut," she said, and she hugged him again.

Then she took his hand. "Come with me."

"Where are we going?"

"You'll see."

She brought him into a room he had seen from the doorway but never entered before. It was a combination den and office, probably where she handled a lot of her business, paid bills, went online. She flicked on the lights and brought him to a closet door, moving aside a large plant stand that blocked it.

"You want to know about my marriage? Fair enough," she said.

She opened the closet door. Inside, Rob saw seasonal coats and jackets, a filing cabinet, and stacks of file boxes. She reached up toward a shelf, strained, and grabbed ahold of a long, flat cardboard box. He helped her bring it down.

She brought it over to a small sofa, and they sat down with the box between them.

She placed a hand on the lid and looked at him.

"These are the remnants of my former life," she said.

She removed the lid. The inside of the box was filled with cards, snapshots, and other mementos of an ended relationship. The first item she showed him was an elegant, white and silver wedding invitation for Shannon Mayer and Walter Strom. Then she brought out several photographs of the two of them. The pictures included photos at a beach with white sand and foamy, blue waves. Shannon wore a blue bikini and deep tan. Her hair was longer, she wore sunglasses on her head.

"My honeymoon in St. Croix," she said.

She pulled out other photographs, including a formal portrait taken at some banquet or fundraiser. The portrait allowed Rob to get a good look at Walter, and he appeared much older than Shannon. He had his arm around her waist. His hair color looked artificially reddish brown, hiding the gray, and his face had deep creases. He was a tall, sturdy man, with striking, blue eyes.

"I was young and crazy in love," said Shannon.

Rob stared at the photograph, both fascinated and hurt to see her so close to someone else.

"How did he pass away?" asked Rob as delicately as he could.

"Please," responded Shannon. "I'm just not ready to discuss it." She began returning the items to the box. His eyes roamed the contents as quickly as he could before she replaced the lid and Walter was gone again.

"Fair enough," said Rob. "I appreciate that you've told me this much."

"Maybe someday we can go into it some more," she said. She reached over and took his hand. "It's very hard for me to talk about right now. I've been trying so hard to put it behind me. It's been very rough . . . I know you wouldn't understand."

"Yes, I would understand," said Rob. "I understand more than you think. A couple of years ago, I almost got married. The fiancée I told you about—the reason we didn't get married is she died. Very suddenly, very tragically."

"Oh no," said Shannon softly.

"It completely devastated me. And the circumstances were really terrible."

Rob told her then all about Beth and the nightmare encounter with the SUV. He took her through the entire day . . . the bike ride, the engagement at the beach, the incredible joy, and then the road rage disaster: the malicious, construction zone sideswipe that sent Beth headfirst into a concrete barrier, breaking her neck, and killing her. He described the subsequent civil suit against the SUV driver and the shocking outcome that left the guilty unpunished. He ended his story there. He didn't need to go on. That was where the story should have ended anyway.

"Oh, Robert," she said, touching the tears on his face. "We really do have a lot in common. We must have been brought together by fate. Two tragic soul mates . . ."

Rob asked, "Your story—you'll tell me one day?"

"Yes," answered Shannon. "I promise."

She embraced him, and it felt good and warm. He held on for a long time. He was in love with her, but still felt he didn't truly know or understand her. He desperately needed more.

Nineteen

Now it was 1:23 A.M. Exactly one minute later than the last time he had checked the digital clock on the nightstand.

For two hours, Rob had been entangled with Shannon on her queen-sized bed, both of them naked, one of them sleeping. She was out, snoring ever so slightly, staying in the same position, on her side, facing him. He kept adjusting, without letting go, unable to get comfortable. He just couldn't sleep.

The intensity of their lovemaking earlier should have sent him into a nice, deep slumber. Following their argument, her big blowup with the salad plate, and the tearful revelations on her den sofa, the mood had strangely segued to aggressive passion and arousal. They didn't even pause to advance from the den to the bedroom. Instead, they tossed sofa cushions on the floor to avoid rug burns (but he got them anyway). Their clothes scattered to the outer rims of the room, leaving them dressed in nothing but their own sweat. After the romping achieved its zenith, they went upstairs to take a shower together, and then the whole thing got started again.

They never touched dessert.

And now she slept like a baby while his mind pounded away with disconnected emotions and jumbled thoughts, criss-crossing like little bolts of lighting. He couldn't shut them out.

He had to know.

What had happened to her husband?

What was her alleged crime?

Why was she wanted dead? And by whom?

Her explosion of rage tonight frightened him. It wasn't the first time he had witnessed an abrupt shift to fury. She remained guarded about her history. There were secrets, and he couldn't wait any longer for her to tell him at her own pace. There simply wasn't enough time.

Rob looked into Shannon's face: the lips slightly parted, eyes shut, hair spilling every which way.

He began to slowly slide away from her. He pulled an arm out. He moved his leg out from between hers.

She made a small sigh, like a little child, but did not open her eyes.

Completely disconnected from her touch, Rob waited several minutes to see if she would react, but there was nothing. Just the slight sound of her breathing and the delicate rising and falling of her chest.

Rob climbed out of the bed as quietly as possible. He put his feet to the floor. He walked softly.

Rob left the bedroom and headed downstairs.

He didn't turn on any lights, brushing his hands against the walls for guidance. On the first floor, the cluttered rooms, with their antique furniture and gift shop paraphernalia, seemed to come alive with witnesses. Little objects threw off big shadows. It was a tangled path. He proceeded in the dark wearing only his boxers. He did his best not to stumble into anything and send it crashing, like the Chinese vase or the easel with the watercolor print.

Why does she surround herself with all this stuff?

He crossed the living room and dining room and entered the den.

What am I going to say if she finds me in here?

He realized he didn't have a decent excuse. Looking for the bathroom? Midnight snack? Screw it.

Rob turned on the small lamp perched at the top of her large, oak desk.

Click.

Not a lot of light, but enough.

He started to snoop around the cubbyholes. He looked in drawers. He found bills, paperwork connected with her store, stationery supplies, a sewing kit, and chewing gum.

Nothing to aid his investigation.

He moved on to the closet. Earlier she had shown him some of the contents in a cardboard box that represented "the remnants of my former life," as she had put it. But they had only skimmed the surface items. Maybe there was more useful evidence buried below.

He moved the plant stand that blocked the closet door. He opened the door and reached high for the large, flat cardboard box.

It was awkward to maneuver and almost slipped off balance in his hands, threatening to send the contents spilling and crashing to the floor. But he did a little dance and kept it under control.

He brought the box to her desk. He sat in her desk chair, placed the box in his lap, and scooted closer to the glow of the small lamp.

He removed the lid.

He pushed aside the items she had already shared with him. He dug into unfamiliar territory.

It still wasn't terribly revealing.

More wedding stuff. Walter's cuff links. His wedding ring. Birthday cards. Photos. More photos.

There were poolside shots of a younger Shannon in a wet, clinging, two-piece bathing suit, posing sexily, practically campy. The pictures were extremely alluring, so much so that he almost wanted to run upstairs and wake her up for number three.

Instead, he kept digging.

He found the program to Walter's funeral: classy, sad, with a listing of names he did not recognize.

The he found a small notecard, like the type that accompanies flower deliveries. The handwriting said, "Dearest Shannon. My heart aches when we fight. Forgive me. I love you always. Walter."

Rob found a few newspaper clippings related to Walter's construction business, including a photo of him breaking ground for a new mall in a far west suburb.

Walter was at least twenty-five years older than she. He appeared to be very successful, wealthy, accustomed to the good life. There were few clues to be gained from his appearance. He was just a regular guy. Handsome, fit, well-dressed. There were clippings and photos of Shannon and Walter and friends at ritzy social events. Walter found plenty of uses for his tux. Shannon was almost always at his side, elegant, a hand on his shoulder or an arm around his waist, beaming, eyes aglow from the flash.

He found a little photo book with pictures from a European trip. He recognized sites from Paris and London. Under the photo book, there were mementos from a variety of excursions: an Italian café menu, a label removed from a bottle of French wine, a love note and goofy doodle on Honolulu hotel stationery, an unsent postcard from Mardi Gras, a World Series program.

Anchored at the bottom of the box, Rob found the largest, heaviest item: Shannon and Walter's wedding album.

They had spared no expense to create a handsome, leather-bound book containing page after page of professionally shot 7×10 stills.

Rob listened carefully for any sounds in the house. He heard none. He placed the box on the floor and studied the wedding album in his lap.

The pages were thick cardboard. He turned them one by one, absorbing every detail of the extravagant event. The reception appeared to take place in a grand ballroom at one of the historic downtown hotels, maybe the Drake?

Walter and Shannon looked truly happy. The friends and relatives were in a celebratory mood. All the traditional shots were covered: the walk down the aisle, the ceremony, the limo ride, the dinner party, the first dance, cutting the cake, removing the garter, tossing the bouquet, and all sorts of giddy people raising their glasses to the camera in a happy toast to the new Mr. and Mrs. Strom.

It was all starting to get rather boring when Rob turned a page and uncovered a photograph that caused him to gasp out loud and break into a cold sweat.

A big happy picture of Shannon in her white wedding gown sharing a laugh with several other women at the reception. There was a blonde, a brunette, and a redhead, all early twenties, in colorful, strapless gowns, probably friends from college or somewhere, nothing unusual.

Except in the background, almost out of frame, Rob saw a familiar figure, suited up, very serious and staring ahead, looking right back at Rob.

It was Trey Wright.

Twenty

Justin Hoyt placed the football on his son's grave, carefully centered against the tombstone, about two feet back on the manicured green grass. He stood back. It was an official NFL Game Ball, double-laced with top quality leather, not some shoddy replica. This was the real thing.

"Tommy, we went into overtime," said Hoyt, "and we evened the score."

It was his first visit since the death of Doug Decker.

The death of Doug Decker. It sounded so good that he let the words roll through his mind a few more times. Death of Doug Decker. Death. Of Doug Decker. Dead. Died.

Knocked out of bounds and off the planet.

After the discovery of the body in the woods by two elderly hikers, the police showed up at Hoyt's home. They asked him easy questions. Hoyt had easy answers. At the time of the shooting, he had been closing a glass deal with a small auto repair chain in Gurnee. He provided the name and number of the owner, Bill

Mellander. The police didn't really treat Hoyt like a suspect. In fact, after the interview, they apologized profusely for bothering him, explaining it was their obligation. One of them asked for his autograph.

The newspaper quoted a police source suggesting that the shooting may have resulted from a drug deal gone bad, or perhaps a turf war with another dealer. The killing did not even make major headlines. A dope peddler shot up in the woods wasn't going to create an uproar in the community. In fact, if you listened closely, you could hear the positive buzz. Good, honest, decent folks were pleased.

Parents were shoving the article in front of their teenage sons and daughters, rubbing their noses in it: "You *see?* That's where drugs get you."

The only people who were upset by the drug dealer's demise, naturally, were the dealer's blood relatives.

"Whoever did this, your days are numbered!" shouted a long-haired, gap-toothed hippie identified as Doug Decker's brother. He screeched about vengeance to any reporter who would listen. "There's going to be payback," he vowed, articulation blurred by a speech impediment that added wrong letters to his words. But his message, to Hoyt's ears, was clear: I'm oily, brain-dead trailer trash just like my dope-dealing kin.

Hoyt had no pity for the killer who shot poison into Tommy's arm and no pity for the killer's family. None at all. If the family really cared, they would have turned that criminal in to the police a long time ago.

The early strains of dawn streaked across the sky. Hoyt checked his watch and knew it was time to leave the cemetery. He had an important appointment to keep.

But he had to go incognito.

Inside his pick-up truck, Hoyt put on a large, floppy fishing hat and big sunglasses. Not a brilliant disguise, but good enough.

He realized he was wearing his trademark snake-skin cowboy boots, possibly a mistake, but then again, so what if he did get spotted?

He was just going for a chat with somebody. Can't a guy chat with another guy?

When Hoyt pulled into the small parking lot, there was only one other car. There were no kids on the playground. It was probably still too early in the morning. The swings moved to and fro in the wind, gentle, with nobody on them.

At the far corner of the park, Trey Wright sat on a bench, reading the newspaper.

Hoyt hopped out of his pick-up truck, slammed the door, and headed over to see him.

Wright looked up as Hoyt's large shadow fell on him.

"The Bengels traded Christian Spann," said Wright.

"Can you believe it?" said Hoyt in his southern drawl. "They get a first-round draft pick, I know, but still . . . leaves one heck of a hole in their offense."

Wright neatly folded the sports section. "Speaking of having a good offense . . . We have some things to talk about. Have a seat." He gestured for Hoyt to join him on the bench.

Hoyt sat. His huge weight caused his end of the bench to creak, lifting Wright ever so slightly.

"I trust you're doing better?" asked Wright.

"I am," said Hoyt. "The vermin has been crushed. He'll never contaminate another child. My only regret is that I did not get to personally witness the light fading from his eyes."

"He will not be missed."

"I want to thank you, Mr. Wright. From the bottom of my heart—"

Wright held up a hand. "Please stop. It wasn't me. It was The Circle. And now the wheel rotates again, and it is your turn to absorb its power and show your strength."

Wright reached under the folded newspaper next to him and brought out a padded envelope.

"The gun?" asked Hoyt, accepting it.

Wright nodded. "Semi-automatic pistol. Eight shots in the magazine. Slide lock . . ."

"I'm familiar," Hoyt said.

"Good."

Wright handed over a manila envelope. "Your assignment. I'd like you to open it here, so I can answer any questions."

Hoyt unclasped the envelope. He pulled out a photograph and a sheet of paper with a name, home and work addresses, and time schedule.

Hoyt stared at the face of Shannon Mayer. She smiled sweetly at him, collar up, thick and tumbling brown hair thrown back behind her shoulders.

"A woman," said Hoyt, surprised.

"A very dangerous woman," said Wright. "Even more dangerous than the drug peddler who killed your boy. Just as that sociopath had to die, this woman must be put to rest so that evil is destroyed and goodness prevails, by any means possible."

Hoyt nodded. "I understand. She will be wiped out. Defeated. The victory belongs to justice."

"You will follow the oath of The Circle?"

"I swear by it."

"You have what it takes to win?"

Hoyt's eyes narrowed. He became consumed by his best game-day intensity, bringing back the aggressive, single-minded focus that drove his NFL career. "I'm going all the way to the end zone, Mr. Wright. That is all I see. Anything in my way gets trampled. This young lady will be on the losing side. There will be no other outcome."

Wright beamed with pride. "Go win one for the team."

Twenty-one

Rob awoke to the chirps of a cuckoo bird. The sounds ended as abruptly as they started, and he realized they were coming from a downstairs clock. Another one of her gift shop items, probably imported from Germany or maybe Switzerland.

The bedroom shades were drawn, but slivers of light still managed to find ways to pierce the room. Rob stirred on the bed, rolled over, reached, and landed his hand on . . . air.

Shannon was missing.

He quickly sat up.

"Shannon?"

No response. Rob tossed aside the sheets and hopped to the floor. He threw on a T-shirt, pulling his arms through the sleeves as he moved to the stairs.

"Shannon?"

"In here. The kitchen."

Rob entered the kitchen, and there she was, in her white robe, fixing a ham and cheese sandwich.

"I'm packing you a lunch for school," she explained sweetly.

Rob smiled. "You don't have to do that."

"I want to. If I remember anything from high school, it's the crap they serve in the cafeteria." She motioned to a small paper sack. "I got you some chips, cookies, and an apple. What would you like to drink?"

"Don't worry about the drink. They have a vending machine in the teachers' lounge."

"You like mustard or mayonnaise on your sandwich?"

"Mustard."

"Done."

Shannon added mustard, lettuce and tomato. Rob watched her take a long, sharp knife from the knife block and cleanly sever the sandwich in half.

She wrapped the sandwich, placed it inside the paper sack, and brought the bag over to the island at the center of the kitchen, where Rob's briefcase rested.

She put down the sack. She started to unsnap the briefcase latches.

The gun is in there. Rob sprung into action. He reached her before she had time to open the second latch.

"Whoa," he said, sliding the briefcase away from her.

Startled, she stepped back. "I was just going to put your lunch in there."

"That's okay, I'll carry it separate," he said. "I don't want it to get mixed in with my papers. You know, mustard on the kid's essays."

She still didn't understand. "But it's—"

So he shut her up with a kiss. A long kiss. He reached inside her robe. Within several minutes, they had both forgotten all about the sack lunch.

He finally had to pry himself away. "I'm going to be late for school."

"I could write you a note," she offered.

"Tonight, we'll pick up where we left off. Remember everything: the hand positions, open or closed mouth . . ."

"You're crazy." She laughed. Then she told him her idea to visit Amour, an adult shop in a neighboring suburb, that night. "You can pick out anything you want me to wear, any accessories, the whole works, as long as I get to do the same."

"Halloween comes early," he said. "I like it. A little trick, a lot of treat."

"Think about what you want me to wear," she said. "You have all day. Don't let it distract you in class . . ."

"Fat chance. I'll have to stand behind my desk, that's for sure."

He remained distracted during the long drive to Evanston. But it wasn't about the outfits. He had returned to his original obsession from the night before.

Walter Strom.

Shannon Strom.

Trey Wright.

What was the complete story? What was she not telling him? Why all the mystery?

He taught his first period class, a "D" performance, then used his free second period to slip into the computer lab. It was crowded, but he managed to kick one of the kids off a PC with "I need to go online. Important teacher business."

Rob opened the Internet browser and called up a search engine.

He typed *Walter Strom.*

He punched Enter.

Instantly, a list of hits arrived. He scanned them. There were various Walter Stroms from around the country entangled with one another.

An insurance agent in Angola, Indiana.

A percussionist for the Phoenix Orchestra.

A news article about a man killed in Chicago.

Bingo.

Rob took a deep breath and clicked the link.

The *Chicago Sun-Times* website filled the screen. A brief article from a couple of years ago.

MAN KILLED OUTSIDE NIGHTCLUB, WIFE HELD.

The sentences under the headline leapt out at him. He read and reread the story, barely able to breathe. He moved his briefcase closer to him.

> A Chicago man was killed outside a Near North nightclub early Sunday morning in a fight with his wife that turned deadly.
>
> Witnesses report that Walter Strom, 56, and his wife, Shannon Strom, 25, began arguing at Bounce, 1601 N. Wells, shortly after midnight. According to witnesses, Mr. Strom accused his wife of flirting with another patron. The confrontation rapidly escalated and advanced outside.
>
> Mrs. Strom told police that her husband beat and kicked her repeatedly in the alley and at-

tempted to choke her. The Gold Coast resident alleges that she hit her husband with a brick to defend herself. The blows to the head killed Mr. Strom, who died at the scene.

Walter Strom founded Willowbrook Development, a local commercial construction firm based in Oak Park.

He is survived by a son, David, 32, of Niles.

"Oh my God," said Rob out loud.

A couple of students turned to look at him.

"It's nothing," he said softly, but it was a lot more than nothing. It was everything.

Rob returned to his search and clicked on several other articles, some of them follow-ups with additional details and later information.

The next article he read was: QUESTIONS REMAIN IN FATAL CLUB BEATING.

The article talked about the police investigation. Shannon continued to assert that she had acted in self-defense. She told police she never intended to kill Walter. She just wanted to save herself. The only witness, a kitchen worker at the club, spoke out on Shannon's behalf.

There was also a quote from David, Walter's son from an earlier marriage.

"This is nothing less than first-degree murder," said David. "I am confident that the courts will bring out the truth."

A third article, dated nearly a year later, described the subsequent trial and jury verdict.

Based on the kitchen worker's testimony and a

medical expert's analysis of Shannon's injuries, including bruises to her throat, the jury concluded that Shannon acted in self-defense. She was found not guilty.

After the verdict, the defendant wept and later released a statement to reporters. "I just wanted to protect myself. I didn't want to lose Walter. Today's verdict does not remove my pain. I still have to live with this for the rest of my life."

"Yo buddy!"

Rob jumped and closed the web browser as Hank strolled over to him.

Hank laughed at the reaction. "What's the matter, you downloading porn?"

Rob turned away from the computer. "Hank, I have an emergency. I need you to tell the department chair I had to leave. They'll have to get a substitute for me, or cancel my classes. *I really have to go.*"

Hank's cheery disposition dropped and he grew alarmed. "Rob—are you okay? What's wrong? Can I help?"

"I have to leave," said Rob, rising from the seat. "I'm sorry to do this."

"Just let me know . . ."

"Thanks, Hank. I'm sorry."

Rob grabbed his briefcase and ran from the school.

Twenty-two

Rob hammered his fists against the large black door. He waited for a response. The door had no window; it was just a steel slab. In fact, the entire front of the establishment, which ran nearly half the block, was a blank wall, windowless.

The only dash of identification came from a big jovial sign with rubbery rainbow letters: B-O-U-N-C-E!

Rob stood before the nightclub where Walter Strom died, not far from the intersection of North and Wells on Chicago's north side. This was the setting for the tragic fight with Shannon. The backdrop for the story she would not share. So it was up to Rob to conduct his own investigation.

He pounded again, and then heard bolts sliding on the other side. The entire door shuddered and opened. A tall, scarecrow-like man stared back, wearing a checkered shirt and blue jeans. His hair was slicked back. He looked young, but wore narrow grandpa glasses on the end of his nose.

"We don't open until four. Try McCarty's—"

"I'm not a customer," said Rob quickly, speech rehearsed. "I'm a writer for the magazine *Modern Woman*. I'm writing a feature about abused women who fight back. I'm on a really tight deadline, and I'd like to include a few paragraphs on the Shannon Strom story. Are you familiar?"

"That was years ago," said the man.

"Doesn't matter. I just need a few minutes. I'd like to talk with someone, like the owner, who can tell me about what happened that night."

"I'm the owner," said the man, adding unenthusiastically, "and I was there that night."

Rob could see the lack of interest in his eyes and pressed further. "Just a few minutes, I promise. There will be a nice plug for your club."

"As a murder scene."

"No—as a scene for heroism. This is a story about a woman who took a stand against domestic violence. She fought back."

"Will there be a picture?"

"Sure," Rob lied. "We'll send a photographer. Do you want to be in the picture?"

He liked that idea. "Maybe standing in front of the sign?"

"Of course."

"All right, come in. I've got a few minutes. But I've got a lot of work to get ready. This is a ball-busting job, it's not a bunch of fun and games."

"Right."

The man introduced himself as Keith and allowed Rob inside.

Keith took Rob through the front section of the

club, which included a small eating area. Normal, undramatic lighting revealed crates of liquor arrivals, piles of sweepings, and various employees moving about, tossing chatter at one another. Keith advanced to a wide-open room with a dance floor and DJ booth. Mirrors made the place appear three times bigger. Groupings of large black speakers sat in silence. Thick, heavy spotlights hung unlit, strung across the ceiling. There was a narrow upstairs balcony around the rim of the dance floor, populated with small tables. A brick wall decorated with slick graffiti art backed up the DJ booth.

Keith brought Rob to one of the loveseats against the wall, shaped in a small curve to bring couples together. Christmas tree lights entangled in fish netting hung above their heads.

As they sat down, Keith said, "This is where they sat when it all started."

"Shannon and Walter Strom?"

"Right. And you should know from the start, I'm not telling you anything I didn't already tell the police. In fact, they could give you a lot more information than me. There was an investigation team. I think I still remember the lead detective's name. I could call him—"

"Not necessary," said Rob. "Just tell me what you know."

"Okay. They had been here a few hours. They came here a lot. I think they lived in a high-rise on Oak Street, one of those ritzy condo buildings with a swimming pool and trees on the roof, you know? So I would see them here from time to time. They dropped a lot of cash. He was a lot older than her, but looked good for his age. They always came together. Sometimes it was all lovey-dovey. Making out like kids. Other times, they would bicker and argue. I couldn't hear the words, because of the music, you know. But you could read it off their faces. It was a love-hate thing. Not that unusual. I bitch with my old lady all the time. But things really got out of hand that night. They knew some other people, or met some other people, I don't know which, but she was talking with this other guy, a young guy. Maybe they danced, I'm not sure, but Walter—it really pissed him off. She was kind of wild and flirtatious. That was her personality. He was always brooding. He was slamming back the drinks—whiskey sours. So basically, she did something to make him jealous with this other guy. I think she put her hand on his butt. Maybe it was all innocent, misconstrued, or maybe she was taunting her husband, I don't know. So she comes back to the table and Walter starts yelling at her. Really yelling, turning heads. He called her a slut. So she throws a drink in his face. They start grabbing and shoving, and my bouncers told them to take it outside. I won't have fighting in my club, even if it's a married couple. People come here for a good time, right? It's supposed to be a happy place."

"So what happened next?" asked Rob. "They went into the alley?

"Right. She storms out of here. She doesn't go back through the front of the bar. She finds this fire exit we have. Over there, under the video monitor."

He pointed and Rob saw it, a door with a bar

across it, with the traditional red EXIT sign illuminated above.

"Take me to the alley," said Rob.

"You want to see where the old man bought the farm?" Keith smirked. "Sure, I get it. Doing your research, right?"

Keith led Rob out of the club and into the back alley. They winced in the daylight. It was a narrow, debris-ridden path of gravel with Dumpsters and buzzing flies. It smelled bad.

"I didn't see it, but apparently they really got into it out here," said Keith, kicking a Slurpee cup out of his way. "Happened right here, on this spot. He started to beat the hell out of her, knocking her all over the place. Kicking, punching, then he tries to strangle her. But she got her hand around a brick . . ."

"So you didn't see this fight?" said Rob.

"No. Heard all about it, though."

"There was a witness who testified . . ."

"Right. That was one of my employees. He came out here to take out the trash and he saw two people fighting, and realized one of them was a chick. He saw this guy choking her and slamming her head against the ground. So he drops everything to run over to help her—but before he gets there, she's clobbering the guy with the brick. She hit him a bunch of times, because he kept coming at her, even with dents in his head. Probably the booze, you know?"

"So then what happened?"

"The guy, Walter, he's unconscious. Shannon and my employee come back inside the club to call the police. I don't think anybody realized at this point that he was going to die."

"What did Shannon say?"

"She was crying, hysterical, you know. Her face was a mess. She had blood all over her shirt. It was pretty awful. I put her in my office because she was freaking out the customers."

"And when the cops arrived . . ."

"The police, an ambulance, the works. But he was dead. They couldn't do anything for him. They put up police tape, sectioned it off. The TV crews showed up. It was a circus for a while. Then the whole thing went to trial. I had to testify, all the stuff I've told you just now, under oath."

"I understand that Walter Strom had a son," said Rob.

"From another marriage, right. I think he was older than his stepmom. The son was totally convinced that she killed him on purpose. He campaigned to press charges. He was certain that she was only after his old man's money. His father was a rich guy. He made millions in construction, building shopping malls. They had only been married for a while. She inherited a load of cash."

"In the millions?"

"I think so. The son was pissed off because she inherited the old man's fortune. She's younger than him and he'll never see a dime of it."

Rob studied the patch of gravel, dirt and weeds where Walter Strom died at the hands of Shannon. He tried to envision her striking him with the brick, repeatedly. It wasn't difficult when he imagined the explosive Shannon who threw the plate of salad . . . the enraged, pink-faced woman who shouted at him after the mini-golf date and stormed out of the bar.

Maybe her violent temper had saved her life.

"The employee who witnessed the fight out here . . ." said Rob. "Do you have any contact information for him? I want to pay a visit. For my story. It would be good to interview the eyewitness. Do you know where I could find him? Is there a phone number or address?"

Keith said, "You don't need it. He's here today. He's still my employee. His name is Elio Rodriguez."

Keith guided Rob back inside the club. Elio was setting up rows of glasses behind a long bar. He was probably in his late twenties, chunky, with a soft face and tightly cropped, black curls.

"Elio," said Keith. "Got a reporter here from a magazine, says he's doing a story about abused women who fight back. He wants to talk about that lady who killed her husband with a brick."

Elio nodded slowly. He stared at Rob.

Keith asked Elio, "Can you talk with him? I'm sure it's just the same stuff you got asked before. Just a couple of minutes."

"That's right," Rob told Elio, as Elio didn't look comfortable. "Couple of minutes, just a few questions."

"I'll leave you guys alone," said Keith. He added to Elio, "If he wants anything to drink, it's on the house."

Elio nodded.

Keith left.

Rob sat in one of the tall chairs lined up at the bar counter.

"Thanks, I really appreciate this," said Rob.

"Where's your notebook?" asked Elio.

"Excuse me?"

"Your notebook. If you're a reporter, how come you don't have a notebook or a tape recorder?"

Rob thought for a moment. Good question. Then he tapped his temple. "Don't need it. It all goes in here."

Elio shrugged. "So what do you want to know?"

"Just what you saw. Did you see Walter and Shannon Strom fighting inside the club?"

Elio fidgeted with a rag, wiping the same section of counter over and over. "No. I mean, I saw some commotion by the dance floor, but I didn't pay much attention. People fight all the time. We have bouncers."

"When did you go out in the alley?"

"Five, maybe ten minutes after they left the bar." Elio had a hard time looking Rob in the eye. His voice was gentle and he appeared shy. "I took out the trash, like I always do five, six times a night. On a Saturday night, I'm moving a lot of garbage."

Rob realized he would have to prompt him. "And the fight in the alley . . . What did you see?"

"Two people fighting. The old guy was just whaling on her. He had her on the ground, kicking her in the back, smacking her. It was pretty bad. It took me a minute to realize he was . . . he was doing it to a lady."

"So you went to go help?"

"I was totally surprised for a minute, and then I saw

him choking her, really hard. She was really gagging, she couldn't breathe. I started to run at the guy . . . and then . . . she started hitting him. I couldn't see it until I got closer, but she had a brick. Man, she was hitting him over and over and over . . ."

"So you didn't get in the middle of it?"

"I didn't need to. That brick stopped him. But if she didn't get to him first with the brick, I would have been all over the guy. If she didn't kill him, maybe it would have been me."

He said it with a rise of passion in his voice.

"That Walter Strom, he was a mean old guy," said Elio. "He deserved to die."

"So you and Shannon went back inside the club?"

"Yeah. The guy was totally out. We went in and called 911. She was really scared. Even though he choked her and everything, she wanted him to be okay. She didn't want him to die. She was crying."

Rob looked into Elio's eyes and asked him, "Do you believe she killed him out of self-defense?"

Elio returned the stare. "Absolutely. I do."

Rob left the night club.

He went directly across the street to a Greek restaurant with posters of racks of lamb in the windows. He found the pay phone in the front entryway and jammed coins into the slot.

Rob called Niles information and asked for the phone number for David Strom.

He had the operator patch him through.

After four rings, a man said "Hello."

"Hello, Trey Wright," Rob said. "Or should I say 'David Strom.' "

The other end went silent.

"I know your story, David," said Rob. "I know your real name. I know why you want Shannon Mayer dead. But she killed your father in self-defense. It had nothing to do with the money."

"She's pulled the wool over your eyes, hasn't she?" stated David bitterly. "She has duped you like everybody else. Well, let me tell you a simple fact. Shannon Mayer killed my father. They had been married one year. She never loved him. She killed him in an alley in cold blood to inherit three million dollars."

"Your father physically attacked her," said Rob. "There's an eyewitness."

"Garbage. Total bullshit. You don't think she paid off that stupid dishwasher to lie for her?"

"No, I don't."

"Then you don't really know her. You know nothing. You didn't see how that bitch treated my father every single day. She used him, she abused him, and she killed him off."

"I don't buy that one bit," responded Rob. "You just wanted me to do your dirty work. That's why you gave me a bogus name and sucked me in with all your self-righteous bullshit. You pulled me in because I was vulnerable. I had the rage, I was hell-bent on vengeance. Then, when I wouldn't go with your plan, you tried to have me killed."

David loudly declared, "Robert Carus, you will not bring down The Circle. You have been corrupted. Like the lawyers, the police, the D.A., the judges, the juries. You are a disgrace. You have been made a fool.

She has blinded you with her good looks, suckered you with sweet lies. You have been seduced by evil. You have gone to the other side. But I will continue to lead the fight for real justice."

Rob felt his voice rise. "This isn't about justice. You surround yourself with victims, claiming to be one of them, but you're not. You're manipulative. You're a phony. Maybe you've fooled yourself. Maybe you've fooled the others. But you don't fool me."

Before David could interject, Rob told him, "I'm telling Shannon about your entire scheme. I am going to tell her how you tried to arrange for her murder. How you tried to have me killed. This game of yours is over."

And then Rob slammed down the receiver into its cradle with thundering finality.

Twenty-three

Rob stomped the accelerator and pulled away from the curb, shooting into traffic with a squealing of tires. He narrowly missed a delivery van. Screeching brakes piled up behind him, followed by a blast of horns. Rob yanked the wheel to the right and swerved around another vehicle, momentarily barreling toward oncoming traffic in the adjacent lane, creating more slammed brakes and horn melodies.

His brown teacher's briefcase sat on the seat next to him. It contained the gun he carried for protection. The semi-automatic taken from the attacker in his apartment building. The weapon supplied by David Strom under the name of Trey Wright.

Rob's fear of the weapon had dissipated over time. He knew he would now use it if necessary, anytime, anyplace.

His absolute number-one priority was to protect Shannon. He had to get to her shop as soon as possible. He was going to tell her everything: His original mission. His discovery about Trey Wright. The secrets of The Circle. The plan to have her killed. His refusal to carry out the order.

After he unloaded the truth, then they would discuss next steps. Maybe it would involve the two of them moving away someplace. Going under assumed names. Whatever it took.

The traffic going west on North Avenue crawled. Rob wanted to leap out of his car and scream at every obstacle. Stoplights showed red every fifty feet. People double-parked, or straddled two lanes, or halted in front of him for last-minute left turns. At one red light, Rob actually snaked across the intersection, gambling that people would rather brake than hit him, and he was right.

But half a block later, he saw a Chicago police car. Fortunately the woman behind the wheel didn't look his way, but if she had known about his driving behavior, she would have given him hell, especially with an unlicensed loaded gun in the briefcase next to him.

Rob made himself obey the traffic laws and stay within a reasonable range of the speed limit. It made him crazy, but he couldn't blow everything now by acting stupid.

Every minute that slipped away before the Kennedy Expressway was agony.

Then the expressway came into view and he rejoiced, swinging onto the on-ramp, which led to . . . more agony.

Typical midweek commuter traffic created a sluggish pace. There would be no fear of getting a speeding ticket here.

Rob used the time to rehearse his speech to Shannon. It would be a long and difficult one. It would take a long time for her to understand. But he would quickly get to the bottom line.

He had fallen in love with her. He didn't want to hurt her. He only wanted to protect her.

No more secrets on either side. This was a new beginning, chapter one, for both of them.

When Rob reached the 294 Tollway, traffic became a little better, then a lot better. The farther he got from the city, the faster he could drive.

Inside half an hour, he arrived in Barrington. As the scenery turned serene, he forced himself to slow down and gather his wits. He pulled onto Main Street, allowed pedestrians to stroll the crosswalks, and casually rolled into a parking space across the street from Charms.

Just seeing the pink awning set his heart racing.

Rob grabbed his briefcase and exited the car.

He crossed the street and walked up to the familiar entrance. A cheerful handmade sign greeted him: OPEN! COME IN AND BROWSE.

Rob opened the door and heard the familiar *jingle* of chimes. He stepped inside.

The sweet odors of scented candles and soaps greeted him. The ceiling fans rotated above, humming pleasantly. He stepped forward into a path lined with birdbaths, wine racks, floor vases, and tabletops of sales items.

He did not see Shannon.

"Shannon?" said Rob. "Shannon, it's Rob."

No response.

Rob circled the store, called her name twice more,

then went to the cash register counter. Her chair sat empty behind the counter.

Then Rob saw the thin, curtained doorway that led to a back room.

"Shannon, are you back there?"

Again, nothing.

Rob slowly circled the counter. He approached the curtain, stopped, and listened to more silence. He stuck his hand through the crack between the curtain and the doorframe and pulled the curtain back, unveiling the room.

David Strom stepped into view, aiming a pistol at Rob's chest.

"Shut up," said Strom before Rob could say a word, "and get in here." Rob saw Shannon standing near Strom, eyes petrified.

Rob froze completely. He gripped the handle of his briefcase.

"Get out of the doorway and come in here, or I will end your life now," Strom said firmly.

Rob stepped inside. The curtain shut behind him. He moved toward Shannon.

"No, get away from her," said Strom. "Other way."

Rob advanced farther into the room.

Strom moved the aim of the gun from Rob to Shannon to Rob again.

The narrow back room had no windows, just counters and shelves filled with merchandise, some of it still packed and in boxes. Large filing cabinets covered one wall. Rob noticed a heavy, solid door that led to the alley. It was across the room, about six feet from Shannon, who stood near a table of untagged merchandise.

Rob remained fixated for a moment on the door to the alley. A getaway route.

He glanced at Shannon. She gave him a helpless look. Rob could see that she was shaking.

Strom waved the gun at Rob, and Rob jumped. "No. Back. Keep moving back," said Strom.

Rob continued stepping backward until he bumped into a small, compact refrigerator.

"Good," said Strom. "Stay."

Strom turned his attention to Shannon. "Your boyfriend has come to rescue you. I think that's romantic, don't you?"

Rob lifted his brown briefcase and placed it flat on top of the refrigerator. Strom immediately turned and shot him a look.

Rob lifted his hands, palms out.

"I don't want you to move," said Strom. "I just want you to listen."

Rob nodded.

"Thank you," said Strom. He continued to alternate the gun's aim between Rob and Shannon. "I was just having a discussion with my stepmother. Strange thing . . . when the mother is younger than her son. That should be a tip off that something just isn't right." He stared at Shannon. "Right, Mother?"

Shannon just glared back.

"There's an old saying," said Strom, "that goes: If you want something done right, you have to do it yourself. It's very true." He shook his head sadly. "Rob, I appointed you to take care of this because I thought you were the best we had in The Circle. You're smart, you're controlled and collected, plus you had the right amount of rage. The right hunger for vengeance. You were the chosen one to handle her."

Rob felt Shannon's shocked expression burn into him.

"She's innocent," said Rob.

"No," replied Strom. "Your interpretation of the facts is misinformed at best. She is guilty of murder. *Murder*, Rob Carus. And now she is sentenced to die."

Strom turned to Shannon.

"Shannon," said Strom. "Would you like to tell your boyfriend here the truth? That you're a crazy bitch?"

As Strom placed his focus on Shannon, Rob dropped his hands to his sides. He slowly brought the hands behind his back. He began to feel around . . . and touched the briefcase that rested on the little refrigerator.

Rob knew he had to act quickly and inconspicuously to open the briefcase and retrieve the gun inside.

"I want to hear you say it out loud," Strom instructed Shannon. "That you never loved my father. That you only loved his money, which you used to buy so many nice things for yourself, like your big house, and this ridiculous, stupid vanity shop." He motioned toward the scattered merchandise still waiting to be tagged and displayed. "All this *crap*."

Eyes fixed ahead, Rob kept his hands working behind him. His fingertips brushed the small knob alongside one of the latches. His touch slipped on and off the knob. He carefully positioned his fingers . . . pressed gently . . . nothing. He pressed harder.

The latch popped with a small *twang*.

"You're the crazy one, David," spoke up Shannon, staring hard at him. "Let's face it. You were the one with the problems."

"Me?"

"Yes, David. You just couldn't cope with having a stepmother near to your own age, young and beautiful. Right, David? That's why you used to come around when your father was at work and fuck me, David. Did you tell Rob about that?" Her voice grew louder. "Or did you leave that part out? Tell him, David. Tell him how you were sleeping with your new mother, and how sick and twisted that made you feel inside."

David snapped, *"Shut up, Shannon."* His grip tightened on the gun. He took a step toward her, pointing the barrel into her face. "Just shut your filthy mouth."

"I thought this was all about telling the truth," she said.

Rob's fingers worked the second latch. He was having trouble. His hands were trembling and slick with sweat. He kept adjusting, trying to make small movements and stay quiet. He could feel the bump of the knob, the outline of the latch, but it was stubborn, stuck. He kept losing his place, slipping off the knob. He pressed harder.

Finally . . . *twang*.

Strom had stepped into Shannon's face now. He

bitterly told her, "I've had enough of your shit. This has been going on for too long. I have no more patience. Goodbye, *Ma*."

He forced the barrel of the gun into her mouth.

Rob opened the briefcase lid. His hands quickly swam inside, shoving papers . . .

Rob felt metal.

Strom's eyes darted off Shannon. He turned and caught Rob fumbling with something behind his back.

Rob began to pull the gun out of the briefcase. He brought his arm around, swinging the weapon toward Strom.

Strom yanked his gun from Shannon, extended his arm straight at Rob and fired.

Rob felt the bullet strike the side of his head, an eruption of searing pain. His gun tumbled out of his grasp and across the floor. He toppled to the ground. He brought a hand to his ear and it quickly filled with blood.

Horrified, Rob looked up from the floor.

Strom still aimed the gun directly at Rob's head, preparing to take a second, more precise shot.

But then Shannon's arm appeared behind Strom, extended, a perfect arc, swooping up, then down, bringing a heavy brass candlestick to Strom's skull with such force that the crack sounded like another gunshot. The impact nearly propelled Strom's eyeballs and tongue right out of his head, and he started to turn, but lost all consciousness, and fell to the ground . . .

. . . and Shannon didn't stop.

She transformed into some kind of raving beast.

Her face turned pink and hardened as she continued to hammer away with the candlestick, sickening *whack* after *whack*, blood shooting in jetstreams in multiple directions, out of Strom's eye sockets, nostrils, mouth, and several brand new openings.

Rob watched in horror, curled up in his own pain and bleeding, wondering if this was the gates to Hell.

Shannon wouldn't stop hitting Strom, and Strom was dead, very dead. She screamed profanity in a raw and ugly voice like someone possessed.

When the beating stopped, Shannon threw the candlestick across the room with a crash.

Rob could see her panting. He sat up, still pressing a hand to his bloody, torn ear, which rang loud and hard.

Shannon stood over Strom, hair wild, eyes crazed. This was the look he had seen before in glimpses . . . except now it was amplified beyond anything he could comprehend . . . a ferocity that had exploded from someplace deep inside.

Strom's head had lost its shape, reduced to a broken, jagged lump of sticky red blood, skull fragments and pink brain. His limbs were forever limp, body crumpled.

Shannon admired her work.

"Like father, like son," she said emotionlessly.

She reached down. She pulled Strom's gun from his fingers.

Rob remained on the floor, stomach jumping, ear on fire, sick from the shockwaves. He forced his eyes away from Strom, a.k.a. Trey Wright.

Shannon approached Rob. She gripped Strom's gun.

Rob looked up at her.

She stared into his face. Expressionless.

"He nicked you good," she said.

"I think it's just my ear," said Rob, "and a cut on the side of my head." But she wasn't listening.

Shannon looked down and saw the gun that Rob had dropped to the floor.

"So you were sent on a mission to kill me," she said, continuing to look at the gun.

"Shannon, no . . ." said Rob.

She placed her foot on Rob's gun.

Abruptly she kicked the gun across the room, spinning it away across the hardwood floor.

Then she pointed her gun directly at Rob.

Rob threw his hands in front of his face. "Shannon!"

"I'm sorry, Rob," said Shannon. "I am truly deeply sorry that you had to get mixed up in all this. You saw and heard some ugly things. But I don't think anybody is going to buy self-defense a second time. It worked well enough once, you know, paying off that dishwasher. Getting him to choke me, getting the necessary bruises on my neck. But this . . . this is a much bigger mess. It's much harder to explain. I have a lot of cleanup to do. You need to go."

Rob felt horror consume every cell in his body. He shook violently. "Shannon, don't do it," he pleaded.

"If it's any consolation, Rob, I did love you for a while. But love . . . is fleeting." She shrugged. "You already knew that."

She pointed the gun at Rob's forehead. "I'll aim careful. I promise it won't hurt. One perfect shot to the brain. No pain, baby. I promise. Be strong."

Rob shut his eyes tight. He felt the blood continue to trickle from his wounded ear, rolling in big drops down his neck. He waited for the shot that would end it all . . . a final, deafening BANG.

Instead, he heard a *jingle.*

Rob opened his eyes.

Shannon kept the gun on him, but turned her head.

Someone had entered the store.

"Hello?" cried a man's voice.

Shannon shot her eyes back at Rob. The gun stayed on him. She still looked entirely capable and willing to finish him off.

"Hello?" said the voice again.

"We're closed!" shouted Shannon.

A long silence passed.

Rob wanted to yell out for the customer to leave. *Save yourself! She'll kill you, too!*

Shannon's finger remained wrapped around the trigger, and the barrel remained pointed at Rob's forehead.

The visitor wouldn't leave. He called out again. "Hello!"

In a low growl, Shannon told Rob, "Don't move." She continued to point the gun at him, while taking small sidesteps toward the curtained doorway that led into the store.

She stood behind the curtain, trying to peek through a crack.

"Yo! Hello!" thundered the voice, louder now.

Shannon kept the gun behind her back. With her free hand, she opened the curtain halfway. She allowed herself to be seen, but blocked the room behind her.

"What is it? We're closed," she said sharply.

A large man, six-foot-four, with a buzz cut, stood at the cash register counter. He spoke in a polite southern drawl. "Pardon me for the intrusion, ma'am, but are you Shannon Mayer?"

Shannon looked him over from top to bottom. She scowled, "And who the fuck are you?"

Justin Hoyt fired a single bullet into her heart and she fell dead to the ground.

As Shannon fell, she tore down the curtain with her. It covered her corpse neatly. And revealed the room inside.

Hoyt saw Rob on the floor.

Rob saw Hoyt.

Hoyt aimed his gun at Rob.

Rob froze. *Oh great, now who's going to shoot me?*

Hoyt kept the barrel pointed at Rob as he moved around the counter and approached the backroom.

Hoyt entered and saw all the blood.

"Holy mackerel," he said. He saw Strom's dead body on the ground. The destroyed skull.

Hoyt looked back at Rob.

"I apologize, mister," said Hoyt, "but now I must end your life."

His finger began tightening on the trigger . . .

In an instant, Rob recognized the snakeskin cowboy boots . . . the towering six-foot-four frame . . . the buzz cut and southern drawl . . .

"Don't shoot!" cried Rob. "I'm in The Circle!"

Hoyt hesitated.

Rob sputtered, "The night at Traveler's Inn. I was there. I'm one of you. I had a mask on. Just like you. The black mask. I came here to kill Shannon Mayer under the orders of Trey Wright. You just . . . beat me to it."

Hoyt looked over at Strom's body. "And who's that?"

"That's Trey Wright," said Rob.

Hoyt's eyes got big. He studied the body for a moment, then shrugged. The face had been pummeled into anonymity. "I guess I'll have to take your word for it."

"His real name is David Strom," said Rob. "She killed him. I got shot in the ear. She beat him with a candlestick. It's been . . . busy back here."

Hoyt nodded slowly. "I'll say."

"I think we better get out of here," said Rob.

"I guess we better." Hoyt lowered his gun. He extended his free hand and helped Rob up.

"Thank you," said Rob. "I'm Rob Carus. I teach high school English."

"Justin Hoyt," said Hoyt. "I used to play football, until I wrecked my knees."

"We've got a real mess here," said Rob, surveying the room. "We need to come up with a plan real quick." He pointed to David Strom's body. "Maybe we should put your gun in his hand. Wipe your prints off first. That way, it'll look like he shot her."

"Before or after she beat his brains in?" asked Hoyt.

"Either way . . ." said Rob.

"I'm just sayin', it don't make a whole lot of sense

for a woman with a bullet in her heart to be able to kill a man like that."

"Then he shot her after."

Hoyt made a face. "After his head was beat in? That doesn't work, either."

Rob became exasperated. "I don't know then. Have you got any ideas?"

"Murder-suicide," said Hoyt slowly, thoughtfully. "She killed him, then shot herself out of despair."

"Shot herself in the heart? That's not logical."

"Then how do we fix this?" Hoyt frowned and put his hands on his hips.

Hoyt and Rob continued to examine the scene. There was blood everywhere. Rob's ear continued to throb painfully.

Finally, Rob said, "Screw it. Let the cops sort it out. Let's just get out of here."

"I agree with you one hundred percent," said Hoyt.

Rob picked up his gun from where Shannon had kicked it. He returned it to his teacher's briefcase. He snapped the briefcase shut.

Rob and Hoyt left Charms.

On his way out, Rob flipped the OPEN sign to read CLOSED.

Twenty-four

An importer named Huck found the bodies in the late afternoon. He had Turkish rugs in his van, only the finest, and Shannon Mayer had told him she would be there, checkbook in hand. When Huck saw the CLOSED sign—at 3:30 P.M. on a Thursday—he didn't leave. He knocked a few times, muttered curse words, and finally pushed on the door. Finding it open, he entered the shop.

Huck went looking for Shannon, which led to a peek into the back room, which led to Huck throwing up all over his shirt.

The Barrington shop double-murder made the lead story that night on the newscasts in Chicago.

Rob watched in his apartment, door locked, shades drawn. He wore a clumsy bandage on the two-thirds of his ear that remained intact, masking the deformity underneath. He gobbled aspirin to keep the pain bearable.

He flipped between newscasts and, at the very least, didn't hear his name.

". . . badly beaten body of . . ."

". . . police investigation underway . . ."

". . . unanswered questions . . ."

". . . exploring a potential connection with the killing of local businessman Walter Strom at a downtown nightclub three years earlier . . ."

". . . speculate that David Strom came to the shop to exact revenge for the death of his father . . ."

". . . but this investigation is a long way from over."

The next morning, before school, Rob drove to the bridge over the Skokie Lagoons. He put on his blinkers, climbed out, and checked for witnesses. Then he tossed his gun into the murky waters. This time he did not even watch it sink. He hopped back in his car and drove away.

A few blocks from the high school, Rob noticed a police car behind him. He checked his dashboard—going the limit, or close enough, anyway—and prayed for the best.

The police car's red and blue lights erupted, flashing and revolving. The police car pushed closer to the rear of Rob's Nissan.

Rob realized that this was it. The end. A life in prison. The closing chapter. He was too tired to run or fight. It was finally time for the law to take over.

Rob pulled to the side of the road. He hoped that none of his students or their parents would see him getting handcuffed on the way to school.

But the police car sped past Rob to another destination.

Rob watched it go. Then he giggled. The giggle became a hearty laugh. A deflation of tension. Then he almost cried.

In each class that morning and afternoon, Rob made his announcement to the students.

Today was his last day.

The timing wasn't too terrible: the school year only had another week-and-a-half left in it. The big stuff was over. He returned all the tests and papers in his possession. Everyone got A's and B's. It wasn't totally random, but close.

He told his classes, "As you know, my fiancée died two years ago this summer. It has been a very difficult time for me. More difficult than anyone could imagine. Sometimes, when things get really bad, it pays to move on to a new environment and start fresh. Start a new page."

When students asked about his bandaged ear, he made up a story about walking into a sign. They couldn't appreciate the symbolism, but he found it apt.

As a final reading lesson in his English Honors course, he assigned *The Ox-Bow Incident*, a study of vigilantism by Walter Van Tilburg Clark. "It is about dichotomies," he told them. "Good and evil, individual belief and mob mentality, order and chaos, law and anarchy, all set against the backdrop of the wild, wild west."

They appeared interested. One kid had seen the movie.

Between classes, Rob distributed his letters. A letter of resignation to the administration. A good-bye note to Hank, promising, "You'll hear from me again." A thank you to the chair of the English department for being so supportive during this difficult year.

Of course, the person who took the news the hardest was Maureen.

She no longer draped herself in gothic gloom. Colors had returned to her wardrobe in recent days. However, her face definitely displayed pale shock at the news.

When class let out, Maureen approached him as he was shutting his briefcase.

"Can I talk with you in private?" she asked.

Rob looked at Maureen and became hit by panic. Maureen held a newspaper clipping about the Barrington murders. The article included a photo of Shannon Mayer.

"Sure," he said, doing his best to control himself from jumping out the window. "Let's wait until the room empties out."

After all the students had left, Rob shut the door. He sat with Maureen at a pair of desks in the front row.

He studied her expression for clues.

She looked troubled.

"I need to tell you something very important," she said.

"What is it?" asked Rob.

She held up the clipping about Shannon. "I know the real reason why your girlfriend got killed."

Rob felt a jolt to his heart. He immediately began perspiring, expecting the worst. "You do . . . ?"

Maureen nodded.

"What . . ." said Rob. "What is the reason?"

"It's because of me," said Maureen.

"Excuse me?" said Rob.

"When I saw you with her at the movies, I made a secret prayer. I wished for her to die. I was so jealous to see you with her. I wanted to . . . get back at her. So for revenge, I prayed that she would die." Maureen looked ready to burst into tears at any moment.

"No, no," Rob reassured her. "It's not your fault. Don't think that way. That's not how things work."

Still despondent, Maureen said, "Why does love hurt so much?"

Rob answered honestly, "I don't know,"

Then Maureen asked, "Mr. Carus, how come all your girlfriends die?"

Rob could only shrug. "Just a lot of bad luck, I guess."

"I'm going to miss you, Mr. Carus."

Rob thanked her. He told her, "Mark my words, you're going to find a boyfriend. A great guy, your own age. You're going to forget all about me. I promise. Time heals everything."

"Where are you moving to?" she asked.

He picked a destination on the spot. "I'm going to teach on the East Coast."

Rob checked his watch and told her he had to get to his final class. Before they left the room, Rob gave Maureen a hug. She beamed. On the way out, she dropped the newspaper clipping into the trash basket.

After his last class, Rob retrieved his boxes from his office. He had packed most of his belongings first thing in the morning. Now all that was left was loading them into his car. Rob said goodbye to the faculty and administrators who came by. He promised Hank he would not lose touch with him.

"Thank you for everything you tried to do for me," Rob told Hank. "I'm sorry if I didn't always appear appreciative."

"I know it's been rough, buddy," said Hank.

"Yeah," sighed Rob. "You don't know the half of it."

In the parking lot, Rob filled his trunk and gave one last look at Evanston Township High.

It was a beautiful day. The skies were pure blue.

Rob pulled out of the parking lot and headed home. He turned on his car radio and punched in his favorite station. At once, a familiar song burst out of the speakers. It jolted him.

Beth's song.

Instinctively, Rob reached to shut it off. But then he stopped himself. He sat back. He felt warmth and smiled.

Rob let the music play.

THE MOON POOL

MAX McCOY

Time is running out for Jolene. She's trapped by a madman, held captive, naked, waiting only for her worst nightmares to become reality. Her captor will keep her alive for twenty-eight days, hidden in an underwater city 400 feet below the surface. Then she will die horribly—like the others....

Jolene's only hope is Richard Dahlgren, a private underwater crime scene investigator. He has until the next full moon before Jolene becomes just another hideous trophy in the killer's surreal underwater lair. But Dahlgren has never handled a case where the victim is still alive. And the killer has never allowed a victim to escape.

TARGET ACQUIRED
JOEL NARLOCK

It's the perfect weapon. It's small, with a wingspan of less than two feet and weighing less than two pounds. It can go anywhere, flying silently past all defenses. It's controlled remotely, so no pilot is endangered in even the most hazardous mission. It has incredible accuracy, able to effectively strike any target at great distances. It's a UAV, or Unmanned Aerial Vehicle, sometimes called a drone. The U.S. government has been perfecting it as the latest tool of war. But now a prototype has fallen into the wrong hands . . . and it's aimed at Washington. The government and the military are racing to stop the threat, but are they already too late?